Fact Check and More Probing Tales

By

James Hanna

Fact Check and
More Probing Tales

By
James Hanna

Copyright ©2022 James Hanna
Published by Sand Hill Review Press
www.sandhillreviewpress.com

Library of Congress Control Number: 2022904961
ISBN: 978-1-949534-30-6 (paperback)
ISBN: 978-1-949534-31-3 (ebook)

Cover images by Gerard Bowlby
Graphics by Backspace Ink.

SHRP
Sand Hill Review Press

To Catherine Barker Hanna

Acknowledgements

FIRST, I WOULD LIKE to thank Antaeus for helping me develop the story line for some of these tales. I would also like to thank Teri Moore for thoroughly proofreading the book and Gerard Bowlby for designing its catchy cover. I would also like to thank Catherine Hanna, my mother, for supporting me in my ambition to become a prolific writer. To her I have dedicated the book.

I am thankful to the following members of my critique group for their input on these stories: Marisa, Elizabeth, Shirley, Vivien, and Teresa. The book is stronger because of them.

Again, a special thanks goes to Mary, my wife, and Tory Hartmann, my publisher, friend, and chief editor.

Thank you for reading Fact Check and More Probing Tales. If you enjoyed it, consider telling your friends or posting a short review on my Amazon author page. Word of mouth is an author's best friend and is much appreciated.

The following stories have previously appeared in these literary magazines and anthologies:

Title	First Published
The Land Fish	*The Rathalla Review*
Life as We Knew It	*Crack the Spine*
Biff Malibu	*Literally Stories*
Do You Do Hits?	*Adelaide Magazine*
The Bog Runs	*Across the Margin*
The Good Pimp	*The Fictional Café*
Urban Cowboy	*Fleas on the Dog*
The Tallyman	*The Chamber Magazine*
Sandy Ajax, We Hardly Knew You	*The Fictional Café*
Did You See the Tasmanian Devil?	*Literally Stories*
Strutting Hog	*Literally Stories*
	Red Savina Review
The Sowbelly Trio	*Adelaide Magazine*
	Literally Stories
How I Done Good in School	*Fleas on the Dog*
How I Got Me Some Standards	*Goat's Milk Magazine*
Pickup	*Scarlet Leaf Review*
The Lottery	*The Chamber Magazine*
	Fleas on the Dog
Contempt	*Across the Margin*
The Keeper of the Abyss	*A Thin Slice of Anxiety*
A Diamond as Big as a Black-Eyed Pea	*N'ig*

Contents

Foreword

WHEN JAMES HANNA asked if I would be interested in writing a foreword to this fine collection, I was honored. I already knew many of the stories within, and I figured that it would be a task of simple dictation by my memory to my fingers.

But it was too late. *Something* achieved sentience and pestered me with annoying questions and observations. The first being, *What is the difference between an introduction and a foreword?*

"Silly Something," I muttered, lighting the day's third cigarette, grimacing from a swallow of unexpectedly-lukewarm coffee, "there ain't one–they are synonyms. Now, go away, you're bothering me."

I don't know, Something mused, *seems to me that Mr. Hanna deserves a foreword written by somebody who knows the difference between a foreword and an introduction.*

"All right, wiseass," I sighed. "What is the difference between the two?"

Me? How should I know? I'm just a 'silly Something.' But I bet if you Googled them you'd find the answer. Instead of Googling, I chose the error-prone human approach, and if this so happens to be more of an introduction than a foreword, you may rest assured that the ignorance is solely my own.

I went with the human approach because whether James is exploring absurd best sellers ("The Land Fish"), the hard-case hopeless ("The Tallyman") or just sending up thoughts to be blasted like skeet by "Mary" ("Biff Malibu"), his writing is a human endeavor created by a sensitive yet ironic artist. *Fact Check and More Probing Stories* also has a deep sense of humor, which, for me, a work must have to be considered valid. Readers new to James will recognize their universe in his works, but they will also come away with new ideas caused by exposure to a writer who isn't shy about telling the truth as he sees it. The good thing there is he might offend some with his viewpoints.

I hope that is so.

Welcome to his universe.

Leila Allison
Associate Editor
Literally Stories UK

The Land Fish

MASON TROUT was a determined but little-known writer. This may have been spawned by the fact that he only read classic literature. When friends asked him what his three favorite books were, he answered without hesitation. "*Moby Dick*, *The Canterbury Tales*, and James Joyce's *Ulysses*." He then would grin like an angler who had caught an eight-pound bass.

"Mason," his wife Jill said one day while he was tapping away on a novel. "Have you ever read a book that isn't a dusty relic?"

"Just what are you asking me, sweetcakes?" he muttered.

"I'm asking," she said, "if you ever read a book not written by a dead white author?"

"Sure," said Mason triumphantly. "The other day I finished *Cold Mountain*, and Charles Frasier is still alive. His allusions to *The Odyssey* are really quite amazing."

"I'm married to a literary snob," she scolded.

Mason shrugged and cracked his knuckles. "We're all snobs about something, cupcake."

"Well, what good is being a *literary* snob if the public won't buy your books?"

"I write for literati," said Mason. "I don't write for the common herd. Did you see the review I just received on *The Pitcher in the Wheat*? The reviewer wrote, 'Mason Trout's use of alliteration goes way beyond the pale.'"

"Most reviewers call your books boring and derivative."

"What would they know?" said Mason. "Reviewers are only failed writers. Do you think they'd be wasting time writing reviews if they were able to write books themselves?"

"Is that any worse than writing books that only snobs will read?"

Mason closed his eyes and counted to ten. For a temperamental scribe in his seventies, he had remarkable self-control. Yes, his wife was the breadwinner, but that did not entitle her to be rude. What right did she have to barge into his den anytime she had a burr in her ass? It was bad enough that the critics panned him and the public ignored his books. The very least his wife could do was to show him a little respect.

"Have you seen today's paper?" Jill asked. "*Book World* mentions your latest novel."

"How nice," Mason grumbled as she handed him the Arts Section. Daphne DuBois, his most blistering critic, had written the review. Holding the paper as though it might burn him, he grudgingly scanned her attack.

A Load of Crap

We have come to expect the humdrum from local author Mason Trout, but his latest effort, Callahan's Sleep, *disappoints even these expectations. Told in what could be generously described as a subliminal stream of consciousness, Mr. Trout captures none of the lyricism of the great work it emulates. The book is neither prose nor poem although it struggles to be both. Verbal hiccuping would best describe what his dreadful book has to offer. And why did Mr. Trout draw a fish and write* fin *at the end of his final chapter? Is he saying we should fly forever in*

Finnegans Wake *like a flock of mindless gulls? I would urge that only insomniacs pick up this mind-dulling book.*

"A load of crap," griped Mason. "Honey, is that what *you* think of the book?"

"Stop asking me that question," Jill said. "You know I never read your books. It's bad enough that I have to live with you without knowing what goes on in your head."

"My use of colons is exquisite," said Mason. "Even *Book World* concedes to that. You won't find anything like it in those Harlequin romances you read."

"If your books do justice to colons," said Jill, "I'll leave you to ponder that thought."

"A load of crap," Mason repeated as Jill breezed out of his den. He could picture Daphne DuBois smirking while trashing *Callahan's Sleep*. What fiendish delight she must have taken in writing that toxic review. You'd think she was something mightier than a critic for a local rag.

He wanted to smear her with honey then pour ants onto her, but his writer's imagination came up with an idea that was far more poetically just. Why not write a book so bad that it will make her squirm for real?

"A load of crap," Mason repeated. "*I'll* give her a load of crap."

*

Setting aside his novel in progress, *To Save a Hummingbird*, Mason pondered the sort of book that might make Daphne DuBois squirm. *Why not a woman's romance?* he decided. *One of those saccharine parodies inspired by* Jane Eyre. *A trashy tale of a forlorn heroine who is rescued by true love.*

Excited, Mason began to write and he soon had two thousand words. The book flowed from him so fluidly that he knew it had to be tripe. Great books do not come so easily. Great books take effort and time. Great books require texture, thought, and poetic connotations. But his fingers scrambled like lemmings as they traveled over the keyboard, and before he knew it, Mason was up to seven thousand words. Forfeiting meals and sleep, Mason continued to write. After a week, he had completed a book of sixty thousand words. Words so hastily written, phrases so soggy and trite, that it was all he could do not to puff out his chest and crow like a rooster greeting the dawn. The book was not crap but diarrhea. It was sure to get Daphne DuBois' goat. He read over the book a second time to make sure he had not missed a cliché.

The heroine, an eighteenth-century beauty born in the Highlands of Scotland, had raven-black hair, the fairest of skin, and eyes that flashed like diamonds. Her name was Megan McCullough, she was wild and temperamental, and she liked to stand on perilous bluffs and let the wind toss her hair. On her twentieth birthday, Megan agreed to marry a wealthy landowner, but on the eve of her wedding, she suffered a terrible accident. While cantering her Arabian stallion across the Highland moors, Megan lost her grip on the reins and the horse ran away with her. When a deer jumped in front of the stallion, causing it to rear, Megan was thrown from the saddle and tumbled down a ravine. She survived the horrible fall, but both her legs were crushed, and she lay for three days in a peat bog until a huntsman came across her.

At this point, Mason suspected most readers would put down the book, so he felt a grim satisfaction as he read it to the end.

On becoming an invalid, Megan called off her engagement. "The loss of my legs I must live with," she told her anguished mother. "But I will not suffer pity as well. I would rather the life of a spinster." "Lord Hawthorne still wishes to marry you," her mother reminded her. "And what kind of wife would I make him?" Megan bitterly replied. "No, never shall I marry unless I can walk down the aisle."

Retiring to a small fishing village on the rugged Scottish coast, Megan spent her days in a shack staring out to sea. The shack was cold and drafty, the porch was falling to pieces, but at least the mutinous North Sea swells afforded her company. One day, her gaze lingered upon a local fishing lad: a simple boy named Angus McNeill who was carrying his nets to his skiff. Noticing Megan sitting on the porch, Angus tipped his rainhat. "Pretty miss, may I be of service?" he said, having instantly fallen in love. "Away with you, lout!" shouted Megan. "Can't you see that I am a cripple?" "Ah, but I have legs for us both," said the lad, and a smile touched Megan's lips.

And so began a friendship that weathered many a storm. Insulted by his kind intentions, Megan scolded the boy like a parrot, but the stalwart lad withstood her tongue-lashings as though they were gentle rains. He brought her the freshest of northern pike, which he fried in batter and beer, and he fetched her bouquets of heather that he gathered in the moors. And when Megan's legs pained her to distraction, he stroked them as though they were kittens. "I know that my legs must disgust you," snapped Megan; the boy only shook his head. "Why must you think such thoughts," he replied. "I know only that you are in pain."

Nurtured by Angus' kindness, Megan recovered some use of her legs, and one day she put her ire aside and made a tearful confession. "I love you, Angus McNeill," she said. "I never planned such a thing." "I love you too, Megan McCullough," he answered. "Even more than I love the sea." The two of them wed in the village chapel and began a fine life together. And, yes, upon their wedding day, Megan walked down the aisle.

So what should I call this piece of shit? Mason wondered as he typed "The End." *What title best captures its mawkishness and relentless sentimentality?* After thinking for only a minute, he titled the book *The Land Fish*.

7

*

Making an exception to her hands-off rule, Jill proofread the book. When she told him the book was wonderful, Mason knew he had written a dud. What better proof did he need of this than a compliment from his wife? A woman who never read anything but formulized, Harlequin trash.

The following month, the book was launched, and Daphne Dubois did not disappoint him. Her review was so scathing, so primal and base, that it seemed like a howl of pain. Smirking like Mephistopheles, Mason savored her every word.

This Fish Should Have Stayed in the Sea

What can I say about Mason Trout that I have not said already? Surely, he stands alone as the most derivative of authors. But at least in his previous failures, he was trying to write something grand—something that might steal the glory of Salinger or Harper Lee. In his latest opus, The Land Fish, *Mason does not even try to do that; he has chosen instead to emulate the worst of Nicholas Sparks. But not even a blaze of bathos can spark this sickening book. For characters as flat as cardboard, look no further than* The Land Fish. *For a plot as corny as Crackerjack, look no further than* The Land Fish. *For dialogue staler than rolls dug out of Pompeii, look no further than* The Land Fish. *This book wallows in its campiness like a mudskipper flounders in muck.*

Laughing, Mason copied Daphne's review and posted it on Facebook. Let the world acknowledge that he had gotten the better of that sanctimonious shrew. Let the world know that his rapier wit had cut off Medusa's head. Let all the world see that woman as a bitch in the throes of a meltdown—a fishwife so vile and volatile that he had played her like a harp.

To keep the joke going, Mason took his book to his weekly critique group: a gathering of writers thoroughly versed in Shakespeare, Proust, and Beckett. After announcing that he had nailed his nemesis, he read them the book's first chapter, but it soon became apparent that the group did not share the joke. *Oh*, their collective stare seemed to say, *so you're writing pulp romances*, and their faces clouded over with the sort of indifference one might show a street musician.

Mason's disappointment continued that evening when he opened up his email. His queue contained dozens of messages from his stable of literary friends: guardians of the creative torch, preservers of culture and standards, bulwarks to the seas of amateurism that threatened to wash over the land. A scribe of historical fiction wrote, "Mason, why are you writing for money? Do you think thirty pieces of silver are worth your eternal soul?" Another, a professor of philosophy, wrote, "How could you do this, Mason? The reading public is dumb enough without you making it comatose." And a well-known essayist on Shakespeare's sonnets wrote only three brutal words. "Et tu, Mason?" he groused, and Mason felt as though he had been slugged.

"What have I done?" muttered Mason, burying his face in his hands. Would his name now rank among such doodlers as Danielle Steele and Nicholas Sparks? Had the book branded him as conspicuously as the red letter on Hester Prynne's blouse? His groans were so deep and labored that they drew Jill into his den.

"Mason," she snapped. "What *is* the matter? Is it something to do with your book?"

"My reputation is toast," Mason moaned.

"Your reputation with whom?"

"The protectors of the flame. The finest minds in the land."

"Mason," Jill said. "I will say this just once, so please *listen* to me this time. Whatever their accomplishments, your friends are like crabs in a bucket. Do you know what crabs in a bucket do when one of them tries to climb out? They latch onto him with ferocious claws and try to pull him back in."

"Better to drown in a bucket than to roam the land a pariah."

"Oh, Mason, stop being so silly," laughed Jill. "You're sounding like Megan McCullough."

*

Had his embarrassment been confined to his emails, Mason might have been able to stand it, but when he checked his book's ranking on his Amazon author page, his shame multiplied tenfold. *The Land Fish* was ranked thirty-fifth among the Top One Hundred Kindle Books, and among the Kindle Romances, it was rated number one. Number one over books with titles like *Bound by a Billionaire*. And even more distressing were the hundreds of Amazon customer remarks. Comments like "I've never been so moved" and "Please write more stories about Megan." Who were these brain-dead dilettantes who had fallen in love with his book? As he scanned the reviews he felt as though he were being eaten alive by zombies.

But Mason's humiliation had only just begun. After the book had been out for a month, an executive from Walt Disney Pictures phoned him. The executive, who sounded like he was twenty years old, offered to buy the movie rights. He also mentioned that Jennifer Lawrence was interested in playing Megan McCullough. Jennifer Lawrence! His celebrity crush! Mason blanched at the sound of her name. Hadn't that wretched book done enough harm without dragging down Jennifer Lawrence? It was only at his wife's insistence that he agreed to look over the contract.

When a contract for ten million dollars arrived in the morning mail, Jill took one look at the figure and slapped a pen into his palm. "If you turn it down, I will leave you," she threatened. "It's high time your writing made money. Since I've supported you for forty years, I'm vested in that book too."

"They want more than just one book," complained Mason. "Hollywood makes series now. That means they want me to write three more Megan McCullough books."

"Well, *write* them," Jill ordered. "It's not like you have anything better to do."

May Jennifer Lawrence forgive me, thought Mason. *May God forgive me too.* Clutching the pen as though holding a snake, he signed away his soul.

*

Although he had become an outcast, Mason kept attending his critique group. And he kept reading chapters of *The Land Fish* to unreceptive ears. He was losing hope that he would get the group to understand the joke, but the mocking stares he drew were better than the trauma of being alone. When alone, he was forced to suffer an even more crushing defeat. When alone, he was forced to realize his abasement knew no bounds. Because, when alone, he was forced to admit that he dearly loved *The Land Fish*. He loved its archaic sentences, its ornamental style, and he loved Megan McCullough so much that she seemed like a long-lost daughter. *Oh, fortune, what have you done to me?* he thought as he sat in his den. *Oh, muse, why did you program me to be a writer of pulp?*

When the movie came out, the guardians of culture descended upon it like locusts. The critic for *The Boston Globe* wrote, "I watched my colonoscopy on television—it was more interesting than *The Land Fish*." The critic for *The Washington Post* wrote, "A beached whale of a movie. This flop makes *Beach Blanket Bingo* look like *Citizen Kane.*" And the critic for *The Wall Street Journal*, in the cruelest jibe of all, stated, "Even Jennifer Lawrence could not salvage this drippy script."

And yet the movie grossed thirty million dollars in its first week of release. Theaters showed it on several screens to accommodate surging crowds, and adolescent girls carried canes so they could feign Megan McCullough's limp. "I love it," gushed Miley Cyrus, Disney Pictures' greatest star, and Megan McCullough dolls soon appeared in Walmarts all over the country.

As though branded with the mark of Cain, Mason would not come out of his den. He shut down his Facebook and email accounts, refused all visitors, and he committed himself to a life of isolation and booze. In booze, he could blur his wretchedness. In booze, he could soften his shame. In booze, he could glimpse the specter of the writer he might have been. At Jill's insistence, he sobered up long enough to attempt to write a sequel, a tale he hoped to call *Megan's Daughters* and infuse with some quality. But his fingers froze as though atrophied when he placed them upon the keyboard, and he returned to the bottle as inevitably as a frog hopping into a lake. His drinking became so heavy, his temper so epic and harsh, that one day Jill came into his den and said she was leaving him. "You were annoying enough as a failure," she said. "In success, you're impossible."

"Success will always elude me," said Mason. "I'm a writer of drivel and crap."

"Don't flatter yourself, Mason. You're no longer a writer at all."

"Better a fruitless life," Mason said, "than one of broken success."

"There you go sounding like Megan again. *Must* you be so melodramatic? I doubt that you would know success if it grabbed you by the throat."

"If I can drink myself to oblivion," said Mason, "*that* would be a success. If I no longer hear my miserable muse, *that* would be a success."

"Fine," replied Jill. "Stay drunk if you must. But you *will* hear from my attorney."

*

After Jill left him, Mason spent three months moping in his den. He no longer bathed or answered the doorbell, he let his hair grow wild, and whenever he felt the urge to write—to tap his creative spring—he lay down on his unmade bed until the feeling went away. Where once he had ridden the rapids of a leaping imagination, he now dwelled in a stagnant swamp in which he hoped to drown.

On the day that his boozing caught up with him and he suffered a fatal stroke, he sighed like a faucet and went to his bed. *At last, at last*, he thought. But he felt no relief as he lay there and waited for death to come. Yes, an otherworldly light was streaming across the floor, but the woman who hobbled toward him seemed the unlikeliest of escorts. Her jet-black hair was as disheveled as his, her eyes were hollow and sad, and she stared at him like a jilted bride as she sat on the foot of his bed.

"Why did you let me go?" Megan asked.

"I had no choice," replied Mason.

She locked her eyes upon his and spoke in a tiny voice. "I cannot fault you for scorning me, sir. I am feral and cruel as the wind. But are my transgressions so loathsome that you would take my life as well?"

She was gazing at him with pity and sternness, yet he felt only unbridled love. Pygmalion could not have loved his statue as much as he cherished this small, unkempt woman.

Her eyes were now sparkling with tears, and a barb crept into her voice. "I had so many adventures to come. Will you write them now, Mason Trout?"

"Does it matter now?"

She frowned like a critic. "Why *wouldn't* it matter, sir?"

She still has her temper, thought Mason, *but I love her in all her moods. Were she my very own flesh and blood, I could not love this woman more.*

"May I quarrel with my daughters?" she asked. "May I lash horses across the moors? May I spread my legs for scoundrels after my husband dies at sea?"

"I'll write them, damn my soul," Mason said. "You'll break a hundred hearts." He knew now he had never been worthy of her, this brave, impossible woman, and he experienced the deepest of gratitude when she chuckled and lowered her eyes.

"Then come, sir, the Highlands await us," she said. She slowly rose from the bed. Taking his hand in hers, she led him toward the light.

Life as We Knew It

MY WIFE, MARY, AND I sit in the living room of our Florida home. We are watching the six p.m. news. The Washington DC police are herding demonstrators from Lafayette Park. The shouts of demonstrators are punctuated by the pop of flash grenades, and lingering drifts of pepper spray obscure them as they retreat. Minutes later, we see the White House occupant standing in front of a church. He is clutching a Bible as though it were a shield.

"That is absolutely surreal," Mary says, but I am not impressed. Since Mary and I retired, I am content to let life pass us by.

"A kleptocrat hiding behind a Bible?" I say. "What's unusual about that?"

"He's so damn artless about it."

I shrug. "His supporters won't care," I say. "They knew he was a rube when they elected him president."

Mary is knitting a sweater, and she pauses to complete a stitch. "Well," she says, "at least karma is catching up to him now."

"Why did karma have to wait for a pandemic?" I say. "Couldn't it have come around sooner?"

Mary goes on with her knitting. "Better late than never."

I turn down the sound on the television. "If karma can't sting with precision," I say, "I think *never* is better than late. Why does it have to kill thousands just to punish Trump?"

Mary, ever sensible, does not look up from her knitting. She says, "Karma will catch up with the protesters too. They're taking the pandemic home with them."

I switch channels but get only more news. Protesters are swarming a highway. "I don't think *all* lives matter to them."

Mary puts down her knitting. "Watch your mouth," she cautions. "Do you want to be known as a racist?"

"I don't want to be known at all," I say, then I recite from "The Second Coming." "'Things fall apart,'" I parrot. "'The center cannot hold.'"

"Again with that damn poem?" Mary mutters.

"What do you have against Yeats?"

"Nothing," says Mary. "But he is kind of stale. That poem's getting beaten to death these days."

I am comfortable with the familiar, so I recite another line. "'The best lack all conviction while the worst are full of passionate intensity.'"

"That poem gives you too much credit," says Mary.

"What do you mean by that?"

"Well, you've *never* been very passionate."

"At least, I'm not spreading disease."

"Maybe not," she says, "but you *are* spreading boredom. A little passion on your part would be welcome now and then."

"Do I have to burn police cars?" I joke.

"That's not what I meant," says Mary.

"We're housebound," I say. "We can't *take* a vacation. Life as we know it is over."

"I *know* we're housebound," says Mary. "But for *you*, that's a bit too convenient. Do you really think you can sit there all day and make no effort at all?"

"Do you actually expect me to recover the past?"

"No, but I expect you to try."

"Well, what do you want me to do?"

"Figure it out," she replies.

*

The next afternoon, I log onto the internet, hoping to reclaim life as we knew it. Our days of carefree trips are done, our days of dining out are done, but I hope to at least find some semblance of a romantic getaway. As if by divine coincidence, a colorful ad pops up. It features a restaurant with a porch light so green that it might have beckoned Jay Gatsby, and a voice you could pour over waffles is making a soothing pitch. *"An intimate dinner for two? No problem. Wines from the south of France? No problem. Candlelight while you dine? No problem. The Auld Lang Syne Bistro has it all, and we even supply the candles. Just combine any items on our menu for a sumptuous three-course dinner. In less than half an hour, your meal will be ready for curbside pickup."*

I slowly scroll down the menu and am impressed by what I see. The menu features pork schnitzel, stuffed salmon, and duck breast with apricot chutney. It lists honey-baked chicken, prime rib with fresh herb sauce, and burgundy beef stew. It has garden and strawberry salads and fifteen types of soup, and for dessert, it offers a choice between butter tarts and chocolate mousse. On top of this, the menu suggests a wine for every course. It lists forty types of wine, all from the south of France, and a lively description and food pairing accompany every wine. For example, Babar Bordeaux is described as a wine with a whisper of boldness—a wine that goes well with schnitzel and prime rib au jus.

I summon Mary to my computer and ask her to check out the ad. "This could bring back life as we knew it," I say.

Mary sits down and scrolls through the ad. "We never knew life this good."

"Shall we pick out a couple of dinners and dine by candlelight?"

"I'm allergic to fish," says Mary, "and ducks are too cute to eat. But I wouldn't mind having a prime rib dinner with maybe a garden salad."

"What kind of dressing?"

"Vinaigrette."

"And for dessert?"

"Surprise me."

"What about wine?"

"Whoa there, stud. You know I never drink wine."

I write down Mary's order and include a butter tart, then I carefully study the menu and decide what to get for myself. When I have made some adventurous choices, I feel like a connoisseur, and I read my selections to Mary as though reciting an epic poem. "Vichyssoise with Chardonnay, burgundy stew with Merlot, chocolate mousse with plum wine—that oughta make a change."

"What kind of change are you talking about? Are you trying to turn into a lush?"

"I'm trying to do something romantic," I say.

"Well, I don't want a romantic drunk."

I explain to Mary that the bottles are small, but she only rolls her eyes.

*

I stay online to place our orders and am stymied by all the instructions. It seems getting back life as we knew it will not be a simple task. First, I have to secure the location of an Auld Lang Syne Bistro near us—it appears that this intimate restaurant is part of a national chain. After securing a local location, I must confirm a pick-up time then I have to list the color and model of the car I intend to bring. I am forced to slog through forty more questions before moving on to the menu—questions so stark and invasive that I should have probably been read my rights. *Did you sneeze today?*

Did you masturbate? Did you wash your hands after peeing? Since a single irreverent answer would probably blacklist me, I answer each of these questions with a watchmaker's care.

By the time I arrive at the menu, my frustration has only begun. Each food item I order lists dozens of subcategories. For example, my request for burgundy stew unleashes this torrent of queries: *Do you have any food allergies? Would you like grain or grass-fed beef? Would you like gluten-free gravy?* The questions go on and on like a nonstop merry-go-round.

After I have chosen the food items, I feel like I've battled a hydra, but when I come to the wine list, my frustration hits a new peak. I must pick from a dozen different brands for every wine I choose; I must also list the year of the wine and the region in France I prefer. *Sorry, not available* pops up so frequently that I make alternate selections as desperately as I might have played Russian roulette. "Mary was right," I mutter. "I should have left out the wines."

It takes me almost four hours to get the order completed. The bill comes to three hundred dollars. I enter my credit card number. I feel like I've passed the bar exam when my order is confirmed.

*

I drive to the Auld Lang Syne Bistro to make my curbside pickup. It is located in a shopping center twenty minutes from our house. The restaurant, which looks like a Tudor home, has an expansive parking lot, and a dozen cars sit in front of the place in numerically marked parking spaces.

I pull into one of the parking spaces and read the instructions on the placard. The message says, *Phone us when you arrive and announce your parking space number. Somebody will be out with your order.* I punch-dial the phone number on the placard.

I only receive a recording. I leave a message and wait, but I do not get a response.

After half an hour, I spot someone rushing from car to car. She is a short, wiry woman wearing a cloth mask that makes her look like a bandit. When she reaches my car, she taps on the driver's window. She steps back as I lower the glass.

"Hon," she says, "this ain't my fault. I only hand out the meals."

"What's not your fault?" I ask stonily.

"The chef didn't show up for work."

"That's not my fault either," I say.

The woman wags her head—she seems put off by my comment. "His wife ran off with her hairdresser, hon. She left him a Dear John note. Ya expect a fella to show up for work after going through something like *that*?"

I listen without sympathy. This is too much information. "Will he be back tomorrow?" I say.

The woman shuffles her feet. "If he doesn't kill the slut—yeah," she snaps. "That's no way to treat your husband. But try us again tomorrow, hon—just submit another order. And ask for me—my name is Jan. I'll make sure ya get real quick service."

"Thank you, Jan," I say.

She dashes to another car.

I decide to drop by McDonald's as I pull out of the parking lot.

*

I return home with a couple of Big Macs and tell Mary about my experience. When she looks at me impatiently, my palms begin to sweat. "The chef's wife eloped with her hairdresser," I bleat. "What can I do about that?"

"I'll *tell* you what you can do," says Mary. "Go online, make sure your order is canceled then never go there again."

"So how will we get back life as we knew it?"

"There must be another way."

When I log back onto my computer, I have serious reservations. I wonder where our country would be if our founders had given up so easily. Infused with the spirit of Jefferson, I resolve to make a stand. For the first time ever, I decide that I will ignore one of Mary's requests. After performing some wrist-stretching exercises to stave off carpal tunnel, I recite the first line of "The Second Coming" as though it's a battle hymn. "'Turning and turning in the widening gyre, the falcon cannot hear the falconer.'"

I make sure my previous order is canceled then I laboriously fill out another, including all the food items I listed earlier in the day. This time it only takes me three hours because I eliminate the wines. When I spot a box marked *Special Remarks*, I express my condolences to the chef—it seems the roaring pandemic has given me empathy. I decide to grant the poor man time to recover from his heartbreak, so I set my pickup hour for eight p.m. the following day.

*

The next evening, I leave the house when Mary isn't looking. I drive to The Auld Lang Syne Bistro and park in one of its numbered spaces. Jan is standing in front of the restaurant like a sentry guarding a fort. When she spots my car, she walks over and salutes me. I roll the window down.

I think she is smiling behind her mask. "Your order is about ready," she says.

"How's the chef?" I ask.

She drops her gaze. "He ain't in a very good mood, hon. He believes in fine dining—not takeout."

"I'm sorry to disappoint him," I say.

Her voice grows sympathetic, or perhaps the mask softens her tone. "Don't let that bother you, hon—I want you to have a nice evening. Besides, this bug ain't gonna last for more 'an another month."

Apparently, Jan is a Trump supporter—who else would believe such crap? I want to expand her thinking, but this is not the time. I don't want to give her a lecture if it might tempt her to spit in my food.

*

Holding a bulging paper sack, I walk through our front door. I carry the sack into the living room where Mary is sipping iced tea.

"Where have you been?" asks Mary. "Oh, don't tell me—I already know. You were out recovering life as we knew it."

"I'm a man on a mission," I say.

"Really," says Mary. "It's just a meal."

"So was the Last Supper."

I dump out the sack on the coffee table and flinch when I hear Mary gasp. Its contents consist of two candles and a dozen fish sandwiches.

"You're kidding," says Mary.

"I wish I were."

"Did you look at the receipt?"

"This isn't my fault," I stammer. "All I did was pick up the meals."

"You *didn't* pick up the meals," Mary snaps. "Not unless you ordered fish."

I grit my teeth like a boxer. "Next time I'll get it right."

*

As I reopen the link to the Auld Lang Syne site, I'm glad that we at least got the candles. This tiny victory sustains me as I fill out a third order. It takes me another three hours to order our original meals, and I console myself by leaving a very modest tip.

22

Mary watches me as I labor. "Are you really this obsessed?"

"The falcon cannot hear the falconer," I say, and I press the checkout button.

Mary shakes her head stoically and makes me sleep on the couch. As I leave the house the next evening, she does not say a word.

I drive back to the Auld Lang Syne Bistro. The parking lot is empty. I should take this as a warning, but I am too focused for that. Instead, I see it as a sign that the service will be fast.

Jan spots me from the restaurant door and strolls out to my car. When I roll down the driver's window, she hands me a ten-dollar bill.

"Keep it, hon," she snaps. "You must need it more than me."

"You'll get a bigger tip," I say, "when you start getting my orders correct."

When I explain about the fish sandwiches, she chuckles behind her mask. "I guess that means that some rednecks got prime rib and vichyssoise."

"You're taking this very lightly," I say.

"Naw, you're gettin' too worked up. You don't need to get this excited about a coupla lousy meals."

"It's not about prime rib," I say. "It's about getting life back as we knew it."

"Ya can't go home again, hon," she says. "Haven't you read that book."

I look at her incredulously. "You've read Thomas Wolfe?"

She places her hands on her hips and scowls. "I also read Shakespeare, hon. I hope that don't upset you. You look like the sort of fella who likes to keep things in a box."

Again, she has given me more information than I care to assimilate. "Why don't you go box up my order," I say. "Make sure you bring the receipt."

"As you like it," she jokes, and she goes back into the restaurant.

Returning five minutes later, she hands me a full shopping bag. The receipt is stapled to the bag and I comb through every item. "It looks like you got it right," I say.

She dramatically slaps her forehead. "Oh, thank god. I don't wantcha missin' out on life as you knew it."

*

I place the food on our coffee table and open two of the plastic boxes. Both boxes contain duck a l'orange. Mary stares in disbelief.

"That's not even on their menu," I say.

"Did you check your receipt?" Mary says.

"I went over every item. I was sure they had it right."

I hand the receipt to Mary. She does not glance at it. "They must have stapled it to the wrong bag. You should have looked inside the boxes."

"Will you settle for duck a l'orange?" I plead

"You know I don't eat duck."

"Well, if we can't get back life as we know it, we may as well settle for duck."

"You eat it," says Mary. "I'm making myself a peanut butter sandwich."

After Mary vanishes into the kitchen, I guiltily devour my duck. It is utterly delicious, but that does not shake my resolve. I am more determined than ever to get my order right.

*

Mary no longer speaks to me—it's like she has taken a vow of silence. But with destiny in the balance, I can put no stock in that. So every day for the rest of the week, I order two meals from the restaurant, and each day my endeavor is thwarted by some karma run amok. On one occasion, Jan phoned me to say the power went off in the kitchen, so most of the food had spoiled and had to be tossed out. On another occasion, she texted that the chef had been thrown in jail. He had violated a stay-away order and beaten the shit out of his wife. On a third occasion, I actually made it as far as the parking lot, but Jan came out of the restaurant and told me that the new chef had just sneezed on my food.

"Why don't you give it up, hon," she said. "Your wife must be fit to be tied. I'm thinking of blowing this pop stand myself and taking an acting class."

"I'll miss you," I said, and I meant it.

"I'll miss you too, hon," she replied.

I gave her a fifty-dollar tip, perhaps to placate the gods, and I drove back home to go online and order two more meals.

Yes, Mary has stopped speaking to me, but what can I do about that? I can hear destiny calling—a summons I dare not defy. So I park myself at my computer and plug away on that site. I know I will get back life as we knew it. Perhaps on my very next try.

The Lottery

A WARM WIND is blowing from the north, and today the air is clear. The air is the color of tea. The air is usually the color of coffee—not the color of tea.

Today, I see trees and grass. The trees are twisted and scaly, the grass is drier than straw. I wish that the air was the color of coffee, not the color of tea. If the air was the color of coffee, I would not see the trees and the grass.

Whatever the color of the air, I can always see into the dome. The dome is huge and bright. The dome has forests and lawns. I see leafy trees and flowers when I look into the dome.

The dome is one mile high, and it must be a hundred miles wide. Birds fly about within the dome—colorful, cheerful birds. There are towering buildings inside the dome, there are roads with buses and cars. There are lakes with fountains and ducks. There is farmland with very tall crops.

I am glad the dome is beautiful, it is where our protectors live. Our protectors are tall with shiny bald heads. Our protectors wear flowing white robes. They do not look like us—we are naked and hairy, not pretty like our protectors.

Our protectors guard our tribe from the trolls that live high up in the hills. If it was not for our protectors, the trolls would come down from the hills. The trolls have razor-sharp claws. Their cocks are harder than stone. They would butcher and rape everyone in our tribe if it was not for our protectors.

Our protectors are kind and intelligent, unlike the horrible trolls. I am very afraid of the trolls—I do not want to feel their claws. Not everybody in our tribe is afraid of the trolls. There are unbelievers in our tribe who are not afraid of them. "Have you ever seen a troll?" they ask us. I have never seen a troll, and that is a very good thing. Our protectors make sure the trolls never come down from the hills.

*

Today, the air is clear. The air is the color of tea. I can see the shapes of the hills where the deadly trolls have their home. I wish the air was darker—I do not want to look at the hills.

My name is Jeremiah—I'm an old man of seventeen. I belong to a tribe that lives outside the dome, and I have no other names. Jeremiah is a very good name. Everyone in our tribe has that name. Even women and girls are named Jeremiah. Our protectors have given us all this name. They say it's a very fine name. They say there will be great love in our tribe if all of us share the same name.

A great many tribes live outside of the dome, but none of them share our name. Our protectors tell us to stay away from all the other tribes. The tribes are very bad, they say. The tribes have cannibals in them. The unbelievers in our tribe ask, "Have you ever seen a cannibal?" I tell them I once saw a cannibal, and he was from another tribe. The cannibal was eating a girl from our tribe. He was gobbling down her intestines, which drooped from his hands like snakes.

I stay far away from the other tribes. I do not like cannibals. I do not like the unbelievers either, but our protectors say let them be. Our protectors say everyone in our tribe should be able to speak his mind.

Inside the dome, there are cows and sheep. Inside the dome, there are farmlands and orchards. Outside the dome, there is dust and rocks. The dust is very dry and the rocks are very hot. There is no farmland outside of the dome. There are no animals.

Our protectors feed us every day—they do not want us to be hungry. Every day, giant vans leave the dome and distribute food to all the tribes. The food is dumped from the vans, and there is always plenty of food. There are apple cores and peanut shells and chicken bones and bread. There are banana peels and corn cobs and watermelon rinds. The food is very tasty. I eat until I am full.

*

Today, the air is the color of tea. It is not the color of coffee. I can see the lights of other domes that are many miles away. There are domes all over the country. There are domes all over the world. I do not want to look at faraway domes, so I turn my head away.

When the domes fight with each other, there is a truce among the tribes our dome feeds. Our protectors tell us to band together, and they give us banners and swords. Even women and children are given banners and swords. Our protectors say we must kill the tribesmen fighting for other domes. They say we should eat their livers because the livers will keep us strong. They say if we eat only the livers, we are better than cannibals.

The unbelievers say there is no glory in fighting tribes from other domes. They say the domes fight each other for sport. They say it is bad to eat livers.

I am proud to have carried a sword and a banner. I am proud to have fought for my dome. I have killed those who fight for other domes. I have eaten their livers too.

*

Today, the air is the color of tea, and protectors walk among us. Whenever the air is the color of tea, our protectors visit us. They come down from the sky in magnificent floats that make a cooling wind.

Our protectors are tall and beautiful. Their eyes are like pools of blue water. They do not stay very long outside of the dome, but it is good when they walk among us.

Our protectors ask us a question when they come to visit us. It is the same question every time. "What will you do for us?" they ask. Their voices are thin and melodious. They sound like wonderful birds.

Once a protector looked at me and touched me on the forehead. I never felt a gentler touch. I never saw bluer eyes. "What will you do for us?" he asked. His voice was musical.

I told him I had killed tribesmen from other domes. I told him I had eaten their livers. The protector looked at me and repeated, "What will you do for us?"

Our protectors are kind and comforting. We love them very much. The women in our tribe have orgasms when our protectors walk among us. "What will you do for us?" our protectors ask the women. Sometimes, they gather up women and girls and fly them back to the dome.

The unbelievers among us say our protectors should stay inside the dome. They say our protectors should never ask us what we will do for them. I tell the unbelievers I would do much for our protectors. Our protectors keep us fed. They give us banners and swords. They protect us from the terrible trolls that live up in the hills.

*

Today, a warm wind is blowing, and the air is the color of tea. Today, our protectors have set up the stage where they have the lottery. Whenever the air is the color of tea, the lottery is held.

There are numbers tattooed on our forearms. My number is 6609. Our protectors spin a big lottery wheel that all the tribe can see. They spin the wheel four times. They call out a number each time. If each of your numbers is called, you will be allowed to live inside the dome.

All our tribe gathers around the stage. It is good to live in the dome. We can better serve our protectors if we are allowed to live in the dome.

The unbelievers say they do not want to live in the dome. The unbelievers have no numbers on their forearms. "We are all of one body," our protectors announce when they have the lottery. But the unbelievers are never selected to live inside the dome.

Today, the wheel spins slowly, and my number does not come up. I have attended the lottery hundreds of times, and my number has not been announced. I know it will not be much longer until my number comes up. I know that very soon I will live in the beautiful dome.

Today, a woman I do not like wins the lottery. She is standing among unbelievers. She has no battle scars. The woman is very lucky to have won the lottery.

*

Today, the air is the color of tea. Today there are devils among us. Whenever the air is the color of tea, devils come among us. The devils put bad thoughts into our heads—thoughts that make us angry. Our protectors tell us that it is unwise to listen to the devils.

I have listened to a devil today, and today I am very angry. I am angry because our protectors gave out many beautiful banners. The banners are bright and colorful, and they flutter like flames in the wind. The banners declare we are all of one body—that is a very good thing. The banners proclaim that our dome will shine brighter than all the domes in the world.

I am angry because our protectors did not give me a beautiful banner. I have killed many tribesmen from other domes. I have eaten their livers too. I have split open the wombs of their women so they will not be filled with bad seed. Our protectors did not give me a banner, but they gave banners to unbelievers. I am very, very angry at our terrible protectors.

The unbelievers tell me that there are no devils among us. They say it is our protectors who put bad thoughts into our heads. They say I should not be angry because I did not get a banner. They say if I keep bad thoughts in my head, I will not win the lottery.

*

Tomorrow has come. A warm wind is still blowing. The air is not the color of coffee—it is still the color of tea.

There will be a lottery today because the air is the color of tea. A few protectors have set up the stage where the numbers are announced. I am no longer angry at our protectors—my thoughts are good once again. Some unbelievers stand beside me while the lottery wheel revolves.

Today I am very lucky. Today my number comes up. The protector who spun the giant wheel called out, "6-6-0-9." Today I will get to live in the dome and better serve our protectors.

The protector who spun the lottery wheel is looking directly at me. His face is like the face of a statue. His eyes are as blue as a lake. "What will you do for us?" he says. His voice is as pure as a flute.

I walk behind the protectors, and we get inside the float. My thoughts are good today. I am sad that my thoughts were not always good. I am glad our protectors are kind.

31

I see the farms and cattle as we land beside the dome. I see the lakes and the butterflies. I see the orchards and birds. My heart is as light as a sparrow. My thoughts are very good.

I leave the float and follow the protectors into the dome.

*

I have never felt a softer breeze. I have never seen brighter colors. I have never smelled the sweetness of flowers. I have never heard voices so gentle.

I see many buildings that are tall and straight, and I see giant temples too. Wonderful signs sit on top of the temples. The signs say *WE ARE ALL OF ONE BODY*. I see carts being drawn by magnificent horses as I walk towards one of the temples. The carts are full of bodies. They are rolling towards the farmlands. The bodies look like they came from the tribes that live around the dome. There are many, many bodies inside the rolling carts.

I know I will soon be among the bodies that are rolling towards the farmlands. I am glad that I will lie with the bodies—I should not have had angry thoughts. I am glad I will join the bodies while all of my thoughts are good. I am glad the unbelievers told our protectors about my angry thoughts.

Soon, my body will nourish the crops that grow so very tall. It will nourish the fruits and nuts that touch the lips of our protectors. I am glad I will nourish the fruits and nuts. I am glad we are all of one body.

Biff Malibu

MY WIFE, MARY, AND I sit on the deck of The Boatyard, a Sarasota seafood restaurant. Since our retirement, we lunch here several times a month. Mary is eating a hamburger because she is allergic to seafood. I am devouring fish and chips, which I have smothered with malt vinegar.

Mary gazes out onto a channel where seagulls soar like kites. She then looks at me and says, "I'd like to pick your brain. If you could go back in time and change one thing about yourself, what is it you would change and how would it have affected your life?"

"That's two questions," I answer. I feel myself starting to sweat.

"Let's not get technical," Mary says. "You may answer them one at a time."

"What would *you* change about yourself?" I ask.

Mary puts down her burger and sighs. "I'd have been more open to people. I'd have been more spontaneous. I hate to think of all I missed out on simply because I was shy."

"I have done that too," I blurt. "I'd have opened myself up a lot more."

"No, you wouldn't have," says Mary. "My sister is right about you. She says you're the most self-protective person that she has ever met."

"I wouldn't be so self-protective," I say, "if your sister didn't pick me apart."

"Quit trying to change the subject," says Mary. "Just answer me honestly. What would you have changed about yourself and how would it have affected your life?"

I am not a proponent of honesty when a tidy lie will do, but this time I have no option except to tell Mary the truth. "I'd have learned to ride a longboard," I confess, "and I'd have changed my name to Biff."

"Biff?" Mary says.

"Biff Malibu. That's a good name for a surfer dude."

Mary rubs her eyes as though the Florida sun has pricked them. "Your capacity to reinvent yourself never fails to amaze me."

"You told me to be honest," I say.

"I guess I asked for that. So how would learning to longboard have affected your life?"

"Every time I caught a wave, I'd have been sitting on top of the world."

"Hmmm," Mary says. "That's pretty poetic. Hey, wait a minute, mister. Isn't that a line from a Beach Boys' song?"

"The Beach Boys oughta know," I say.

"The Beach Boys never surfed."

"Maybe not," I reply, "but they sure were spontaneous. Drive-in theaters and cha-cha burgers were lifelong values to them."

"They celebrated all that is shallow. Is that what you want to do?"

I shrug. "Why not be shallow if it keeps life simple and fun?"

"Does it have to be as simple as that?" Mary says. "Please tell me again how learning to surf would have affected your life."

"I'd have ridden the breakers at Mavericks. I'd have learned how to shoot the tube, and I'd have taken my pick of the beach bunnies after winning a trophy or two."

"Beach bunnies?" says Mary. "What are those? Are you by any chance referring to women?"

Since Mary has dismissed me as callow, I have nothing more to lose, so I sing a couple of bars from "Surfer Girl." ". . . We could riiide the surf together while our looove would grooow. In my woody, I would taaake you everywhere I go."

"Amazing," says Mary, salting her fries. "I can't believe how banal you are. I ask you to be honest and you give me a fantasy."

"I'm an author," I say. "My business is to create fantasy."

Mary points to a vinegar stain on my chin. After I pick up my napkin and wipe it away, she says, "So *when* would you have written your books?"

"Whenever the surf was slack."

Mary sighs like a schoolmarm on Monday. "Think about what you just said," she replies. "Think of how your book covers would look. *The Siege: A Prison Riot Redefines Justice* . . . by Biff Malibu. *Call Me Pomeroy: A Novel of Satire and Political Dissent* . . . by Biff Malibu. Would anyone have taken you seriously?"

"I'd have been too shallow to care."

"All right," says Mary. "I'm calling your bluff. So why don't you longboard here?"

"Have you seen the waves in the Gulf?" I say. "They aren't even two feet high. The only time I could surf in the Gulf would be during a hurricane."

"Okay, so why didn't you surf before we moved here from San Francisco?"

"I was a probation officer—remember? When would I have found the time? But, thinking back on it now, I wish I had *stolen* the time."

"If you had surfed in California, would you have adopted that stupid name?"

"Of course, I'd have told my probationers that they could call me Biff."

"Do you think they'd have taken you seriously if you'd let them call you Biff?"

"Maybe not," I say, "but I'm sure they'd have complimented my tan."

Mary rolls her eyes and returns her gaze to the channel. "It's amazing to think how much *less* there is to you than meets the eye. Out of all you might have changed in yourself and all you might have accomplished, you'd have chosen to turn your life into a perpetual holiday."

"Shall we change the subject?" I ask her.

"Yes, let's talk about something else."

As Mary stares at the water, I ponder my buoyant soul, and the thought of my life as an endless summer does not disturb me at all. Mary will bring up this subject again—she still hopes to straighten me out. But I see no reason to dwell upon that because somewhere the surf is up.

Do You Do Hits?

I AM A MAGNET for strangers. They approach me in airports, subways, and bars, and they tell me their most compromising secrets. I never solicit these revelations; in fact, I would rather they left me alone. As a compulsive reader, I wholly prefer the company of books. *The Iliad* and *Moby Dick* are such durable friends to me that I prefer reunions with Achilles and Ahab to making a live acquaintance. But strangers tell me their stories— why I do not know. And they tell me stuff that they say they keep hidden from family and friends. Perhaps I ought to warn them that I'm a very poor guardian of secrets, that whatever scripts I find useful, I will mold into tales of my own. So be careful what you tell writers—it may bite you in the ass.

I will now betray the confidence of a fellow named Finian McFaddle. I met him in a sandwich bar in San Francisco's Mission District. A waitress had just brought my order, a hamburger and fries, when he sat at the table beside me—a bald, middle-aged man with a chin so weak that he looked like a giant mole.

"How's the food?" he asked me before I had taken a bite. His voice was thin and whiney, the voice of a practiced complainer. I suspected that if I had told him that my burger was raw, he'd have gladly bawled out the waitress.

Not waiting to hear my reply, he scooted his chair next to my table. "Sheesh," he said, "the service in here is like waiting for Godot."

Were it not for this hint of a literary mind, I'd have taken no interest in him. But his mention of my favorite play made a cloying impression on me. Otherwise, I would have made an excuse to finish my lunch in peace. I would never have put my burger down when he said he had stories to tell me. I would never have stifled a chuckle when he said that his name was Finian McFaddle.

Sadly, he made no mention of Beckett's hapless tramps, perhaps because he considered himself no less intimate with the absurd. His voice bore a wounded assurance that the stars were out of whack, and that he had no choice but to bend my ear to set the record straight. He preceded each of his stories with a guarantee of his victimhood, a claim that suggested that Jesus alone was less deserving of his fate. "Now I was just walking around," he kept saying, "minding my own damn business, and you aren't gonna believe what happened to me next." He described how he'd been a target of several robberies, and he said any crackhead with a knife or a gun considered him an easy mark. "Sheesh," he said, "it's not as though I live in Hunter's Point. I live in the goddamn Sunset District—it's not even a bad neighborhood."

I said, "Do you ever do anything else?"

"Whaddya mean by that?"

"Anything other than walking around minding your own damn business."

"What are ya, some kinda comic?" he snapped. "Ya think I asked to be mugged? Why are you acting like a prick when I'm telling ya sensitive stuff?"

I said, "Why are you bragging about being a victim?"

He plucked a napkin from the dispenser and used it to blow his nose. "It's like what they say about rape," he said as he balled the napkin up. "If ya can't do nothin' about it, it's smart not to put up a fight."

"Who says you can't do something about it?"

He rolled his eyes and sighed like a furnace. "Don'tcha think I tried? The last time I got robbed, I enrolled in this goddamn class. A class called *Verbal Judo and How to Survive a Threat.* I found it on the internet and thought it was worth checking out."

"Was it worth giving up your martyrdom for?"

"Stop being a wise guy," he said. "I gave the fucking class a try, but it didn't work out too well. Shit, you're just not gonna believe what happened to me next."

*

Having resigned myself to being his hostage, I did not expect further abuse. I did not expect Finian McFaddle to ask me to pay for his lunch. But after he flagged down a waitress and ordered a Rueben and garlic fries, he said, "Lend me a jackson, buddy. All I got is a buck."

I said, "That's too much."

He wagged his head. "You some kinda cheapo?" he said. "Do you think I'm the kind of person who won't leave a respectable tip?"

Not wanting to force a scene, I gave him a ten and a five. "That ought to do it," I said. "Not a dollar more."

He tucked the money into his shirt pocket and snorted like a mule. "Ya got no savoir-faire, buddy," he said. "That won't leave much for a tip. Shit, I don't know why I'm bothering to talk to you at all."

After the waitress served him his lunch, Finian began to fidget. He took a bite of his Rueben and said, "The corned beef's too dry." Setting the sandwich aside, he picked up one of his fries.

"Lighten up, buddy," he muttered as he popped the fry into his mouth. "You a reporter or somethin'? Ya look like you're gonna take notes. I'm lucky the press didn't crucify me for what happened to me next."

"I left my pen at home," I said, and that seemed to satisfy him. Shoving his plate aside, he started to tell me the story.

"It all began with that goddamn class. It was held in the Richmond District in the local YMCA, and I hadda pay an Uber driver to get there 'cause parking is a bitch. I also hadda shell out thirty bucks just to get enrolled—just to walk into this room fulla losers and give up half a day of my life.

"Well, the class was run by this woman with diarrhea of the mouth. She gave us a long-winded lecture that was mostly about body language, then she said if ya wanna stop being a victim, you gotta change people's perception of you. Ya gotta take charge of the situation, so they won't keep pulling that crap. Then she spoke about verbal judo, which is nothing but running a con. The trick, she said, is to fool folks into doing what you want 'em to do."

"Like getting them to pay for your lunch," I said.

"Naw, it ain't quite as easy as that. She had us do some role-play so we could master the techniques, then she gave us each a certificate and sent us on our way.

"Now I got Scottish blood in me, so I know how to value a buck. I put the receipt for the class in my wallet—damn, that was thirty whole dollars. I was gonna scream for my money back if that bullshit didn't work."

"How did you plan to test it out?"

"I was gonna walk around, minding my business, and wait for some punk to rob me, and then I was gonna stare him down and put that crap to use. The proof of the pudding is in the eatin'—that's what I always say. And speaking about eatin', are you gonna eat those fries?"

"Why don't you finish your own?" I said.

"They got too much garlic in 'em—I shouldn't have got 'em with garlic. Say, gimme yer fries if you're not gonna eat 'em. I gotta cleanse my pallet."

I passed my untouched plate to him, and he gobbled down my fries. He then belched into a napkin and went on with his story.

"No one gyps Finian McFaddle," he said. "I'm too good at pinching a dollar. But I walked around the Sunset for five whole days, and nobody tried to rob me. So I started strolling around the Tenderloin where it's easier to get rolled. But even in the Tenderloin, nothin' happened to me. There were gangs all over the place, selling drugs and talking shit, but no one tried to shake me down. You'd 'a' thought I was a leper.

"Well, one night I strolled 'round the Tenderloin 'til three o'clock in the morning. Shit, I was gettin' so frustrated, I was about to tear up the receipt. But just before I called it quits and dialed myself an Uber, this kid wandered up to me, and he was holding a handgun. If it weren't for the gun, I'd 'a' laughed at him—he was just some sad little bozo, and his pants were draggin' so bad that I half-expected him to trip. 'Your wallet, please, mister,' he said, and I almost felt sorry for him. His eyes were bloodshot and crusty, his cheeks were acne-scarred, and his gun, a nine mil Glock, was shakin' in his hand.

"'So you want my wallet?' I said to him, and he nodded like a parrot.

"'My baby momma she's sick,' he explained. 'She needs some medicine. I wouldn't be doing this, mister, if it weren't for my baby momma.'

"I handed the punk my wallet and he stuffed it into his pocket, and that's when I decided to change his perception of me. 'Do you do hits?' I asked him. 'I'm lookin' to hire a hitman. There're some folks I wanna have wasted 'cause they keep on fucking with me.'

"Well, the little punk just looked at me like I was speaking Chinese. 'I just want some medicine, mister,' he said. 'It's for my baby mama.'

"I said, 'I'm gonna ask you one more time, so get the shit outta yer ears. What I wanna know is if can I pay you to do hits.'

"'Mister,' he said, 'I don't know nothin' 'bout that.'

"'Then you're worth nothing to *me*,' I said. 'Now you can stick me up for chump change, or you can earn yourself some real money. How are you gonna play it, son? I haven't got all night.'

"The kid just looked at me funny like he still didn't know what to say. Even for a robber, he didn't seem particularly bright. 'Who you be, mister?' he finally asked, and he started chewin' his lip. His teeth looked kinda old like he'd been smokin' too much crack.

"Now I hadda tell him my real name 'cause my wallet was in his pants pocket. He had only to check my driver's license to find out if I was lying to him. So I looked at him like he was a bug and I was thinkin' 'bout squashin' him flat. 'My name is Finian McFaddle,' I said, 'and I'd like my wallet back. I also wanna know if you got the balls to do hits.'"

*

When our waitress passed by our table, Finian ordered a glass of iced tea. "Make it sweet, blondie," he said, "and don't skimp on the ice."

He asked me to lend him another five dollars, and he cursed when I shook my head. "What ya loaned me will leave 'bout a dollar once I pay the check. Even if I throw in the buck in my wallet, that won't be much of a tip. One plus one is just two, buddy boy—ya want me to look like a miser?"

"Just tell me the rest of the story," I said.

"Paaatience, paaatience," he crooned. "All this goddamn talking has given me cotton mouth."

The waitress returned with a glass of iced tea and planted it on our table, and Finian took a lingering sip then wrinkled his mouth like a prune. "*Paw*," he snapped. "It's too damn sweet. She musta put cough syrup in it."

"Are you going to finish your story?" I said.

"Quit naggin' me, buddy," he snapped. "I'll finish it a damn sight quicker if ya show some courtesy.

"Now the little punk handed my wallet back and he said, 'Who you want dusted, mister?' I told him he could start by smoking the mayor, and I'd pay him five grand for that. I ain't sure why I put a hit on the mayor—that was kind of a rash thing to do. But in the heat of the moment, I couldn't think of any other way to take charge.

"The kid's eyes got bigger 'an doorknobs, and he put his gun back in his pocket. He said, 'Why you speakin' to me 'bout that? If you got that kinda money, mister, you could hire some Mafia dude.'

"I guess the kid needed confidence, so I decided to stroke his ego. I invited him to this all-night diner so we could discuss a deal. After we both ordered breakfast, I said I'd give him a trial. I told him to return to the diner tomorrow night, and I'd hand him a thousand dollars. I said he would get the other four grand after he knocked off the mayor. What I didn't tell him was that I'd be waiting for him with the cops.

"Ya know, that kid was so fucking dumb that I got him to pay for my breakfast. I told him I needed the cash in my wallet to take an Uber to the bank. I said I expected great things from him, and we bumped fists to seal the deal. And then I went home and had the best night's sleep I had in years."

*

Pausing in his monologue, Finian pointed at my plate. "Ya gonna eat that burger?" he asked me. "Ya haven't taken a bite."

"You may as well have it," I said. "You've already eaten my fries."

"Don't act so high and mighty," he snapped. "It's gotta be cold by now."

He called the waitress back to our table and handed her my plate. "Give it a sizzle, Sugar Tits," he said. "I like my hamburgers hot."

"Will you finish the story?" I asked him. "What happened to that kid?"

"Can ya wait another damn minute?" he said. "I gotta take a piss."

Before I could answer, he rose from the table and shuffled towards the john. I considered leaving the restaurant, so he wouldn't squeeze me for a bigger tip, but he owed me the rest of the story—I had paid for it with my lunch. Suppressing my better instincts, I waited for him to return.

"Lemme give ya a warning," he said as he ambled back to the table. "Someone pissed on the floor of that bathroom. Ya don' wanna go in there."

"Your burger is ready," I told him. "Sugar Tits warmed it up."

He sat back down at the table and picked the burger up with one hand. "Ya mind if I eat it first?" he said. "I don't want it to cool while I'm talking."

He took a bite and made a face. "It's overcooked," he groused, but he devoured the burger in several more bites than leaned back in his chair.

"All right," he said, "here's what happened. The next day I went to the Tenderloin Police Station to set a trap for the kid. I walked into the station and I bellied up to the counter, and I saw this gray-haired sergeant nodding off behind the bulletproof glass. So I hammered on the glass to wake the asshole up, and I told him, 'My name is Finian McFaddle. I wanna file a report.'

"Well, the cop stared at me like he knew my name, and he handed me a report form, and while I was scribblin', this dyke detective came waddling up to me. She was holdin' her cuffs in a pistol grip and clicking the strands into place, and she looked so goddamn grouchy that she hadda be on the rag. I said to her, 'Sister, would ya mind not breathin' down my neck?' And she said, 'Would you mind dropping the pen, sir, and putting your hands behind your back?'

"Well, before I knew it, I was wearin' the bracelets and she was reading me my rights. I said to her, 'What's the charge?' and ya wanna know what she said? She said, 'Conspiring to assassinate an elected official. We have a witness, sir.'

"I said, 'Who do ya think you're messing with, sister—some rube off a turnip truck? I've got a master's degree in English, and I'm gonna sue you seven times over.'

"The dyke said, 'Congratulations, sir. I have a doctorate in jurisprudence.' The bitch thanked me for coming into the station and saving the cops some trouble. She said the city's tactical unit was tryin' to hunt me down.

"She fitted me with leg irons then frog-marched me out to this squad car, and she told me to watch my mouth as she shoved me into the back seat. I told her I needed to take a pee, but she didn't give a shit. She just sat there waiting for backup, and soon a whole buncha cop cars pulled up. Next thing ya know, I was getting booked in that jail on Seventh Street."

*

Digging his thumbnail into a toothpick, Finian peeled off a sliver of wood. He then used the sliver to pick his teeth, smacking his lips as he worked. "The trouble with toothpicks," he said, "is that they make 'em too damn big."

45

After paying his check with the money I gave him, he kept on picking his teeth. When the waitress handed him his change, he gave her a sporty wink.

"How did they find a witness?" I asked. "There was only you and the kid."

"The kid *was* the witness?" said Finian. "Can you believe that crap? He went to the Tenderloin Station and dropped a dime on me."

His nostrils flared as he told me this, then he waited for me to reply. I said, "You shouldn't have hired the kid without checking his resumé."

"Yeah," said Finian, still picking his teeth. "He was just a little pussy. Ya know, he was even sitting in court when I went for my arraignment. The judge told the little fucker that he was a mighty fine citizen."

I said, "Why would some punk in the Tenderloin decide to become a snitch?"

"All I can say," said Finian, "is that one and one ain't always two. But at least the kid came to his senses by the time my case went to trial. He didn't show up for the hearing, and the court couldn't locate him. But I spent three months in the slammer before the judge dismissed the case."

"Maybe the gangs put a hit on the kid."

"Naw, that ain't what happened. After they let me outta the hoosegow, the little shit robbed me again. It was only a coupla weeks later and I was sittin' in Golden Gate Park, and that same damn kid came up to me and pulled a gun outta his pants. 'I need some money, mister,' he said. 'My baby momma she's sick.' He didn't even recognize me, he just pointed the gun at my chest."

"Did you give him some verbal judo?" I asked.

"Fuck that," Finian said. He wiped his mouth, rose from the table, and put down a two-dollar tip. "I gave the kid my wallet and figgered I'd got off cheap."

The Bog Runs

Author's Note: Fifty years ago, feeling like a prisoner of the American Dream, I took a job on a cattle station in the Never-Never. The memory of this indiscretion grows stronger every year.

THE MOMENT I STEPPED OUT of the Land Rover, I was assailed by hordes of flies. Ravenous, sweat-thirsty bush flies that covered my face like a mask. The flies were my first impression of Birdstone Station, a remote cattle outpost in the Top End of Australia's Northern Territory. The station consisted of a drab cookhouse, a squalid drovers' barracks and a corral filled with spindly horses. It did not impress me as much as the flies.

"How long until you get used to them?" I asked Jim Cooper, the rangy head stockman who had picked me up at the Darwin Airport. He was a weathered man with a permanent squint, and he had driven me two hundred miles to this remote, forbidding place. Most of our drive was on a graded dirt road through an endless scrub of tea trees. Fascinated, I watched as big red boomers and blue-tinted does leaped out of the path of the Land Rover and thud-thud-thudded away to vanish among these slender paperbark trees. Would this be a cure for the restlessness that had made me drop out of a midwestern American college, catch a tramp freighter to Australia and talk a cattle company in Brisbane

47

into flying me to the Top End? I had lied when I said I was a cowboy, and I had hoped to get away with the lie. As I swatted at the flies, I now realized the worthlessness of my deceit.

"How long?" Jim Cooper said with a laugh. "Mate, you never get used to them."

"They're enough to drive you mad," I said, spitting a fly off my lips.

"My oath," said Jim, "but if you weren't mad to start with, you wouldn't come here in the first place. Even the abos don't hang around long. We used to have a crew of blackfellows—blokes who were *born* to the land. The bloody lot of them went walkabout a couple of days ago."

"Why would they want to go walkabout?"

"Only an abo knows," said Jim. "They go walkabout all the time. The only reason we hire them is that no one else suits the land."

Will this cure my suburban boredom? I wondered as my eyes drifted back to the scrub. The impenetrable sweep of paperbarks was a bleak yet thrilling sight. Perhaps I would still find less to be missed as a drover in the Northern Territory.

"It's not civilization," I conceded. "Or anything close to it."

"Forget about being civilized," said Jim. "Only madness will help you out here. Besides, there's nobody on this station but us and a drunken cook."

Had I come too far? I speculated as I tried not to breathe in the flies. *In my quest to find an adventure, had I fallen into an abyss?*

As though reading my mind, Jim shook his head and patted me on the shoulder. "Mate, the Outback has no use for the nonsense that brought you here. If you listen closely to the land, you oughta hear it laughing at you."

"Maybe it will look better from horseback," I said. I was not unfamiliar with horses, having grown up riding them in Brazil

48

when I was a State Department brat. Was it my love of horses that had spurred my wanderlust?

"Crikey," Jim replied. "If your horse steps in a pig hole, you'll get thrown and break a leg. After that, you'll either die of thirst or the wild pigs will eat you up."

Was he teasing me? I wondered. I attempted a joke of my own. "What if I take a canteen and a shotgun?"

Jim snorted and rolled his eyes. "If you regard the Outback too lightly, mate, there's a lot more ways you can die. A water buffalo might gore you, a bush fire might suffocate you, or you might get so lost in the scrub that you'll ride in circles all day. Unless you have a blackfellow with you, you won't last long out there."

"Suppose I go walkabout too," I said. "Maybe I'll run into one."

"We still have a job to do here," said Jim. "You don't need to go looking for blackfellows—they'll come to us when they're ready."

A hint of movement caught my eye, distracting me from the flies. It was a sand-colored wallaby inching toward a creek as though undecided if it would drink.

"So we're not going to muster cattle," I groused.

"Not 'til the abos get back," said Jim. "Two white blokes aren't enough to handle a mob of untamed cattle."

"When do you expect them back?"

Jim popped open a tin of tobacco and rolled a cigarette. Tremors in his calloused hands suggested early Parkinson's disease. "A week or two—no worries," he said. "The buggers always come back. When they're done with their bloody walkabouts, they want to earn money for grog."

"So what's this job you have for us?"

"The bog runs," Jim said. "That much we can manage. We'll do the bog runs, mate."

*

The following morning, we started the day with a breakfast of bully beef. A surly cook fried it up for us and served it with beetroot and tea. He also made us some bully beef sandwiches, which he tucked into brown paper bags.

As we settled into the Land Rover, I commented on our breakfast. "How come we have to eat spam?" I said. "We're on a cattle station."

"Have you seen the cattle here?" Jim muttered. "They're nothing but hide and bone."

The Land Rover jounced aggressively as we traveled beside the creek. Jim said we were heading towards Darkie's Hole, one of the farthest paddocks on the station. Steering the Land Rover skillfully, he maneuvered it through a village of termite castles—towering, reddish structures that looked like ancient ruins.

"I wish I was back on the Alice," said Jim. "This country belongs to the pigs."

He was referring to Alice Springs, a cattle town in the Territory's Red Centre. In the days to come, Jim would talk frequently about the stations near Alice Springs. That his wife had died on one of these stations, her blood poisoned by an ironwood splinter, did not diminish the reverence with which Jim spoke about the heart of Australia. "But I left the Alice after she passed," he said. "That was over a year ago. A drought killed so many cattle that there wasn't much work to be found."

"What was her name?" I asked.

"Ileana," he said, "but that's a bit of a mouthful. I called her Helen for short. Now I've had better pokes from the lubras, but we were married for almost three years. And all she could do was nag me about going to live in Brisbane. I finally told her she could go with me blessing, but she passed before that could happen. An ironwood splinter, the size of a pin—that's what did her in."

We rode for an hour in silence then entered a sweeping, fenced paddock. Emaciated cattle watched me suspiciously when

I opened then shut the gate. As we drove on, we passed through savannah dotted with eucalyptus brush, and an emu sprinted alongside us as though challenging us to a race. The country was so epic that the paddocks all had names. "We just entered Horse Paddock," Jim explained. "The next one is Flying Fox Paddock. Around noon, we'll come to Darkie's Hole and that's where we'll check the bogs."

*

When we spotted a dingo, Jim cursed and brought the Land Rover to a stop. The dingo was lying by a patch of cane grass, which was no more than a stone's throw away. It perked its ears and looked at us as though we were alien beings.

Retrieving a high-powered rifle from the boot, Jim aimed at the gaunt, yellow dog. "This three-oh-three will bring him to justice," he said as he steadied his aim. "Dingoes are the only buggers I know who will kill for the sport of it."

The gun boomed—the dingo yelped then trotted into the cane grass. "Got him," said Jim. "He'll die in there once he finds a hole to lie down in."

Jim put the Land Rover back into gear, and we continued towards Darkie's Hole. "In Queensland, they put up fences to stop them," he said. "But no fence ever stopped a dingo from killing a mob of sheep."

"How long since you were in Queensland?" I said.

Jim scowled. "Not long enough. I served two years in Boggo Road Jail—that was twenty years ago. After I served me time, I left that bloody state for good. Been in the Territory ever since."

"Why were you put in jail?" I asked.

"Queensland has too much law," said Jim. "The coppers charged me with the rape of a minor, but a fair go is what it was—a little Tasmanian whore who lied about her age. She did five other blocks before she fucked me then she tried to charge me a tenner for sloppy seconds. The tart ran straight to the cop shop when I wouldn't cough it up."

I nodded with genuine sympathy, not doubting Jim's tale for a moment. Instead, I could only envy his fierce independence of spirit.

Entering Flying Fox paddock, we drove through a towering fig-tree grove. The sinewy bark of the fig trees looked like bodies blended in wood. Jim downshifted the Land Rover to a crawl and guided it through the trees.

A burst of piercing shrieks announced our arrival in the grove. High above us, the sky was black with countless flying foxes. The racket they were making suggested that Judgment Day had come.

*

I opened a final gate when we arrived at Darkie's Hole. The paddock was a mudflat with a scattering of billabongs. As we rolled towards one of the billabongs, I was struck by a rotting aroma, a smell so penetrating that it grew difficult to breathe.

The billabong was a mile in length and as wide as a football field. It was littered with cattle that had come to drink and sunk to their shoulders in mud. Mobs of feral pigs were feeding on the cattle, pigs as black as the tar-colored mud that held the cattle fast. The pigs bounded across the mudflat as we approached the billabong, and a falcon rose above them, emitting its prehistoric cry.

Jim drove along the bank of the pond, inspecting the helpless cattle. Most appeared to be dead or in various stages of dying. A few were lowing plaintively and struggling to free themselves, but the majority looked as passive as Hindu monks in prayer.

"Look at their shit," Jim advised me. "That will tell you which ones might be saved. If the shit is old and crusty, the bugger is long-past saving. If the shit is fresh, that means the poor sod might have a bit of a chance."

Many of the cattle had been partially eaten, including some that were still alive. Jim parked beside a trembling bull and handed me the .303. The beast had several deep wounds where the pigs had gobbled its flesh, wounds that shrank then expanded as the animal labored to breathe. I looked at his shit. It was drier than wood.

"Do the right thing," Jim said.

I held the rifle as though it might burn me. "How do I do the right thing?"

"Stand over the bugger then trace an X between its horns and its eyes. Shoot in the middle of the X. That'll do the job."

Having never shot anything before, I sat as though paralyzed. I then slipped out of the Land Rover and slogged towards the beast. It looked at me indifferently as I hobbled through the mud.

My heart hammered as I stood over the animal and traced the imaginary X. I pointed the rifle at the center of the X and took a shallow breath. As I pulled the trigger, I flinched as though slugged. The gun did not make a sound.

"Take off the safety," Jim called.

I released what I thought was the safety and aimed a second time. The gun spoke as I squeezed the trigger, the butt slammed into my shoulder, and a hole the size of a penny appeared in the forehead of the beast. The animal shuddered as though electrified then died with a passive grunt.

"Good on ya, mate," Jim called, but I did not feel worthy of praise. Instead, it seemed that I had done something so vile it could never be repaired. If ordered to do such a job today, I'd have handed back the gun.

We continued our drive along the billabong, and I executed a dozen more cattle. Each time I traced an imaginary X then shot the beast in the forehead. With each successive killing, the job grew easier.

Finally, we came upon a heifer that appeared to be salvageable. She was struggling furiously in the mud, and her shit was olive green. At Jim's direction, I unhooked a steel cable from a winch bolted to the bull bar then I waded into the muck and looped the cable over her horns. The heifer bawled and stiffened when Jim activated the winch. Seconds later, she slithered out of the mud as though the pond had given her birth.

I unhooked the cable from the animal's horns—she lumbered to her feet. Her eyes were bright with fury, and she kept bawling as though possessed. When she dropped her horns and charged me, I tried to leap aside, but a horn scraped my chest so deeply that it felt like the tip on a knife.

In an instant, Jim jumped from the Land Rover and grabbed the heifer's tail. When she turned and tried to hook him, he shouted, "You bloody, mongrel bitch!" He skillfully yanked the tail—the animal collapsed in a heap—then he wound the tail under a hindquarter and spread the legs apart.

"Come here and hold her," Jim ordered. "I'm gonna fetch the snippers. Mate, next time you turn loose a bogger, make sure you first shorten its horns."

I gripped the animal's tail. "You might have *told* me that first."

My remark—an attempt to be witty—was like whistling in a morgue. It could not compete with dying cattle, the carnage wrought by the pigs or a stench so overpowering that it almost enveloped us.

Jim halved the beast's horns with a huge pair of pruners while I kept pulling up on the tail. When Jim was done with the pruning, he told me to let the animal go.

"She has no fight left in her," Jim said, and we walked back to the Land Rover. "She'll sit there awhile and then she'll probably bog herself again."

He turned the winch back on. The cable retreated like a snake. As we drove away, the heifer watched us with uncomprehending eyes.

*

We hauled several more cattle out of the billabong as the afternoon wore on. I snipped off the tips of their horns with the pruners before Jim turned on the winch. After the winch hauled the beast from the mud, I nervously freed what was left of its horns. If the animal rose and charged me, I followed Jim's example—leaping behind it, grabbing its tail then jerking it off its feet.

"You'd think they'd be grateful we saved them," I grumbled as we continued our drive around the pond.

Jim snorted then spat through the driver's side window. "We're *saving* them for the slaughterhouse," he said, "if we ever get them there. Mate, you're a bit of a yobbo if you expect them to be grateful."

"They don't *know* they're going to be butchered," I insisted, "and it's better than being eaten by pigs."

"So you'd rather those poor, bloody bah-sterds got eaten by people instead?"

We followed the bank of the Daly River as we headed back to the station. It was a huge silty waterway, a quarter-mile wide, that wound towards the Timor Sea. Jim stopped the Land Rover whenever he spotted a beast bogged in the riverbank, and I scrambled down the thirty-foot embankment and hooked the cable over its horns. The horns plowed ruts into the dirt as the animal was dragged up the slope, sometimes to clear the top of the bluff and lie panting on the ground, other times to topple back into the river, its skull popped off like a bottle cap. The corpse, sweeping downriver, would vanish in a boil of water, dragged beneath the surface by saltwater crocodiles.

"Now those crocs won't attack you on land," Jim said, "so you don't need to worry about them. Not unless you're as small as a wallaby, you don't." Despite this assurance, I studied the water whenever I hooked up a beast. When I spotted floatage, I convinced myself it was a log from a mangrove tree. I was always surprised when the "log" changed direction then moved against the current.

A blood-red sunset reddened the clouds when we finally got back to the station. My pores were itchy from bulldust, so I took a dip in the creek. A flock of magpie geese scolded me as I plunged into the water—their primeval cries as old as the dawn of time itself. The creek was cool and cleansing, so I splashed about for an hour, but the fetid stench from the billabong remained in my lungs and throat.

*

The next morning, Jim tossed a few packs of cartridges into the boot of the Land Rover. "We're going to have a bit of a pig cleanup," he said after he slipped behind the wheel.

As we headed back to Darkie's Hole, I looked stoically at the land. It was not a place of promise—a place to be hustled or tamed. As we jounced along, I could almost swear that I heard it laughing at me.

Jim talked about his departed wife as we traveled alongside the creek. "The Red Centre was driving her troppo," he muttered. "I don't think she could have survived it. So I said she could leave with me blessing, but a splinter took her life."

"I'm sorry you couldn't save her," I said.

"She wasn't a bad sort," Jim replied.

Once we were back in Darkie's Hole, Jim told me to reload the rifle. The pigs had returned to the billabong and were feasting on the bogged cattle. A few of the cattle were bellowing as the pigs tore into their flesh.

JAMES HANNA

I slipped a magazine into the .303 then I tucked a clip into the chamber. Closing the bolt, I felt a delicious thrill of anticipation.

"I'll run them down and you shoot them," said Jim. "Do you think you can manage that, mate?"

"Let's do it," I said. I felt no compassion for the gluttons we were about to kill. As I watched them tear into the cattle, I knew I would have no trouble shooting them.

Jim flattened the accelerator, and we charged the billabong. The pigs scattered in clusters across the flat. We bore down on the largest group.

A huge boar with an injured hind leg was limping behind the rest. I freed the safety and took careful aim as we captured ground on him. Before I could shoot, Jim swerved towards the boar and struck him with the bull bar. Squealing with terror, he bounced off the bar and collapsed on my side of the Rover. I fired—missed. The boar lumbered to its feet like an old man getting out of bed. Hooking blindly with one of his tusks, he lunged in our direction.

Panicked, I ejected the shell and fired a second time. The slug slammed into the snout of the boar, and it rolled onto its back. The boar started squealing so lustily that I felt I had pumped life into him. I kept firing, my hands shaking so badly I could barely control my aim. The slugs thwacked rhythmically into the pig as though I were beating a carpet.

Once the boar lay still, Jim gave me a bit of advice. "Take your time shooting," he said. "You're wasting too many bullets."

"I was shitting my pants," I protested.

Jim chuckled and watched me reload. "If you shoot them behind the shoulder, you won't have that problem, mate."

We continued to chase the pigs and caught up with a bunch more. Most were sows with litters of piglets scampering behind them. Following Jim's instructions, I shot some behind their shoulders. In less than a minute, several more pigs lay still upon the ground.

Jim stopped the Land Rover and frowned. "The sucklings too," he instructed. "The dirty, little runts will starve without their mums."

As I watched the litters of piglets crowding around the dead sows, some vestige of conditioning made me put the rifle down.

"Pity won't help them, mate," Jim said. "Here, I'll show you what needs to be done."

Matter-of-factly, Jim picked up the rifle and inserted a couple of clips. He then stepped out of the Rover and shot the piglets one by one.

After he had killed the piglets, Jim said. "Let's have ourselves a smoko." He leaned the rifle against the Land Rover and gathered a few sticks of scrubwood. Placing the sticks in a teepee-shaped pile, he set them ablaze with a lighter. We squatted while the crackling wood heated water in a billycan.

That this netherworld included a tea break was puzzling to me. The Outback, in all its darkness, had ingested me with such ease that I felt undeserving of anything that might give me a momentary break. But the water started to jump in the billy, and Jim dropped in a handful of tea leaves then he fetched a couple of pannikins and filled them with boiling tea.

My hand trembled as I accepted a pannikin. I took a sip of tea. It tasted so bitter, I spat it out.

"Would you like some sugar?" said Jim.

*

We ran the bogs for several more days, and the chore seemed increasingly futile. What cattle we managed to save usually bogged themselves by the next day, but Jim seemed fiercely determined to salvage what beasts he could. We also kept slaughtering pigs, and at first I aimed over their heads. But when I saw them eating the bodies of the swine we had already killed, I lost all restraint and shot as many as I could. After a week of bog runs, I was weary and disgusted. "You know," I said, "only Sisyphus has a task that's worse than ours."

"I don't know the bloke," said Jim, "but he must have a cunt of a job."

We stopped working the bogs the next morning when the aboriginals returned to the station. They were a rail-thin lot with sunny demeanors and tribal scars on their chests. I gave them a nod and they gave me their friendship—it was as basic as that. And they turned out to be the most charitable people that I had ever met. They helped me catch my horses when we prepared for the morning musters, and they rescued me whenever I managed to lose myself in the scrub. I reciprocated by cantering behind them as they chased down enormous scrub bulls. They would jump from their saddles and topple the beasts by jerking on their tails, and if a bull got away then charged them, I would lift them onto my horse. They called me bungi—their word for mate—and they grew closer to me than brothers.

I did not evolve into much of a stockman—I rode too poorly for that—but at least I could stick to the saddle when we rounded the cattle up, and at least I could amble behind the herds and coax the stragglers along. And I grew adept at spurring my horses away from pig holes and feral boars, and one day I hung on when a spooked Appaloosa tried to buck me off.

But the Outback had killed me as surely as my adventures had set me free. Whenever I think of the bog runs, I still hear it laughing at me.

The Good Pimp

WHILE SITTING IN A Starbucks on Mission Street, I met a splendid pimp. The breakfast crowd had dispersed when he ambled into the restaurant, and he gave me a friendly nod before sitting down at the table beside me. He was a towering man with a heavy, black beard and a menacing scar on his cheek, but his eyes were as kind as a minister's and softer than poached eggs. "Good morning," he said, his voice as smooth as butter. He was toting a leather briefcase, which he placed upon the floor, and he gazed at me like a spaniel hoping to gobble a tidbit.

"Have you tried the strudel?" he asked me. "All my girls love the strudel. I assure you it's the finest in all of San Francisco."

Having already sampled the nut bread, I was about to leave the restaurant, but the fellow seemed so amiable that I chose to stay and chat.

"If *all* your daughters like it," I said, "I'm sure it's as good as you say."

"Not my daughters—my *girls*," he replied. "Sir, I work as a pimp."

He was gazing at me so warmly that I felt neither shock nor distrust. But I wasn't sure just how to reply to what sounded like a confession. "I take it you have no daughters," I muttered tonelessly.

He waved at a passing waitress, catching her attention. "Two strudels," he said. "My friend here will join me."

Removing a cell phone from his briefcase, he read some text messages. Afterward, he muted the ringer and tucked the phone into his pocket. "I manage twelve girls," he said. "They are *such* a lot of work. But my guilt would be unbearable if I walked away from them."

"Maybe they'd be better off," I suggested.

"How I wish that was true," he replied. "But that would only happen if I were a terrible pimp."

I said, "I don't care for prostitutes. Not even well-managed ones."

He chuckled. "I'm aware of that, sir. I've been in this business for thirty years. I know how to spot a john."

"So what do you want from me?"

He reached over and patted my wrist. "Sharing my burden with strangers refreshes me, my friend. That and reading the Bible, I try hard to be worthy of it."

When the waitress returned with two plates of strudel, setting them down on our table, he sighed like a kettle, fished into his pocket and gave her a twenty-dollar bill. He seemed to be disappointed that strudel didn't cost more.

I said, "For a pimp, you sound very conflicted."

He took a large bite of his strudel and wiped a crumb from his lip. He said, "I long to give it up—I'm *so* tired of being a pimp. But I tremble to think what would become of my girls if I lay my burden down."

"Could they keep the money they earn?" I asked.

He said, "That would be a disaster—they would only spend it on crack. That's why I pocket their earnings and give them my heart instead."

"Isn't that rather presumptuous?"

He shrugged. "Their families want nothing to do with them, they cannot hang onto their boyfriends. And so, it falls to a pimp to meet all their emotional needs."

"That's a pretty big burden for pimps," I said.

He replied, "It's a cross I must bear. If left on their own, my girls would be helpless—the streets would eat them alive." He plucked a napkin from a dispenser and blotted his sweat-beaded brow. "No, I could never forgive myself if I ever abandoned my girls."

"What makes you such a wonderful pimp?"

"I always put my girls first. I buy them the best of contraceptives, so they won't pick up a disease. I have a doctor check them out three times every month. My door is always open to them whenever they have a problem. Oh, the stories they tell me, but I listen to them like a priest."

"You let them screw strangers," I blurted.

"They would do that anyway."

"You make money off their bodies."

"That isn't my mission, sir. My mission is to keep them healthy. My duty is to keep them safe. I love my girls like daughters, and I guard them with my life."

I did not wish to savor the novelty of sympathizing with a pimp—not even a pimp as personable as this one appeared to be. I pushed my strudel away from me and told him I had to go.

"Finish your strudel first," he begged. "I assure you it's very good."

"You've told me more than I need to hear."

"But you haven't heard half of it, sir. Every Christmas and Easter, I throw my girls a party. Once a month, I rent a bus and take them for a drive along the coast. And, oh how they love the movies, we go every Monday night. I treat them to buckets of popcorn and all the soda they can drink."

"How can you say you buy them treats when they provide the money?"

He looked at me with wounded eyes then spoke as though I had slugged him. "How can you ask such a question?" he said. "Do you know that I'm the most sought-after pimp in all of San Francisco? Do you know that hundreds of girls have begged me to take them into my fold? But twelve girls are all I can manage if I am to do my darlings justice. Although it breaks my heart, I turn many girls away."

"Have any of them ever left *you*?" I asked.

He smiled. "That happened just once. Since you haven't finished your strudel, would you like to hear the story? The story will surely convince you that I am the finest of pimps.

"Her name was Judy, and she was a beautiful but very headstrong girl. She had only been turning tricks for a month, and she had so much to learn. One day, she called me a bloodsucker, and said she would not work for popcorn. She insisted I give back the money she'd earned, and she said she was leaving me. Well, I paid her back every penny she'd earned and a hundred dollars more. I said she had my blessing even though she had spoken to me so unkindly. I warned her that the streets were too perilous for a girl to work on her own.

"Three months later, I spotted her at the corner of Turk Street and Polk. Her arms were littered with track marks, her eyes were darting like lizards, and her nose had been broken so many times that much of her beauty was gone. I insisted she tell me what happened to her, and she wept as she poured out her heart. She told me how she'd been beaten, she told me how she'd been raped, she said she lived in fear for her life every day she was on the street.

"Well, I gave the foolish girl a hug, and I kissed away her tears. When I agreed to take her back again, she cried like a newborn child. I bought her a satin evening gown to replace the rags she was wearing, and I took her on a dinner cruise to celebrate her return to the flock. The other girls were angry when I told them

I'd booked her a cruise. 'Why should she get a cruise?' they cried. 'She treated you like a pig.' I told them not to be angry, I told them instead to rejoice. 'Your sister was lost and now is found'—that's what I said to them."

"Your kindness sounds plagiaristic," I said.

"Is that such a bad thing, my friend? Would you rather I scorned the Gospels and left her to die on the streets? Sir, I'm not that kind of man."

"I get it," I said. "You're a wonderful pimp—the best in all the city."

"Please finish your strudel," he said. "I have a favor to ask of you." He opened up his briefcase and removed a ream of fliers. "If you would pass out just a few of them, I will be your servant too."

Up to that moment, the fellow's delusions had struck me as insular—the haven of a complacent crook sentimentalizing his crimes. But the content of the fliers suggested his fantasies had no such bounds. He was unapologetically running for city councilman.

"You're kidding," I said.

"My friend," he replied. "Why would I kid about this?"

"You're a slaver," I said. "A parasite. You live off of women's bodies."

"No, my friend, I am more like a seed that has fallen on thorn and rock. If cast upon fertile soil, where the sun will not shrink my roots, I will produce a bounty a hundred times greater than what I am yielding today. Think of it, sir, all the whores in the city will fall under my protection. They will get the best of medical care, they will live in safety and ease, and the police will no longer throw them in vans then haul them off to jail."

"I can't believe you're serious," I said.

"Why do you question me, sir? Do you think I lack pity because I'm a pimp? Do you find me insincere? Do you doubt that I love my girls like Jesus loved Mary Magdalene? You said you don't care for prostitutes. Be glad that somebody does."

Pushing his chair back, he shook my hand. His grip was like that of a python.

He said, "You're a very good listener, my friend. You have lightened my load a great deal. You could ease it even further if you pass out a few of those fliers."

Not knowing how else to get rid of him, I told him to leave the fliers. I had no intention of passing them out, but I did not wish to deride him further. If this sanctimonious man was a fool, he was clearly his own fool, not mine.

"Thank you," he said. "There's so much to get done. But finish your strudel first."

As he walked out of the restaurant, I looked at the stack of fliers. Selecting one, I folded it up and tucked it into my pocket. I had to admit that I had just met a very splendid pimp.

Urban Cowboy

I AM HYPERVIGILANT. I have an exaggerated flinch response. Whenever I lock a door, I go back and check it three times. These are the emotional limps I acquired while I was a San Francisco probation officer, a job that let me boast that I was an urban cowboy. So consoling was this image that my PTSD seemed secondary; even today I would venture to say that my glory was cheaply bought. How proud I was of my duty belt, my handcuffs, my two-way radio. How proud I was of the Glock 40 that I usually kept in my locker at work. I even affected a lazy drawl and walked with a gunfighter's swagger, and at times I kept a cheroot clamped between my teeth.

When Mary, my wife, said I looked like Clint Eastwood, I was quick to correct her. "You could say he looks like *me*," I replied. "I'm a real peace officer. Clint Eastwood is shooting blanks."

"Well, maybe you shouldn't be so cocky about putting people in jail."

"Nabbing bad guys goes with the job," I drawled. "I can't get hung up on it. I don't try and understand them—I just tie and throw and brand them."

"Hmm," she said. "That's kind of profound," then recognition dawned on her face. "Hey, that's the theme song from *Rawhide*," she scoffed. "That TV show in the sixties where Clint Eastwood got his start."

"Yeah," I said, "but it's my song now. I *deserve* it more than Clint Eastwood."

Sometimes people would ask me how many arrests I had made. Whenever this happened, I feigned nonchalance and said, "Maybe two or three hundred." I spoke without inflection, as though reciting a grocery list, and I did not bother to mention just how the arrests took place. When it came to the ticklish business of putting people in jail, the San Francisco Probation Department was averse to taking risks. We never made our busts on the streets where bystanders might intervene; instead, we lured our clients to the probation department and arrested them in teams. No rough and tumble for us, no roping and throwing for us. Why risk a bruise or a fractured skull when a timely lie would suffice? So whenever I received a complaint that one of my clients was misbehaving, I conjured up a pretense to bring him to my office. Usually, I would ask him to report for a piss test or to sign some paperwork, but when it came to pathological stalkers I had a more original line. Most of them had rescue fantasies where their victims were concerned, and I shamelessly exploited their delusions to get them hooked and booked. For instance, a stalker once told me that his victim was being abused by her father, so I called the stalker on his cell phone when I learned he was lurking outside her home.

"Jimmy Wong," I said when he answered my call. "I need you in my office at once."

"What's happenin', Mister Hanna?"

"Your girlfriend's in trouble—we have reason to believe that her father's still molesting her. I need you to tell me everything you know about him. I want to lock that pervert up."

In less than fifteen minutes, Jimmy Wong knocked on my office door, and I was waiting for him with a pair of detectives from the San Francisco Police Department.

"Not again," Jimmy said as we hooked him up.

"Thanks for reporting," I said, and I gave him a pat on his shoulder as we perp-walked him to jail.

Yes, I was more conman than cowboy, more bluffer than buckaroo. And I compulsively kept the odds in my favor when I cuffed a client up. My odds grew ridiculously high one day when I was taking a sex offender to jail—a client who attempted to bolt after I collared him for possessing child porn. I was accompanied by two burly detectives from the San Francisco Sex Crimes Unit, and the client broke away from all three of us as we entered the jail sally port. The moment he was loose, a dozen deputy jailers, responding to an alert signal, poured through the electronic jail door and wrestled him to the ground. When I thought of Clint Eastwood single-handedly gunning down three or four bad guys, I had to admit that fifteen to one were not very sporting odds.

On one rare occasion, I left the building to bust a client who lived in Oakland—a former head nurse on probation for stalking a woman she barely knew. She had been spotted outside of her victim's home cutting the telephone wires, and she had failed to report when I called her on her cell phone and tried to trick her into coming to my office. Since this woman seemed dangerously nuts, I teamed up with an Oakland task force—a gang of deputy sheriffs assigned to an apprehension squad. They were a cavalier, good-natured lot with a gallows sense of humor. "Oh shit, that's my sister," one of them said when I showed them my client's mug shot.

Had I made a deal with the Devil by so overplaying my hand—by summoning an entire posse to bust one mentally ill woman? If so, I received the Devil's wages when we broke into her rented room. My client was not there so I could not hook her up, and a search for weapons produced only a penknife and several enormous dildos. When I told Mary about this adventure, she offered a joke of her own. "A pack of armed and dangerous vibrators!" she laughed. "Did you tell them to drop their batteries?" Fortunately, the woman was picked up that evening by a cop from San Francisco's Mission Station. He had spotted her casing the victim's home and arrested her without incident.

Many of my arrests were attributable to another's reputation—a brawny deputy sheriff whom most of us called Pac-Man. He was a huge Filipino dude who worked on San Francisco's Fugitive Recovery Enforcement Team—an outfit known as FRET because it made the bad guys sweat. Pac-Man had a couple of martial arts black belts; he had been shot or stabbed seven times, but he relentlessly combed the city to nab criminals on the run. Whenever I first met with a client, I always mentioned Pac-Man. "If you get in trouble," I said, "surrender to me right away. If I have to put a bench warrant on you, you'll have to deal with Pac-Man. Believe me when I tell you that you don't want to mess with Pac-Man." This spiel was remarkably effective in getting clients to turn themselves in. Probationers spooked by the thought of an ogre would buzz my office phone. When they mentioned a drug charge they may have caught or a complaint they might have suffered, I said, "Make it easy on yourself or you know who's gonna getcha." These clients would dash to my office and put their hands behind their backs. On their way to jail, some even thanked me for saving them from Pac-Man.

So why, with all my precautions, did I suffer PTSD? Perhaps it was due to the threats I drew from clients who could not take a joke. On one occasion, a batterer spat at me while we were standing in open court, and he swore he would make me pay for using a fib to lock him up. Fortunately, this fellow was a resident alien from Ireland, and the Department of Homeland Security deported him back to the Emerald Isle. On another occasion, a stalker I nabbed was released after only two weeks, and he tracked me on the internet as soon as he got out of jail. The client was on probation for harassing a famous movie actress, and I had busted him after he sent her an email promising to cut out her tongue.

Although she was subpoenaed, the actress did not come to court and testify, so the judge released the ingrate to continue his rampaging ways. *U R not God*, he emailed me, *U R gonna dispear*. At least, his misspelled threats gave me a small consolation. I could claim to have the same stalker as a glamorous movie star.

To my credit, I never took stress leave although my nerves grew increasingly raw. Far better a gaucho's aura than the shame of a doctor's note. So my swagger grew bolder, my drawl became thicker, and I feigned a range rider's squint. And I chewed upon my cheroots until they were worn to nubs. "Ayup," I said to Mary before catching the Caltrain to work, "gonna lasso me some doggies and throw 'em in the pen."

"Is that what you call them—*doggies*?" she said. "Those poor souls you put in jail."

When I said that's what cowboys call cattle, she suggested I turn in my spurs.

One day, my office partner and I were taking a drug offender to jail—a shrimpy little fellow who had tested positive for cocaine. As we herded him through the jail parking lot, Pac-Man pulled up in his van. After giving us a friendly wave, he opened the door to his van, and a half-dozen bad guys stepped out of it and accompanied him to the jail. They were linked together with chains, and they walked like a string of horses. He had caught them single-handedly, all in a morning's work.

My bravado left me as quickly as water circling a drain. How could I keep my swagger after seeing a muster like this? Here was your true urban cowboy; here was your lord of the range; here was the windburned vaquero I had so brashly pretended to be.

Pac-Man looked at me and my lone, little doggie, and then he laughed generously. "Mister Hanna," he said, "are you trying to put me out of work?"

The Tallyman

YOU DON'T KNOW ME, but I know you. I'm the one who notices when you ignore a bum begging for quarters. I'm the one who sees you when you cut someone off in traffic. Don't think these matters are petty because you are not on my list. The only reason I have not come for you is that you are not worth my time.

So what is my name? Better you should ask me, *What is my name to you?* Now if I haven't come for you, my name could be Tolerance. But if you turn into some kind of big shot, you might know me as Nathan Skudder. Tycoons and honchos tremble at the mention of Nathan Skudder. So choose your transgressions carefully—you don't want to know me by my true name. Stick to sins better handled by churches or traffic courts.

Just who do I bother with? you ask. *Who is worth my time?* Nobody—the sword I carry is only fit for the Devil himself. But I stoop to noticing lying moguls who steal other people's ideas. I notice hacks who praise only what's common and let geniuses die in the dust. And I'm very aware of starlets who pretend to be what they aren't—those playing the role of heroines while acting like Hollywood whores.

Do I dispense justice swiftly? No, that would be an indulgence. Justice is better served slowly with discipline and restraint. Unless the noose tightens gradually, unless the blade is delayed, the transgressor will escape the full measure of the punishment he deserves.

Do you wonder where you will find me? You will find me where ideas are stolen. You will find me where prodigies weep. You will find me where truth is brokered by bandits then trampled underfoot. I am persistent but honorable, so please remember this: if I should ever come for you, I will look into your eyes. I will not give my sword to a surrogate nor hide behind a desk. That would deprive me of stature and you of your fullest deserts.

Can you outsmart me? you wonder. No—I am far too intelligent. I have the mind of a seer, and I read two books a week. Not the sort of drivel that poisons the public mind, but masterpieces accessible only to those with expanding souls. Thank god, my mother passed at my birth and I was raised in an orphanage: the place was so cruel and alien that it fostered my kinship with books. I may hide behind the persona of an unkempt derelict, but I am intimate with all the classics. I can recite *The Faerie Queene*. Spenser, Shakespeare and Milton are like bosom friends to me. It is *their* collective spirit that I pour into my art. It is their unsullied wisdom upon which I have honed my wit. So do not try to outsmart me or pierce my searing light. That would be like a pygmy shooting arrows at the sun.

Now since I am the hunter, it falls that I also am hunted. But the moguls that hunt me are cowardly; their faces are always well-hidden. The women that hunt me are only brave when their captor is celluloid—when they star in such abominable productions as *Queen of the Amazons*. No, moguls and whores will not hunt me themselves—they will only send surrogates. They cannot wield a thirsty blade, and guns make them pee their pants.

So who is the one that hunts me? He is called the Tallyman— he told me that in a dream. I have only seen him a couple of times, but I know he is after me. The Tallyman is honorable; he is also very brave. His reputation precedes him because he almost always catches his prey. I would not hunt the Tallyman although he is hunting me. I only hunt those that lack honor. Moguls and Hollywood whores.

*

My pursuit of the Tallyman's patrons was decided long ago. After all, it is scripts that rule us—scripts that determine our lives. My scripts are those of an oracle and an author ahead of his time. The moguls are scripted to feed upon scraps like pilot fish trailing a shark. I have sent the moguls a dozen fine screenplays—not a word do I ever hear back. They are shallow swimmers—these moguls. My drifts and currents elude them. They are no more capable of fathoming my depths than a sink might contain an ocean. And yet they peck at my art in the manner that seagulls might strike a beached dolphin. Lines and passages I have composed turn up in the trashiest of films: regrettable chestnuts like *Spiderman 3* and *Maleficent Mistress of Evil*. Ah, rivers that start in heaven end up in the vilest of swamps.

Does the Tallyman seek to kill me? Of course, but how happy that would make me. Am I not a quixotic tramp? Do I not have a martyred soul? If my quests remain true then the day when I die will be better than the day I was born. We are born to innocence and sorrow, but we may pass on to omnipotence. But although I admire the Tallyman, I choose not to be grateful to him. I do not wish to be indebted to one who would cut my throat. And so I concede to the pettiest of scripts: the instinct to flee like a squirrel. What mockery our instincts make of us—we are no more developed than insects.

But back to the subject of comeuppance—the message I wish to deliver. Do I ever make exceptions to those I have vowed to destroy? Yes, but I only did it once. Remember that starlets are spellbinders—they are skillful in their deceits. I once emailed a starlet whose name I won't mention, but suffice it to say that she touched my heart while performing from one of my scripts. I was also impressed that she emailed me back and called me her sweetest fan. Was she worthy of me—no, she was not—but with her I was charitable. I decided the pleasure of bedding her was worth her theft of my work.

Oh, chicanery, your name is woman. Oh, deceit your name is Eve. Not a month went by before she appeared in a flick with a bedroom scene. Not even the lustiest of centaurs, not even a mongrel in heat, not even the commonest of sluts went at it harder than she. It was bad enough that she had betrayed me by fucking a far lesser man, but she did not show the slightest embarrassment in putting her lust on display. I vowed that my revenge would be total, I swore my rout would be sweet, and yet I knew that the cruelest of vengeance would hardly level the books. In every way conceivable, that bitch had stolen from me.

And yet, she bewitches me still, she still has a hold on my heart. When I showed up in the Mission District where she was seeking unmerited glory, I was holding a bouquet of roses instead of the knife she deserved. As usual, my knife was strapped to my shin, but it was not intended for her. From her, I only wanted a smile or maybe her hand on my cheek. I wanted only the merest acknowledgment of what she owed to me. So deep was my degradation, so paralyzed my heart, that I wished only to join her worshippers and cast myself at her feet.

A film crew was stationed on the street, and its members were waiting for her. No patron of manners—she. No fan of decorum—she. She was content to keep them waiting, but this was clearly her right. Her debt was only to me, and I wanted just a crumb. A friendly glance would do me. Or the merest nod of her head.

Two security guards were looking at me as I wandered onto the set. A couple of paunchy thugs who were not worthy of being her protectors. "Hey runt, where ya think yer goin'," one asked me. He was looking at me as though I, and not he, was a boil on the face of humanity.

I showed the greatest of patience as I uttered my reply. "I don't *think* I'm going anywhere," I said. "I am sure of my destination."

"Get outta here, you little bum," he yelled, "or you'll end up in the gray bar hotel."

It was not enough that he had interrupted me, he had insulted me as well. And yet my patience endured as I drew the knife from the sheath on my shin. A bullet between the eyes is what that lout deserved, but I am a merciful paladin and do not take vengeance upon pigs. I presented only the tip of my knife, which I held at a discreet distance.

The pair drew their service revolvers so quickly, you would have thought I was Osama bin Laden. "Drop it," said one, but I clutched the knife and said, "Gentleman, please let me pass." We stood there for several seconds—the most improbable of champions. They, a couple of wannabe cops who hoped I might make them heroes. I, who wished only to place a bouquet at the feet of my beloved. But had the brutes filled me with bullets, the glory would have been mine. Remember, there is no better passage than one spawned by romantic ends. Heaven will ring with cheers of the righteous while seraphim carry you home. *Oh, let me like a soldier fall upon some open plain. My chest expanding to the ball to wipe out every stain.* This Joycean ballad filled my mind as I waited for them to shoot.

But I was struck down not by a bullet but a bag from a beanbag gun. And my chest did not expand to it—I was hammered in the groin. In my quest for epic glory, in my zeal to dwell among angels, I had somehow misjudged the weapon one of those assholes was holding. Cheated, I lay upon the ground as angels passed me by. Not even a cherub will stoop for a warrior felled by a beanbag gun.

*

75

I was not alone in the paddy wagon as I rode to the city jail. Sitting on the bench across from me was a tall, cadaverous man. His eyes were the eyes of a hunter, calculating and alert, and his nostrils swelled like those of a tiger picking up a scent. At first, I did not recognize him because he had grown a full beard. A master of disguise is the Tallyman, and for this, I respected him more.

"Don't let it be here," I said, an appeal to his better angels.

The Tallyman shrugged and raised his hands—his wrists were chained like mine. But his hands were thick and sinewy, and his knuckles were bigger than walnuts. At any given moment, he could have torn off his restraints, so I borrowed a line from Sir Walter Scott, which I hoped might keep him at bay. I said, "Do you know that beasts of game the privilege of the chase may claim?"

His brow knotted into a furrow, he licked his lips like a wolf, and his breath boomed through his nostrils like a black, approaching storm. Thankfully, he did not bare his teeth—they would surely have dripped like stalactites, but his thoughts bore the shock of electricity when they buzzed inside my head. *It will not be here*, he answered. *That would cheat us both.*

Thank god, he was unlike his patron—she who had stolen my art. She would have cut my throat in a second had she the sand to do her own work. No, the Tallyman has standards, he will not slaughter me like a hog. He surely knows the depth of my grief and how totally I have been robbed.

*

I have been booked many times in the San Francisco County Jail, so I felt no discomfort when the cop who arrested me returned me to its bowels. No, I stood like John the Baptist, whose martyrdom rivaled my own, and I did not blink as the booking camera captured my likeness once more. "Nathan Scudder," muttered the booking sergeant. "Whoja threaten this time? Seems every time I turn around, they're hauling you in here again."

He showed not a flicker of interest as he filmed my fingerprints, he did not even bother to glance my way as the arresting cop patted me down. No, only the Tallyman pities me enough to cut me some slack. Only he knows the torment I suffer from those who have pilfered my work. And where had the Tallyman gone to? I did not spot him inside the jail. He must have vanished into the city to hunt me another day.

The following week, I hung my head as I stood before a judge. It is best to show some humility when you stand before the bench. If you lie and pretend to be humble, the courts will turn you loose; if you shout out the truth like a prophet, you will meet a prophet's demise.

The judge, some fool with a face like a monkey, was reading my psych report. The report had been prepared by a jail shrink—a clod with bottle-thick glasses and breath that stank of garlic. The jerk had interviewed me for only five minutes before putting a brand on my soul. No doubt, he had described me as a paranoid schiz—psychiatrists love those words. There is not a seer under the sun whom a shrink will not scar with that term. Were Jesus to return for the second coming and preach salvation to the masses, I have no doubt the psychiatrists would call him a paranoid schiz.

The judge put down the report and squinted at me. "So you're hounding celebrities again," he said. "Nathan, are you taking your meds?"

I nodded like a bobblehead. "Four times a day," I said.

In fact, I was palming my meds and flushing them down the toilet in my cell. No brain-dead existence for me. No life without vision for me. It is better to soar like an eagle and be ostracized from the flock than to hop about with shattered wings and feed in garbage dumps.

I pled to a charge of aggravated assault, and the judge gave me three years of probation. He also ordered me to stay away from that vampish, thieving slut. She who had raped my very soul while wallowing in lust, she who teased me like a siren then abandoned me without a thought. I bowed my head like a beggar and agreed to the stay-away order. But why did the court not order *her* to free her talons from my soul?

And there you have it. By bowing my head, I was allowed to return to the streets. I was permitted to wear the mark of Cain and live in the Land of Nod.

*

I am wholly convinced that the only place for an honest man is jail. But I am not an honest man—I am deceitful and slippery and sly. "Be cunning like the serpent." Were these not Jesus' words? And so with our Savior's blessing, I hide my true face from the world.

But the probation officer they gave me this time, a stringy fellow from Kenya, was skeptical of me when I reported to his office after taking my leave of the jail. "Meester Skudder," he said in clipped English, "how come you accepted probation? According to your presentence report, you're a vicious, little bum. You live on public assistance, you have never held a job, and you've had twenty arrests for terrorist threats and brandishing deadly weapons. Eet will just be a matter of days, my friend, unteel you are back in jail."

"Have you *been* in jail, sister," I asked him because he was already pissing me off.

"*I* ask the questions," he answered. "And eet's Meester Oneybuchi to you."

"Well, ask yourself if you're leading a life of quiet desperation? As a minion to the philistines, I suspect that is the case."

"Quoting dead authors won't help you," he snapped. "Do you think I have not been to college? Do you think I have not read Thoreau?"

"I don't think you read him well enough to know that he was a fraud. He stayed only two years in that cabin of his, he was dumb enough to burn down a forest, and if he had spent more than one night in jail, he'd have accepted probation too."

Ooglybuchi, or whatever his name was, pushed his spectacles up the bridge of his nose. All the time we were talking, he kept adjusting his specs on his nose.

"You seem well-read," he said, "so how come you can't stay out of jail? You are thirty years old, sir—isn't it time you showed a bit of sense?"

"Jail is a good place to contemplate," I said. "I learned that from Thoreau."

Ooglybuchi pinched his nostrils and said, "We are off to a bad start, Meester Skudder. Please come back in one week for a pee test. I must make sure you are taking your meds."

*

"Simplify, simplify, simplify," said that wordsmith of the woods. I'm not sure why he said it three times, but it's still advice I follow. And so I live in a subsidized room in the Dalt Hotel on Turk Street—a room with nothing in it but a bed, a chair and a cot. Except for the noise tenants make in the hallway, I have no distractions at all—that's why I have written a dozen scripts of exceptional quality. Scripts that I mailed to Warner Brothers and Universal Studios.

Upon returning to my simple abode, I took a refreshing nap. Afterward, I picked up my iPad and googled my beloved. I check on her once or twice a day to see if she has repented—it would be callous of me to punish her if she is in the throes of regret. But she gave me no hint of contrition—no nunnery did she seek. She was sitting in a restaurant on Mission Street, batting her eyes like a hooker, and telling a fawning reporter the plot of her latest flick. Word for word, it was the exact same script I had mailed her studio three months ago.

"Bitch!" I shouted. "Pickpocket! Have you no shame at all?" I cursed her for more than a minute—even after my throat was raw, even after some jerk in the room next to mine started banging on the wall. Let him bang—this was no time for etiquette, this was no time for restraint. This was the hour to give her some part of the grief she had given me. *Tit for tat*, I always say—is that not the way of the world? And since her tit was off-limits to me, I was determined to make do with tat.

She must be stopped, I reasoned, *but how?* An idea popped into my head. I grasped the restraining order the court had served on me, and I dabbed it with a bit of Wite-Out then interchanged our names. She would not know the order was a forgery when I pressed it into her palm. She would only think that she no longer had license to shatter my peace of mind.

Oh, genius, your name is Skudder, I thought as I hurried out to the street. No wonder I had written so many fine scripts. No wonder she was stealing from me. Yes, she deserved to be pimp-slapped, but a restraining order would do. After all, she could no more withstand my genius than a moth might resist a flame.

I dashed to the movie set on Mission Street where they were reshooting a couple of scenes, and I caught a fleeting glimpse of her as I elbowed my way through the crowd. Oh, to feel the touch of her hand as I gave her the restraining order. Oh, to hear her apology as I unburdened my grief to her. An apology over dinner would do. We could share a bottle of wine.

The two piggish, security guards stood in my path while she disappeared into a trailer. A will-o'-the-wisp on gossamer wings could not have vanished so quickly.

"How about a filet mignon?" I shouted before she shut the door.

"How 'bout some black-eyed peas," said one of the guards as he pointed the beanbag gun at me.

In my haste, I had forgotten to bring my knife, so I offered no resistance. No, I stood as still as the statue of David while this cop I know cuffed me up. "Skudder," he said as he set the strands, "when are ya gonna learn?" He was overweight and out of shape, and he wheezed as he patted me down. Was he the best the police had to offer? I sighed and shook my head.

"My cross is not to learn," I informed him. "My cross is to shine and be scorned."

"Far as *I* can tell," he drawled, "you got no cross at all. Not unless being a public nuisance can be counted as a cross."

The guard with the beanbag gun snorted and said, "Whadaya gonna do with him, Abe? This is the second time we hadda deal with him this month."

The cop shrugged. "Chew him out then let him go. I ran his name—he's clean. All I can book him for is trespass, and the DA won't prosecute that. Hell, the DA won't prosecute anything that ain't a felony."

The guard slung his bean thrower onto his shoulder and spoke as though he'd been cheated at cards. "That's San Francisco for you," he said. "If he comes back again, we'll call you."

"If he comes back again, kick his ass," said the cop.

The cop pushed me into the cage of his patrol car then drove me to Pier 39. After he let me out of the car and took the bracelets off me, he said, "You'd be in San Quentin, Nathan, if the DA had any balls. It's a pain in the ass to keep busting you just so the courts can let you go."

"It seems payback eludes us both," I said as I stood there rubbing my wrists. "But if it's any consolation, you put on those shackles too tight."

"Whadaya want?" snapped the oaf. "A goddam apology?"

"I'll let it go this time," I warned him. "I have other things to do. But the next time you bruise my wrists, I'll file a complaint on you."

How nice it was to have the brute by the balls—to grin while he glared at me. When one is a suitor of light, good fortune will be his bride.

"Do me a favor," the cop said. "Stay here and feed the seagulls. I don't have the patience to bust you a second time today."

Like a dog with his tail between his legs, he got back into his squad car, and I felt like I had slain Goliath as I watched him drive away.

Since doing God's work made me hungry, I took the asshole's advice. I bought a bread bowl full of chowder, found a bench on Pier 39 and tossed some crust to the seagulls while I sat there eating my lunch.

*

I hate to admit it, but sometimes I feel a bit sorry for that cop. I secretly call him Sisyphus because their tasks are much the same. I am the boulder that dude has to roll up a steep hill every day—the boulder that bounces back down the hill the moment it gets to the top. So I decided to give him a break and stay out of his hair for a while. I decided to return to my spartan abode and work on a couple of scripts.

I walked no further than the Embarcadero subway because it's a pretty long hike back to Turk Street. As usual, the fare booth was empty, so I hopped right over the turnstile. There are indignities I do not stoop to, and one of them is paying train fare. Since the world owes me a million dollars, I should ride in limousines.

As I sat on a bench on the southbound platform, waiting for the train to arrive, I got the sudden feeling that someone was shadowing me. Turning my head, I spotted the Tallyman standing beneath the exit sign. He was taller than a grenadier, his skin was fish-belly white, and he was looking at me like a bill collector about to knock on my door. He turned his eyes away from me when I stared in his direction, but he followed me onto the subway and sat down on a seat opposite mine.

As we sat face to face, the doors hissed shut and the train pulled out of the station. *Would it be now?* I wondered, and my heart began to thud.

He stroked his beard and smiled at me, a smile that did not reach his eyes. I could spot the bulge of a dagger behind his seedy coat.

"Will you give me time?" I asked him. "I'm the pigeon, not the hawk."

His measured stare suggested that my time was running out, but he held his hand up politely and showed me the face of his watch. A generous huntsman was he, an enduring sportsman was he. Yes, space and time the stag would get ere hound was slipped or bow was bent. I sat through several station stops, plotting my escape. When the train pulled into Civic Center, I bolted through the doorway.

*

"I went to the woods," said that braggart, Thoreau, "because I wished to live." Well, I had no woods to go to, but I certainly lusted to live. So I adopted another strategy to elude the Tallyman. Whenever I heard loud footsteps in the hallway outside my room, I quickly opened my window and escaped to the street below. Whenever I went to the post office to mail out new scripts, I varied my route and kept checking behind me to make sure I was not being followed. Even when I returned to the probation department to keep my appointment with Ooglybuchi, I entered the building through the back entrance and rode the jail elevator up to his floor.

"Meester Skudder," said Ooglybuchi as I sat in the chair by his desk. "I have a police report on you. Eet seems you violated your stay away order before eet was even entered into the system."

"Ya gonna arrest me?" I asked him.

He shrugged. "There would be no point in that, sir. I could charge you with violating your stay away order, but nothing will come of eet. Your victim won't show up to testify, and the court won't enforce the subpoena. Movie stars get stalked all the time—they never show up in court."

"That's because they hire assassins," I said, and I mentioned my nemesis. I said only Melville's leviathan, a creature purer than snow, had suffered a hunter as relentless as the one pursuing me. I said I would deem it a favor if he locked me up for a while.

"On what charge, Meester Skudder?" he asked. "Have you committed a more serious crime? Unless you assassinate someone yourself, the courts will not keep you in jail."

"Piss test me," I said desperately. "I haven't been taking my meds."

"That I cannot do either," he said.

"You *promised* to piss test me," I insisted.

He shrugged. "That was last week, Meester Skudder. Due to a recent budget cut, we lost our contract with the lab."

"You're supposed to represent justice," I bawled, "and you're sitting there making excuses."

"May I be blunt, Meester Skudder," he said. "I am buried in cases, the courts here are useless, and there *is* no excuse for you."

"So you're abandoning me to a garrotter. A slayer of prophets and scribes."

"Meester Skudder," he said, "I'm not interested if someone is on your trail."

84

"Lock me up, fool!" I shouted. "Is there no justice under the sun?"

Ooglybuchi adjusted his specs on his nose then patted me on the wrist. "Do not worry, Meester Skudder," he said. "I think justice is coming for you."

*

Am I a hypocrite? you ask. Well, since the law is toothless, I choose to break it at will. *So why,* you ask, *should I expect the law to shelter me?* To this, I reply that there are greater laws than the pablum dispensed by the courts. There is the law of retribution, the Code of Hammurabi, the apocalyptic justice pronounced in the Book of Revelation. "Behold a pale horse!" its author screamed to the robbers, the swindlers, the whores. And who sits upon that horse but I whom the angels have decreed. And yet, I am more dupe than destroyer. And yet, I am more patsy than prince. And yet, I seek only a particle of the pound of flesh I am due. So if the law ever musters an ounce of gumption, a scrap of fortitude, is it not unreasonable to demand that this scrap be given to me?

But since the law is a pussy, I must slink through the streets like a hound. Since the law is a joke, I must hide away like a leper. Even when I am sleeping, I don't have a second of peace. I have the same dream night after night, and I wake up in the coldest of sweats. In my dream, I wander city streets beneath a crescent moon. There is not a person anywhere—I am utterly alone. Finally, I come upon a massive whore who is standing under a streetlamp. She is drunk with the blood of poets, she is black with leprosy, and at her feet lie the severed heads of Chaucer, Milton and Proust. "Who are you?" I cry. She grins like a fat cat. "You know who I am," she purrs. She then lifts her dress and spreads her labia, and her hole is a bottomless pit. "Come, come," she says in a voice warm as piss. "I have plenty of room for you."

Oh, wretched dream, you have turned me into a craven malcontent—you have forced me to endure law's delay and the scorn of despised love. Like Hamlet, I must suffer the slings and spears of fortune run amok—a buffer to only the darker afflictions that lurk beyond the grave. So I continued to endure the theft of my lifeblood, I continued to hide behind dumpsters, I even refrained from proclaiming my love to she who had shredded my heart. But, finally, I suffered such a blow to my pride that I could keep silent no more.

*

Am I a narcissist? you wonder now. Of course, but where is the rub? The moguls, directors and Hollywood harlots are boasters far greater than me. Consider the tedious galas we are forced to endure each year: the Oscars, the Grammys, the Golden Globes, the Hollywood Film Awards. These are but a few of the accolades they heap upon themselves. And where am I in these celebrations of ostentation and pomp? I am the pitiful ghost at the feast, I am the hobo at the door, I am the footman left out in the cold while the fires of foppery blaze. So do not hold me in contempt when I confess my self-love to you. Were it not for the laurels I grant myself, I would gather no glory at all.

You now wonder, *Am I a masochist?* I assure you the answer is no. But at times I indulge in self-flagellation that sinners alone should endure. Why else did I recently watch the Oscars on the television in my hovel? Why else did I sit through three fucking hours of speeches and phony applause? Had I been staked to an anthill with a desert sun searing my eyes, I would not have suffered a greater ordeal than enduring those endless awards. But at least that monotonous marathon afforded me her true measure. At least, I could fathom her cheapness when she accepted the Best Actress Award. Batting her eyes while freezing her smile, she tossed out kudos as though they were dimes. She thanked her director, she thanked her producer, she thanked her grandfather. She thanked her mother, her hairdresser, and half the men she had fucked. Had the master of ceremonies not intervened and ended the charade, I have no doubt she'd have thanked her chihuahua and Siamese cat as well. But not a word did she spare for me, her rock, her stalwart Pygmalion—the muse that had made her prize possible by supplying the script to her flick. This was the final outrage, this was the proverbial straw, this was the withering climax of my winter of discontent.

"Whore!" I shouted. "Charlatan!" I spared her no insult. But when the dimwit next door started pounding the wall, I banked my consuming rage. To plan my reprisal, to serve vengeance cold, I decided to take a walk through the streets and let the night air clear my head.

It was a measure of my desperation, a gauge to my discontent, that I strode the streets for an hour and cursed her with every step. Wouldn't the Tallyman nab me if I abandoned the rules of the chase—if I failed to duck into alleys or hide behind dumpsters and parked cars? No, I think not—he would allow me a moment of vulnerability. He would know that compassion was due to one so cheated as me.

I managed to talk myself out of my fear, but I froze when I spotted him. He was sitting on a bench in Jefferson Square Park, watching me like an owl. He seemed to be embarrassed, as though he were late for a date, but the pallid cast of a street lamp made him look as pale as a ghoul. Did he know I did not want his pity? Did he know I did not want his shame? Did he know his maudlin sympathy had only diminished me more?

"*Earn* your thirty pieces of silver!" I shouted. "Don't sit like a crow on a fence!"

It seemed like an act of charity when he slowly rose from the bench, when he reached into his jacket where his dagger surely lay.

Were courage not so fickle, I would have offered him my throat, but my bravado fled me as quickly as water down a drain. *How tall he was,* I marveled. *How glowering his eyes.*

I ran like a hunted rabbit. I ran like a greyhound on crack. I ran because my only choice was to run away or fight. Oh, Father in glorious heaven, have we no greater options than these? Are we disallowed thought or reflection? Are we disallowed nuance or calm? Oh, great and mighty progenitor, your script has made fools of us all.

*

Fight or flight. Such despicable choices should not have a season at all, so when I returned to my room, I vowed to mitigate my ire. Yes, the wrath of Ezekiel guided my hand as I wrote her another email, but because I still loved her dearly, I tempered the prophet's resolve. I made no mention of ravishing her or slashing her ivory throat. I promised her I would do no more than cut off the tip of her tongue. After all, was she not a victim as well? Were others not pulling her strings? Had the moguls who had hijacked my gift not plundered her beauty as well?

I pressed the send button, releasing the email as though I were freeing a dove. And then I buried my face in my hands and wept for both of us.

*

After several more days of hiding in alleys and ducking behind parked cars, I received a text on my cellphone—a message from Ooglybuchi. *Rejoice, I must put you in jail,* it read. *Please report to me at once.* Relieved that my keeper had developed a spine, I hurried down to the Hall of Justice, and the wings of destiny lifted me as I mounted the stairs to his office.

"Meester Skudder," Ooglybuchi said as I sat on the chair by his desk. "I have no choice—the probation chief *insists* that I lock you up."

He seemed almost apologetic as he removed a pair of handcuffs from his desk, and I felt a seer's obligation to set his mind at ease.

"Consider it prophecy," I replied, and I offered him my wrists.

Ignoring my gesture, he adjusted his glasses and showed me the police report. "So why deed you threaten to cut out her tongue?"

"Ezekiel would want nothing less."

"And what do *you* want, Nathan Skudder?" he asked.

"If it's all the same with Ezekiel," I admitted. "I would rather not cut out her tongue."

Was it my abiding love for her that had forced this concession from me, or did I simply wish to keep her intact so she could keep on performing my scripts?

"*Bravo*, Meester Skudder," Ooglibuchi replied. "That is very smart thinking, my friend. She may win another Oscar and give you some credit this time."

The chuckle in his voice annoyed me, and I'm not a man easily mocked, but I strained to control my temper as I held out my wrists once again.

"Lock me up," I insisted. "She can win all the Oscars she wants."

"Put those hands *behind* your back," he said, as he clicked the strands into place.

After he had secured my wrists and set the safety locks, he said, "I weel make a prophecy too. You'll be out in a couple of weeks."

*

Two weeks later, I puffed out my chest as I stood before a judge. I even curled my lip so I would look like a public menace.

The judge, an old woman too small for her robe, reminded me of a vulture. Her eyes combed the spectators' section as though she were searching for carrion.

"Is the complainant here?" she cawed.

"No, your honor," the court clerk replied.

"Was the complainant served the subpoena?"

The clerk rose from her desk and handed the judge the receipt of service.

"Celebrities," the judge muttered as though uttering a dirty word. "Why do they bother to file charges if they choose not to show up in court?"

She tossed the probation report aside then glanced in my direction. "You are free to go, Mister Skudder," she snapped. "I don't want to see you here again."

"Keep me in jail," I pleaded. "I'm not *free* to go anywhere."

"What are you trying to say?" she snapped.

"Captain Ahab is after me."

"I'm sorry about that," she chided. "Go file a police report."

I lingered at the podium and checked out the gallery. Although the courtroom was packed, I spotted him right away. He was sitting on a pew near the doorway and he appeared to be asleep, but his eyes popped open the moment the bailiff led me toward the holding tank.

"Is it assured?" I called to him.

It's in the bank, he replied, and he winked like a conspirator before the bailiff locked me back up.

As I sat by myself in the holding tank, I trembled like a hare. *Should I have called the judge a cunt?* I wondered. *Would that have delayed my release?* At that moment, it seemed that my whole life was nothing but missed opportunities. So tight was the grief that gripped my chest, so barren the drought in my soul, that when Ooglybuchi entered the tank, I was glad for his company.

"It seems you're an oracle also," I said as he sat down on the bench beside me.

He sighed as though chastised and said to come see him as soon as I was out of jail.

"How hospitable of you," I snapped. "Are you going to serve cookies and tea?"

"Meester Skudder," he said. "I have accommodated you as much as the law will allow."

"The law is a pussy."

"Even so," he replied, "you are living on borrowed time. My friend, do you really believe there is no justice under the sun?"

"Is that another prophecy?"

"It is merely an observation. In Kenya, a parasite like you would have disappeared a long time ago."

"The lot of all prophets," I grumbled.

"It is the lot of all stalkers as well."

"Lock me up or I'll kick your ass."

He smiled and lowered his eyes. "My friend," he said, "you hide among shadows. Your threat is an empty boast. How can I save you from phantoms when you are already a ghost?"

*

I was let out of jail that same morning and met my destiny right away. He was standing outside the main gate, writing into a notebook. The moment I stepped from the sally port, he put the notebook away. He then gazed at me, and his eyes were as injured as those of Banquo's ghost.

"Is it assured?" I asked him again.

It's in the bank, he replied.

I sprinted to Valencia Street then hopped aboard a bus. I was determined not to perish without my dagger in my hand. Far better a Viking's haven, the island of Valhalla, than to have no oasis awaiting me when I entered the void to come.

Arriving at my tenement building, I dashed into my room. I then snatched my knife from under my pillow and named it Providence. If Beowulf can name his blade, why not I? Was I facing a beast less unearthly? Had my date with darkness not come? When fighting the reaper, it is best to look him fearlessly in the eyes—to let him know that the dusk he inhabits is trumped by the darkness in you.

Was I hoping a warrior's resolve would frighten him away? Was I gambling that he had no stomach for the ringing of steel striking steel? If so, my hopes dissolved the moment I hopped through my window. He was waiting for me on the sidewalk, a taco in his hand. So unaffected was he by my bluster that he was having a casual lunch. But the hunger in his eyes remained as he munched his taco. Clearly, his appetite would not be sated by such pedestrian fare. I did not doubt that when he finished the taco, he would feast on my heart as well.

I ran to Golden Gate Park, but I spotted him under a tree, so I caught a bus to Chinatown where I hoped to buy some time. When I spotted a Buddhist Temple, my heart leaped like a fawn. Why not ascend to Nirvana instead? That would not be a difficult task. Surely, I was a worthy candidate for selflessness and light. Had I not led a life of self-denial? Had I not suffered for my faith? Had I not loved a sinful woman in a manner both generous and chaste? Yes, Nirvana would do me just fine, so I hurried into the temple. As I knelt upon a prayer mat before the holy perch, the statue of Buddha looked down upon me and smiled like a happy drunk.

After an hour, I strode from the temple, suffused with a heavenly glow. He was waiting for me on the sidewalk, but his gaze was inhibited. His eyes seemed to say, *I will not take your life when your soul is filled with light. No, not when an angel might claim you. Not when you're primed for great flight.*

"So how will I find my deliverance?" I shouted.

It's in the bank, he said.

Was that a riddle? Was that a challenge? Was he still making sport of me? Or was he simply waiting for me to devolve before he cut out my heart? Whatever his thoughts, I knew that I would not get another chance.

"How much longer?" I hollered.

It will be soon, he replied.

As I dashed down the street, I struggled with the mystery of his words. *It's in the bank?* Was this something more than a cruel and mocking jibe? The world owes me a million dollars, and I have never collected a cent.

It was not until I spotted a Wells Fargo branch that I finally unlocked the riddle. Whipping my blade from the sheath on my shin, I dashed into the building. "Give me your assets!" I hollered. "Give me your liberty bonds!" The young lady I grabbed as a hostage reminded me of her. Her tits were as shapely, her ass was as taut, her shriek seemed frozen in time. She even batted her heavy eyelashes as though they were butterfly wings. But this time, I would not be dissuaded. This time, I would not be fooled. I kept the knife against her throat until I heard a police siren wail.

How fitting it was that Officer Sisyphus burst into the bank. His pistol was out of his holster, and he pointed it at my chest. When I let my blade clatter upon the floor, he grinned like a lottery winner.

"This time we gotcha, Skudder," he said. "Put cher hands behind yer back."

*

So where am I now? you ask. I'm at the Federal Medical Center in Ayr, Massachusetts. It's a therapeutic correctional facility twenty miles from Walden Pond. I am here for ten years, a stretch that puts Thoreau's petty sojourn to shame. The feds could have given me *more* time, but they thought I was out of my head. Oh, irony, thy name is Nathan. Oh, stealth thy name is Skudder. My mind was never clearer than when I pretended to rob that bank.

"Simplify, simplify, simplify," were that hermit's most famous words. And there is nothing more basic than a cell on a lockdown range. A bunk, a cot, an impenetrable door—what more do I need than these? I now work in such a fever that I produce thirty pages each day. I do not even stop my production to go to the exercise yard.

Ah, nemesis, you now worry me less than the fleas that nip at my art—the insects my fiery pages will turn into cinder and dust. Their cowardliness cannot contain me. Their plots cannot stop my pen. Because I am no violable genius. I have thwarted the Tallyman.

Sandy Ajax, We
Hardly Knew You

THE WORLD BASEBALL LEAGUE was born in the sixties in our suburban home in Virginia. My kid brother and I invented it on a sweltering Fourth of July. It was a heroic invention—a vehicle by which two nerdy kids might share the aura of champions. Armed with dice, meticulously drawn charts and a cardboard baseball diamond, Robbie and I commanded the destinies of twenty baseball teams. We played daily throughout the long hot summers—up to six games a day—and we tweaked team standings and player averages after every game. So absorbed were we in horsehide heroics that we rendered the summers neither long nor hot.

Our rosters consisted of four hundred individual players each represented by a 2" by 2" square of cardboard. Batting averages, fielding percentages, slugging potential and base-running speed were recorded on each of these squares along with the name and number of the player. To avoid the stigma of favoritism, we recruited our teams liberally. Movie stars, politicians, and demagogues were included among the players—each with his respective stats. Even so, we did have a favorite player: a switch-hitting, rawboned youth whom we named Sandy Ajax. Although he was a made-up character, he was entirely real to us.

So enthralled were we by the World Baseball League that it had become hallowed ground. Everything else—sleeping, eating, jacking off—were pallid distractions we had to fulfill to return to our field of dreams.

Although Robbie and I are now in our seventies, we still live out our glory days. When we meet at family reunions in Rehoboth Beach, Delaware, we reminisce about the World Baseball League. I might ask him, "Do you remember that triple steal I pulled off in our first World Series?" Robbie might say, "Do you recall the trade we made in '64—when I gave you Willie Mays and Hitler in exchange for Joe DiMaggio. Joe got hot and hit four home runs in a division playoff game."

My wife Mary is less than enchanted by these lively conversations. "You were a couple of dorks rolling dice in a basement and pushing cardboard squares around. Don't you have anything better to talk about than that?"

When I assure her the World Baseball League is worthy of reliving, her stock reply is, "Have fun, you two. I'm going to the beach."

One day, when Mary returned from the beach, she left her towel on the porch. "Don't bring your beach towels into the house," she ordered. "They're too sandy."

Robbie's eyes grew distant as though he were listening to faraway music, and I knew instinctively what he was thinking about.

"Yes, I remember him too," I said as I watched his eyes brim with tears.

We were thinking, of course, about Sandy Ajax, who lasted only one season. Of all the stars we commanded in our pursuit of epic glory, not one of them shone brighter than that stalwart, tireless lad. Sandy got his start playing sandlot baseball somewhere in Oklahoma, and his prowess was such that he was eventually recruited by one of Robbie's scouts. As graceful as a gazelle, as unassuming as a spaniel, Sandy turned Robbie's hapless Potomac Patriots into a World Series contender. I remember his flowing, golden locks as he slammed fifty-seven home runs; I remember his blazing throws from left field as he cut runners down at the plate. He captured our hearts with the ease with which he stole thirty bases, and even though he competed against my teams, I loved him like a brother.

But Sandy's glory was fleeting because the baseball gods took him away. You see, each season, a player took his chances against the injury chart. If his manager rolled snake eyes, that meant the player had pulled a hamstring, a sprain that would keep him out of action for seven games. It also required the player to survive a second roll of the dice. A second roll of snake eyes kicked his injury up a notch: it meant the player had broken his leg and would miss an entire season. Still, a third roll of the dice was required to fully define his injury, and if snake eyes was rolled a third time, it ended the player's career. It meant that a beanball had brained him and put him into a coma.

The chances of rolling three consecutive snake eyes are one in forty-six thousand, but when Sandy was matched against the injury chart, Robbie rolled snake eyes three times in a row. I recall Robbie's stunned expression as he looked at those damnable dice—it was the same look he had on the day that Alfalfa, his pet gerbil, died. "C-c-an't we forget the rule," he stammered. "It will only be for this one time."

"No," I said as the chill of winter paralyzed my heart. "If we fail to apply the rule, it will make the game inauthentic."

I recall Sandy lying in a hospital bed with an IV stuck in his arm. I remember the doctor telling us that only fluids could keep him alive. I recall that fateful day Robbie and I decided to pull the plug—we howled like abandoned puppies as we watched Sandy's life drain away.

We cremated his square in a matchbox, and our tears nearly put out the flame. Afterward, we scattered the ashes in the stream behind our house. "Let's keep this short," I told Robbie as the stream swept the ashes away. "If we mourn him by his worth, our grief will never end." Still, we played every subsequent game as though we were in a trance. The ghost of Sandy hung over us with every toss of the dice.

"Yes, I remember him," I repeated as Robbie wiped a tear from his eye. Even though sixty years had passed, Sandy's glory was still alive.

"Why, oh why!" cried Robbie.

"It was those goddamn dice!" I replied.

Robbie slapped his forehead as though punishing himself for tossing the dice. "Oh, Sandy, we hardly knew you," he said, and he once again started to cry.

*

"What happened, did somebody die?" Mary said as she burst back into the room. The sound of our wretched sobs had bled the color from her face.

"Not in our memories," I replied. "Sandy Ajax will always live there."

"Sandy Ajax? Who are you talking about?"

"The most promising rookie of all," I replied, "and his star had just started to shine. He'd have broken every record if those damn dice hadn't cut him down."

"You're starting to babble," said Mary.

"What of it?" I replied. "Do you know he was batting .384 when that injury chart took his life?"

"My god!" Mary cried. "The way you were bawling, I thought he was somebody real. But you're blubbering over a character from that ridiculous baseball game."

"Don't talk that way about Sandy," I snapped. "You never saw him play. He could even hit a knuckleball—that's hard for a rookie to do."

"He was a stupid piece of cardboard," she said. "I don't *need* to know more than that. What am I going to do with you two if you won't stop making things up?"

I felt no need to apologize as I watched Mary storm from the room. I could only respond to those arbitrary dice that had shattered our field of dreams. Even now my heart aches like a migraine and my grief is too raw to command. *Oh, Sandy, we hardly knew you,* I thought, and I buried my face in my hands.

Did You See the Tasmanian Devil?

WHEN I MENTION that I once spent a year in the island state of Tasmania, people look at me with interest and ask me the same question. A question as patented as Coca-Cola and as reflexive as a burp. "Did you see the Tasmanian devil?" they say. They are probably thinking of that Looney Tunes critter that talks in growls and grunts—not that poor, diseased marsupial that is practically extinct.

In my early twenties, I took a ferry to Tasmania to make a stab at writing. I had been roaming Australia for several years, taking jobs as I found them, when I suddenly felt a need for some creative solitude. I was looking for a lonely retreat where I could draft some stories—a hermitage that would rival Thoreau's hallowed cabin by a pond. I had no thought whatsoever of spotting the Tasmanian devil.

Eventually, I found my spot in the sequestered village of Bridport. It sits on the northern tip of Tasmania and is now a golfing haven, but at the time it was a rustic fishing port with few inhabitants. I rented a bungalow by the sea for thirty dollars a week, and I stocked up on tinned meat and pancake mix to make my meager funds last. As I sat by a fire in the bungalow and outlined my first stories, I could not resist the notion that I was one up on Thoreau. After all, the sound of crashing breakers made Walden Pond seem dull.

Most days, I strolled an isolated beach with sand the color of snow. The beach was utterly barren—not a house stood anywhere, and I felt as though I had been transported to some prehistoric time. As I walked the shore, my first fictional characters bubbled into my brain—not fully-fleshed spirits but embryos that would develop over time. They were much like the early lifeforms that once crawled from the primal ooze.

Of course, I now have readers who say some of my characters are primitive still. After reading my first novel, *The Siege*, a woman just shook her head. "Your point-of-view character is immature," she carped self-righteously. "He's without a doubt the most cynical person that I have ever met."

"How could he be cynical?" I protested. "He was born in a place of stark beauty."

When I told her about my early days on the rugged Tasman coast, her face predictably brightened and she looked at me with awe. "Oh, what an adventure," she exclaimed. "How brave you were to do that. Did you see the Tasmanian devil while you were living there?"

"I did not see the Tasmanian devil," I said. "Nor was I looking for it."

Her eyes glazed over. "My goodness," she said. "What an opportunity you missed."

The singularity of her interest was such that I volunteered nothing more. I did not mention that I interrupted my scribblings to work on a lobster boat. This was an actual adventure, an experience that tempered my soul, a thrill far greater than whatever rush a marsupial might provide.

The boat, a tiny fishing craft with a battered, rotting hull, swayed back and forth like a pendulum with every roll of the sea. "Point the prow at the waves," my skipper called out whenever

I took the wheel. "If them buggers hit us side-on, we're gonna capsize for sure." It was probably our good fortune that the hull leaked constantly; the seawater sloshing about in the hold gave some ballast to the boat. But the snarl of the combers, the groans of the hull and the wanton peppery wind convinced me that I had braved elements I was not equipped to survive.

On one occasion, I lost my footing and toppled into the deep. I was clutching a thirty-pound lobster pot, which I was about to heave over the gunwale, when a whitecap pounded the deck so hard that I staggered like a drunk. So swift was my loss of balance, so sudden the lurch of the deck, that I was still hanging onto the heavy pot when I plunged into the brine. Strangely, I did not panic as I bobbed among the swells; I instead felt the sort of solace that a child in a cradle might feel. It was only after my skipper had tossed me a rope and hauled me back onto the deck that my teeth began to hammer so hard I thought they were going to break. But I was feeling the chill of deliverance, not the threat of a watery grave, as though I had somehow been snatched from a womb and tossed into a bracing world. Weeks later, after we harbored in Bridport, I knew that the sea owned me still. Spoiled by the rise and fall of the waves, I was unable to walk on land.

It is hard to describe the intimacy of almost drowning at sea, but decades later, at a family reunion, I made a feeble attempt. After telling a distant cousin about my dip off the Tasman coast, I was greeted with a callow gaze and again that knee-jerk question. "Cool," he replied, "but what I wanna know is if you saw the Tasmanian devil."

"I wasn't looking for it," I snapped. "I was on a lobster boat."

Thinking back on my cousin's query, I should have kept my temper. I should have known by then that high adventures are isolated affairs. This solitude applies no less to excursions of the mind: the seclusion I felt in my bungalow where I devoured dozens of books. But, although I lived like a hermit, I had the best of company: Hemingway, Faulkner and Joyce became like personal friends to me.

It was only the shouts of some women who worked in the village cannery that prevented me from finding an entire port within myself. I heard their siren voices one day while taking one of my strolls; they had spotted me during their lunch break and their summons rang in my ears. "Over here, luvy!" "I want some of you!" "Come see me anytime!" These brassy solicitations were enough to break the spell of great authors, and I decided to forgo my hermitage to gather some low-hanging fruit.

That night, I went to the local pub where I spotted one of them: a large-bosomed woman with tattooed forearms and thick disheveled hair. She was sitting alone at one of the tables, nursing a pitcher of beer, and she looked in my direction with frank, disarming eyes.

I approached her and bowed like a courtier. "Ma'am," I said in a honeyed voice, "would you spare this orphan a chat?"

She studied me with a furrowed brow, unsure what to make of me. "How come you talk like a poof?" she said finally.

"I'm learning to be a writer."

She shrugged and belched like a cannon. "I think you're a happyjack, luv. That's a bloke who shags poor sheilas then goes on his merry way." Despite her misgivings, she accompanied me back to my bungalow. "You're a one-night stand, luvy," she muttered as she undressed by firelight. "I just wish I wasn't enough of a trollop to know that about you for sure."

We coupled with an intensity that rivaled the toss of the sea. And the following morning she said, "That was fun, but a hubby is what I need."

"How about I fix you some pancakes?" I offered.

She laughed and walked out the door. A few days later, I ran into her inside the village store. "I'm an easy fuck, luvy," she told me. "But that's as far as it goes. I'm not loose enough to give my heart to a bloody happyjack."

Was she a disposable pleasure to me? I think all women were in those days. But I had no wish to dispose of her quite so quickly as that. Although I was not the marrying sort, she had claimed me like the sea. Fifty years later, she still remains my favorite fantasy.

Recently, while swapping stories with a stranger in a bar, I remembered the moan of the Tasman wind and could not help mentioning her. I said, "I gotta tell you about this woman I had in Tasmania."

Indifferent to my nostalgia, the stranger cut me off. "Tasmania," he said. "Hey, did you see the Tasmanian devil there?"

"I did not see the Tasmanian devil," I said. "I think it snuck up a tree."

Once again, I had been reminded that adventures are solitary affairs—that the year I had spent in Tasmania was not tame enough to be shared. So I no longer talk of Tasmania and the tempest it planted in me. And, wherever that critter is hiding, I am happy to let it be.

Single-Leg Pickup

MY WIFE MARY AND I sit on the back porch of our Florida home. I am anticipating the deepening blush of a fiery Florida sunset. I am not expecting the question Mary asks me out of the blue. She asks, "If you could go back fifty years and meet yourself when you were eighteen years old, what advice would you give to your younger self?"

I answer without hesitation. "I would tell my younger self to practice the single-leg pickup."

"Just *what* is the single-leg pickup?" she says. "Some stupid wrestling move?"

"It's a takedown," I explain. "When I wrestled at Washburn Military School, I did not have a signature takedown. If I had developed the single-leg pickup, I'd have scored a lot more points."

"How many points did you need?" she says, and her voice begins to drag. Weren't you undefeated one year? At least, you keep telling me that."

"I was unbeaten my junior year," I remind her. "Thirteen wins, not a single loss, and one match that ended in a tie. If I'd used the single-leg pickup, I might have won fourteen straight matches."

"So that's what you'd tell your younger self—to develop a wrestling move? No life lessons, no words of wisdom—just a silly wrestling move."

I am immune to Mary's derision when I relive my high school wrestling career, so I do not hesitate to enlighten her on the sport. "The single-leg pickup," I explain, "is *not* a silly move. Now the fireman's carry might have been dumb—I could have put myself on my back. But the single-leg pickup would have been perfect for me because I have that extra reach."

"My god," Mary says "I always suspected that you were superficial. But what you just revealed to me amounts to a whole new low."

"Does it?" I say. "My younger self would have shrugged off sage advice. Why not give the brawny lad something he could actually use?"

"Hmm," Mary says, pretending to think. Her chin rests upon her knuckles. "That remark is either incredibly deep or extraordinarily shallow."

"I would also tell my younger self to keep up the laser stare."

"What is the laser stare? You've never mentioned that."

"Right before my matches, I would stand at the edge of the mat. And I would fix my opponent with an unblinking stare that said *your ass is mine.* When the match began, I often saw fear in my opponent's eyes—all because I had spooked him with the good ol' laser stare."

Mary rolls her eyes and says, "You are digging your hole even deeper. Isn't there something more reflective you might say to your eighteen-year-old self?"

"That oughta do it," I answer. "I'm not a man to waste words."

"You're a writer," says Mary. "You've written five books, and your books have won awards. Do you think the person you are today is someone inclined to waste words?"

"In my books, my words aren't wasted," I say. "And I want to keep things that way. My younger self was a meathead who read nothing but *Spiderman* comics."

Mary says, "I was actually impressed with you when we met at that singles' dance. Now that thirty years have passed, I'm having second thoughts. I'm starting to think that maybe I overrated you."

"That's no reason to diss the single-leg pickup."

"Speaking of pickups," says Mary, "what were *you* doing at that dance? Were you searching for a life partner or an empty one-night stand?"

"I wasn't searching at all," I reply. "Before you spoke to me, I was beating off the babes with a stick."

"So what you're telling me," Mary says, "is that you were still trying to run up the score."

"I didn't *have* to try," I say. "When I told them about my jock days, they were putty in my hands."

"If you had mentioned your jock days to *me*," Mary says, "we would not be sitting here today. I'd have written you off as a man-child who was living in the past."

"But what a past it was," I say.

"Was it really as great as all that? What happened in your senior year? You never bring that up."

I confess that, during my senior year, my record was four wins and two losses, and that one of my wins was a forfeit from the Virginia School for the Deaf and Blind.

"Did the laser stare stop working for you?"

"It wasn't that," I reply. "One of the schools we competed against put a ringer in my weight class. A neanderthal named Bubba Stone who couldn't put two sentences together. The school gave him a wrestling scholarship because he was supposed to have been rated fourth in the nation."

"It seems," Mary says, "that you were counting on life not catching up with you—that you really believed you could conquer and crow without ever paying a price."

"I wrestled him twice," I tell her. "The first time was really bad. He pinned me with a cradle after scoring thirteen points. But our second match was a different story. He only beat me ten to five because I executed the Peterson Roll. Right before the final buzzer went off, I had him on his back."

"How do you even remember all that?"

"How could I ever forget? Do you know what my coach told me after I almost pinned the jerk?"

"Something profound, I'm sure," Mary says.

"It was profound enough," I reply. "He said I came within a cunt hair of pulling the upset of the year."

*

The sun is now mahogany red. It covers our faces like paint. Silence hangs like a pendulum before Mary speaks up once again. "Have I had as much impact in your life as some dullard named Bubba Stone? Did I take you out of your bubble and bring you down to earth?"

"Am I down to earth?" I ask her.

"You may have one foot on the ground. But if you keep bragging about what a stud you were, I won't credit you with even that."

Since a quote from the Bard might rescue me, I recite two lines from *The Tempest*. "'Where the bee sucks, there suck I. In a cowslip's bell, I lie.'"

"You suck all right," says Mary. "Don't think you can hide behind Shakespeare."

"At least consider that time-honored quote before calling me superficial."

Mary looks away for a moment then she looks back and nods her head. "All right," she says. "I considered it. And I'm calling you superficial."

"Then 'merrily, merrily I shall live now under the blossom that hangs from the bough.'"

"I'm going into the house," Mary sighs. "You can just sit there under the bough."

Since Mary's snits are fleeting, I am content to sit on the porch. Thirty years of behaving my age has not dimmed my callow torch. I can still sense the specter of conquest; I can still hear the buzzers and cheers. And I had come within a cunt hair of pulling the upset of the year.

Strutting Hog

The highway is for gamblers, better use your sense.
Bob Dylan

YOU ARE ALIVE to the moment—nothing more. And the moment is not alive to you. The shrunken path you walk, the fogbanks swirling around you, the overgrown forest that slows your stride offer neither cheer nor condolence. Rather they make you feel perishable, as though you have stumbled here in your sleep.

You have no memory—for that you are grateful. Memory has no place in this land of fog and shadow. Its mood is not one of reminiscence but pure and utter sameness. Anything smacking of ego would seem like a sacrilege.

Travelers pass you along the trail, traipsing in the opposite direction. Occasionally, they glance at you, and then they look away. Their faces appear to be carved out of wax, their movements lack commitment. They are as defeated as the branches that droop from the ancient trees.

You trudge along the narrow path, but you journey without destination. Not even the sight of a ramshackle mansion allows you a sense of arrival. If the winking sign can be believed, the mansion is a hotel. The sign says Rooms Available and emits a frigid light.

*

Seeking a change of solitude, you stroll into the mansion. The foyer is full of people, but none of them speaks to you. Since the people are as passive as corpses, their snub is a consolation. You do not want to converse with them, you do not want to hear their laments, you want only the sterile bearings a hotel room might offer you.

You belly up to the front desk where a pimply clerk is sitting. You tell him you would like a room. "A room," he repeats, he pronounces the word as though it might infect him. "Yes," you say. "I would like a room." He says, "How do you know you would like a room? You haven't seen the rooms." "All right," you reply, "I would not like a room, but I want one anyway." "You want a room anyway?" he bleats. "I'm calling the manager."

He punch dials a cell phone, while shaking his head, and mutters into the phone. Soon a fat, sweaty man waddles up to the desk and gives you a practiced smile. "He would like a room," the clerk says to him. "But he has not seen the rooms."

"If you haven't seen the rooms," purrs the manager, "how do you know you would like one?"

"I'm here for a room," you argue.

"My good man," the manager says, "that isn't the reason you're here."

The conversation is so convoluted, you decide to leave the hotel. But the manager seizes your elbow before you walk out the door. "We had almost given up waiting for you," he says in a buttery voice.

You feel guilty. "What am I late for?" you ask him.

"Late?" he exclaims. "Why do you think you are late?"

"You said you were waiting for me?"

He laughs. "Come, come. You know why you're here."

Gripping your elbow like a jailer, he guides you down a hallway. You arrive at a room with an open door—a room thick with cigarette smoke. Inside the room, a half-dozen drab men sit hunched around a poker table. You hear muffled bids, an occasional cough and the skeletal clatter of chips. As your eyes adjust to the lighting, you notice an empty chair at the table.

The manager rocks back on his heels and nods like a marionette. "The game has no beginning," he says. "The game will never end. Yes, my friend, we were waiting for you, but please don't think you are late."

That the room is not unfamiliar to you affords you no relief. It smells like blackened cabbage, it resembles an old movie set, and the fellows sitting around the table look like castaways.

"Where is he?" pipes one of them, picking his cards up.

"Who do ya mean?" says another.

"The Hog," the first speaker says. "Anyone know where he is?"

Nobody speaks except to voice bets. The clatter of chips tickles your ears. After a minute somebody says, "I saw him a week ago—or it might have been a month."

You stand as though bound, but you are forced to concede that this room is calling to you. You do not want to sit at the table. You do not want to place any bets.

"Come, come," says the manager, "please take your seat. You have *credit* at this table."

The manager shepherds you into the room. You sit down in the empty chair. In front of you is a generous stack of hundred-dollar chips.

"Is that him?" someone says, nodding toward you.

"Who?" says another.

The speaker, a man with a harelip, says, "Is that Strutting Hog?"

All eyes at the table appraise you, but you utter no reply. You nervously finger your stack of chips. You wait for the cards to fall.

Somebody says, "Bullshit, that isn't him."

"I dunno," says the man with the harelip. "It's hard to tell in this light."

"Deal," someone says impatiently.

The man with the harelip shuffles the deck and flips two cards to every player. The men are playing five-card stud with a hundred-dollar ante. Each player is dealt one card face-down, four face-up, and can bet after each up card is dealt. It is a poker game for purists, but the game is not at all pure. After three rounds of betting, you notice five kings on the table. Harelip, who has two of them, gives himself one more.

You nudge the man beside you. "He's got to be cheating," you whisper. "A deck only has four kings."

The fellow says, "So what? It's his deal, ain't it?"

You hang onto your chips, disgusted, as Harelip deals the final round. He gifts himself an ace and shoves all his chips into the pot.

Everyone folds but a man with four deuces who matches Harelip's bet. Harelip turns over his down card—the card is another king. "Read 'em and weep," he laughs.

The other, a man with a broken nose, flips over his down card—a deuce. "Five deuces beat four royals," he crows. Chuckling, he rakes in the pot.

Harelip leaps to his feet, grabs the man's hand. "You cheated. I saw you cheat," he protests.

"That's enough," the manager says. "Please lose with some dignity." Pulling a revolver out of his pocket he shoots Harelip between the eyes. Harelip drops like a sack of grain, he looks like he has a third eye. You gasp as a glittering puddle escapes from the back of his head. The men at the table don't look at the corpse; they study their cards instead. As the game continues, two thugs wearing black drag the body from the room.

The man with the broken nose sweeps the cards up and passes you the deck. "Wanna deal, pardner?" he offers. "It costs five hundred clams to deal."

You tell him you have no desire to deal.

"Everyone deals," he snaps. "You wanna piss him off?"

"Who?" you ask.

The man sighs like a furnace. "Pardner, don't pretend you don't know who I'm talking about."

"I ain't seen him in over a month," someone says.

"He'll be back," says the man with the broken nose. "The Hog always comes back."

The cards are coarse and grainy. Some are flecked with blood. You throw five chips into the pot and deal quickly. You want to get rid of the cards.

You give one card down and one card up to everyone at the table. Although you have dealt yourself two aces, you fold on the first round of betting.

*

You play a few more hands before you grasp the full stakes of the game. Whenever a player runs out of chips, he stands up and raises his hand. At that point, the thugs in black frog-march him out of the room. After a pistol shot rings out, play at the table resumes, and someone else ambles into the room and sits down in the vacated chair.

Your tower of chips is shrinking. You have not placed a single bet. The player beside you, a man with a stutter, says, "Buddy, he ain't g-gonna like it."

"Who?" you ask.

The man shakes his head. "You *k-know* who I'm talking about. He don't like a fella that s-sits on his cards. He likes to win more than your ante."

Someone else says, "Ya don't gotta worry. I think he's in New York."

"I bet he's in Brussels," another man says. "He likes the festivals there."

The man with the stutter nudges you and says, "Buddy, he ain't g-gonna like it. When he shows up, he's gonna chew you out for s-sittin' on your cards."

You have a full house, jacks over queens, so you chuck some chips into the pot. You lose to a fellow with kings over aces and instantly regret your bet.

The game drags on for hours—hours that melt into days. You win a few hands, you lose a few more. You play the game ethically although everyone else is cheating. Because of this, you do not win big although you manage to stay alive.

You look forward to the bathroom breaks, which you are allowed to take every two hours. You look forward to pausing long enough to eat a complimentary sandwich. And every twelve hours, the men in black escort you out the door. They take you to a nearby room filled with cots, so you can catch up on your sleep. But sleeping is impossible because the pistol shots wake you up.

*

After a week, it happens. A side door creaks like a coffin lid opening, the poker game comes to a halt. The man with the broken nose says, "I toldja he'd come back."

You smell him before you see him. The odor makes you gag. As you hold your nose, an enormous man swaggers into the room. His mouth has the pout of a baby's mouth and looks ready for squalls and bawls. His brow is locked in a permanent frown; his eyes are beady and hard. He studies each man at the table with undisguised disdain then he reaches into his pocket and slaps down a handful of chips. "Gentlemen," he booms in a bullying voice. "We're gonna play Last Man Sitting."

The players all bow their heads; some of them make the sign of the cross. The men in black shout, "Last Man Sitting!" They drag a huge chair to the table.

After the big man squeezes into the chair, you glance at the man with the stutter. "Is that him?" you ask.

"Is th-that who?" the man says.

"Is that Strutting Hog?" you murmur.

The man glares at you and whispers, "*You bet*, but you didn't hear that from me. Oh no, oh no, oh no," he repeats. "You d-didn't hear that from me."

The big man is staring right at you. His face grows as red as a plum. His body odor assaults you like a wave of lethal gas. "Boy!" he booms, "I don't wanna believe what I been hearin' 'bout cha!"

The man's face is broad and impenetrable, like the faces on Mount Rushmore. You feel as though he is appraising you from a very lofty height.

"What are you trying to say?" you ask. Although everyone else at the table is bowing, you do not lower your eyes.

The big man is gazing at you as though he has known you all your life. The mockery in his eyes makes you feel like a phantom at a feast. The man softens his tone and says, "Listen up good. I ain't chewin' my cabbage twice."

"Just tell me what you heard," you say, still refusing to lower your eyes.

"I heard you was sittin' on your cards steada playing the game like yer s'ppose to. I always knew you was a pussy, and now you're provin' me right."

"Am I here for your approval?" you ask.

The man puffs up like a bullfrog—he has reached the end of his patience. "Hang onto your chips!" he thunders. "I'm gonna take my time with you!"

He reaches into his pocket and produces another deck of cards. "It'll cost a thousand dollars to deal," he says. "Anyone wanna deal?" When no one replies, he laughs like a magpie. "All right," he says. "It seems as though I'll be doin' all the dealing."

He throws ten chips into the pot. "Last Man Sitting!" he shouts. "No one else gets to sit at this table—not 'til the game is done." Without bothering to shuffle the deck, he clumsily deals the cards.

It takes you only seconds to notice that the man is an artless cheater. His sausage-size fingers grope awkwardly as he fishes cards from the bottom of the deck. His beady eyes linger like bailiffs as he studies the backs of cards. And when he flicks a card from his shirtsleeve, the movement lacks precision. It looks as though he is shaking a booger from his hand.

Nobody at the table objects as Strutting Hog wins all the pots. They obediently match his bets, they silently lose their chips, and as he rakes in pot after pot, they sit like crows on a fence. Whenever someone runs out of chips, he timidly raises his hand, and the men in black grab ahold of him and march him from the room.

You sit there, your pulse beating faster with every pistol shot. You refuse to match Strutting Hog's bets. You refuse to play his game. You refuse to relinquish any advantage to this foul-smelling barn of a man.

One by one, the losers are marched out of the room. You watch them pass through the doorway; you flinch when the pistol barks. Soon, the only ones left at the table are Strutting Hog and you.

*

Strutting Hog is now sitting behind a towering pile of chips. You have only a handful, and you clutch them like golden coins. "Who are you?" you mutter.

He shakes his head, his jowls wobble like pudding. He says, "Boy, you *know* who I am."

"What spawned you?" you say.

He yawns like a hippo. "Son," he says. "I ain't gonna tell you if you don't know the answer by now."

He stares at you like a hanging judge. "I'll tell ya this much," he says. "This game was arranged a long time ago, before you was even born. So quit actin' like a pussy and bet on the cards you been dealt."

You reproach yourself for your questions. There is only one puzzle to solve. If you wish to survive, you must find a way to clean out Strutting Hog.

"Deal," you say.

He doles out four cards. You get a king and an ace in the hole. Strutting Hog has a king showing. You match his bets and you win with three kings, but you know he is toying with you.

"Deal," you repeat. Again you win, he has dealt you three jacks and two aces, which beats his pair of threes.

You play a dozen more hands, and you win every one of them. You know it is all a set-up—that he's just building you up for a fall. But after an hour your pile of chips is the same size as Strutting Hog's pile.

You throw ten chips into the pot and say, "All right, I'm buying a deal."

He chuckles and hands you the deck. "Serve 'em up, Pussy," he says.

You deal the first four cards, and then you pause to consider your bet. Strutting Hog has an ace on display. You have the king of spades showing. You peek at your down card—the queen of spades. Could this be a possible straight flush?

Strutting Hog counts out a hundred chips and places them into the pot. You cringe and match his wager, you do not even hesitate.

In all poker games, there's a pivotal hand. You know this will be the hand.

You give Strutting Hog another ace then you put your third card on the table. When you see that your card is the jack of spades, you feel profound relief. Your straight flush is still alive, and it's open at both ends.

You know Strutting Hog is still toying with you when he says, "Your next card is free." He winks like a conspirator and grins like a henhouse fox.

Without placing a bet, you deal two more cards. Your heart leaps into your mouth. Strutting Hog gets another ace. You inherit the ten of spades.

"Your next card is gonna cost ya," he says. He counts out two hundred chips and shovels them into the pot. "Too rich for your blood?" he taunts.

You are tempted to fold, but you know you can't fold. You know you must play out this hand.

"I'll see you," you mutter. You match his bet and deal the final two cards. A king falls to Strutting Hog. You get a bullet. You get the ace of spades.

Your heart pounds like a mallet. Your mouth is as dry as lint. This is your moment—you have him beat. You will not get this chance again.

You do not want to make him suspicious. You want him to think you are bluffing. You push your remaining chips into the pot. "Five hundred grand," you announce. Your voice is squeaky, your hands are trembling, but this is just an act.

When Strutting Hog snorts like a racehorse, you know the suck has worked. "All right, little pussy, let's see 'em," he says. He dumps all his chips into the pot.

You turn your down card over, revealing your royal flush. You wait for the men in black to come and take this oaf away. But the men in black do not enter the room, and Strutting Hog is still grinning. "Boy," he says, "do you think I didn't know you had that straight flush?"

"How did you know?" you ask him.

"'Cause I marked every card in the deck."

He turns over his down card, an ace, and says. "Four bullets beat a straight flush."

"Four aces *don't* beat a straight flush," you protest.

He snaps his fingers. The manager enters the room, hands him a burlap sack. Strutting Hog rubs his hands together then sweeps all the chips into the bag. He says, "Son, you shoulda learned the *rules* before you played this game. If I say four aces beat a straight flush, that's how it's gonna be."

When he hoists the bulging sack over his shoulder, he looks like he's toting a bomb. But he gives you only a warning scowl as he saunters out the door. His odor lingers behind like a presence. It fills the entire room.

You feel like you've been in a car accident. You feel as though you have been mugged. Although you are the last man sitting, the men in black come for you.

*

The thugs muster you into the hallway. It is cluttered with ripening bodies. The manager is there, he looks at you nervously. He is fiddling with his tie.

He reaches into his jacket, pulls out the revolver, but hesitates to shoot you. He lowers the pistol and says, "My good man, it seems you are free to go."

"Why am I free to go?" you ask. You feel only fleeting relief.

The manager coughs, he is clearly embarrassed. "It wouldn't be honorable to shoot you," he says. "Not when you won the game."

Being free to go is not good enough. You want your winnings back. You say to him, "Give me the gun."

The manager shrugs and hands you the gun. "Many have tried," he says.

You tell him, "That doesn't matter. I'm placing him under arrest. If he doesn't come along peacefully, I'll put a slug in his head."

The manager places his hand on his heart. "I understand, sir, I do. You are not the first to pursue him."

"Where is he?" you ask.

"He's in the casino. Remember that many have tried."

You search the hotel until you find the casino. Strutting Hog is not there. You hear that he is in the lounge, but you do not find him there either. You search the entire hotel, but there is no sign of him anywhere. A waiter says, "He's in Bakersfield. That's a half-mile down the road."

You leave the hotel. You are back in the fog. You walk with determination. You soon arrive at Bakersfield, but Strutting Hog is not to be found. A policeman tells you he just left town and went to Riverdale.

You walk on through the thickening fog. The path is wider now. You know you will catch him and bring him to justice. Perhaps in the very next town.

The Sowbelly Trio

MY WIFE, MARY, AND I sit on the front porch of our Florida home. Mary is feeling nostalgic, so she asks me a syrupy question. I never feel very comfortable when Mary asks me such questions. I am not good at providing the sort of answers women like to hear.

Mary asks me, "What's your favorite song?"

I think for several seconds, and then I shake my head. "Am I supposed to have a favorite song?"

"Hey, don't get defensive," says Mary. "You aren't *required* to have one. But not many people reach their seventies without having a favorite song."

"What's your favorite song?" I counter.

"Oh, that's easy," says Mary. "It's 'Both Sides Now' by Joni Mitchell. I sang that all through college back in my flower-child days."

"How does it go?" I ask her.

Mary quotes a line from the song. 'So many things I would have done, but clouds got in my way.'"

"Ya gotta watch out for those clouds," I say.

"Now don't change the subject," says Mary. "Remember that two-man band you belonged to thirty years ago? And how you dragged me to those county fairs, so the pair of you could perform? Out of all songs you and Big Al played, you must surely have had a favorite."

Big Al is the name of a social worker I knew when we lived in the Hoosier State. A bluegrass aficionado, he liked to play the banjo, and we eventually formed a two-person band we called The Sowbelly Trio. Big Al sang and picked his banjo while I accompanied him on the harmonica. We actually taped a few "albums," and we hawked the tapes at county fairs. People said our sound wasn't bad, but we needed someone to play bass.

"I like every one of those songs," I tell Mary. "Bluegrass was like a first love to me. 'Foggy Mountain Breakdown,' 'Fox on the Run.' They don't write them like that anymore."

"Quit stalling," says Mary. "What I want to know is what's your *favorite* song?"

I think a bit longer then shake my head. "It's going to be hard to pick one. We did make several albums."

"Yes, I remember the names of those albums. They were really pretty silly."

"*High on the Hog, Second Litter.* What's so silly about those names?"

Mary laughs. "You know, I don't think you took that band seriously at all. But I'm serious now, and what I want to know is what's your favorite song?"

"My favorite song?" I mutter. I can feel myself starting to sweat. "Well, if I have to have a favorite, I guess I'd pick 'Cotton-Eye Joe.'"

"'Cotton-Eye Joe'!" exclaims Mary.

"It's hard to beat 'Cotton-Eye Joe.'"

"Who *was* he? A runaway slave?"

"He might have been one to start with. But now he's a metaphor."

"You and your metaphors," says Mary. "A metaphor for what?"

"The things we cannot control," I say, and I sing the tag lines from the song. "'Where did you come from, where did you goooo? Where did you come from, Cotton-Eye Jooooe?'"

"Out of all the songs you might have selected, you had to choose 'Cotton-Eye Joe.'"

"It's a very popular song," I reply. "There are over a hundred versions of it."

Mary sighs. "That just makes it worse—metaphor or not. I *forbid* you to pick 'Cotton- Eye Joe' as your favorite song."

"Why can't I have 'Cotton-Eye Joe'?"

"If we're going to ask questions," says Mary, "why did you call yourselves The Sowbelly Trio when there were just two of you?"

"It's a catchy name. It made folks perk up and listen. Besides, we didn't think it would be long until we got ourselves a bass player."

"But you never did get one, did you?"

"Well, you might have helped us out. Didn't you play the guitar back in college when you sang that song about clouds?"

Mary laughs despite herself. "Yes, I played the guitar, but I also have my pride. I would never, ever have joined a group called The Sowbelly Trio."

"Too bad. You might have improved our sound."

"That seems like a pretty lost cause."

"We may have been struggling," I answer, "but we were never lost."

"All right," Mary says, "quit stalling around and pick another song."

"How about 'Pig in a Pen'? That fits the image we had."

"How does that go?"

I clear my throat and sing the chorus bars. "'Wellll, I got me a pig back home in a pen and corn to feed him ooooooon. All I need is a purty little girl to feed him when I'm goooone.'"

"You're not helping your cause," says Mary.

"What's wrong with 'Pig in a Pen'?"

"Those have to be the most sexist phrases I have ever heard."

"That song has different levels."

"One level is quite enough. No woman is going to stay home all day just to feed some bumpkin's pig."

"Pigs have personality," I say. "They're also a lot of fun. That's why we chose to name our band The Sowbelly Trio."

"That won't get you off the hook," Mary says. "Now pick another song."

I think for several seconds then decide on a Rascal Flatts number. "How about 'God Bless the Broken Road that Led Me Straight to You'?"

"Nice try," Mary says. "But I'm not buying it. It sounds like a pig in a poke."

"Does that apply to my favorite songs too?"

"I'll leave you to think about that."

Mary leaves me sitting alone on the porch, and I once again feel myself sweat. Do I really wish to part company with the songs that had won my heart? No, I must keep them alive to me—they are too much a part of my soul—so I slip my cell phone from my pocket and give Big Al a call.

Big Al is glad to hear my voice and to relive our bluegrass days. He says our band spread a whole lot of joy although it never amounted to much. He suggests we get back together soon and do a little jamming. If we can find ourselves a bass player, he says, we could go back on the road.

How I Done Good in School

HI, MY NAME IS Toby Dawes. I'm a farm boy from Putnam County—that's in the middle of Indiana. You probably ain't never heard about me because I don't make much of an impression. But I did become a tad famous last year when Pa took me to a whorehouse in Michigan City. That was for my seventeenth birthday, and that's where I became a man. The whore Pa bought me, Brandi, told him I done real good. She said I gave her the best thirty seconds that she had ever had. She said I made her cum three times, and Dad he gave her a hundred-dollar tip for showin' me the ropes. Before I left the whorehouse, the madam gave me a Jonathan apple, and she said a cocksmith like me was welcome back any time.

As we was driving back to Putnam County, Pa gave me a bit of a lecture. He said to me, "Toby, now that you've had the real thing, I hope you stop stealing my cock books." Well, I've still been swiping Dad's porn, but I also been writing to Brandi. I told her that, when I got my driver's license, I'll drive up to see her again. I told her I'd like to take her to a tractor pull before we got back to screwin'. Brandi she wrote me back and said I'm a real sweet boy. She said if I took her to a tractor pull, she might give me a golden shower.

Well, I ain't particularly fond of showers, but that don't matter nohow. I just wanted to mention Brandi 'cause she's my best accomplishment. But I'm also real good at shootin' rats at the Putnam County Dump. I'll bet if I laid 'em side by side, you could count up two hundred rats. I'm hopin' one day that I can teach Brandi the art of shootin' rats.

But this story ain't about killing rats neither. This story is about last summer when I done good in high school. I ain't never done good in school before 'cause I don't apply myself. That's what Ma says anyhow, but I see it real different. As I see it, there ain't no point in learning stuff like science or math. It ain't gonna help you shoot a rat or bleed a buffalo catfish. And if ya walk around spountin' knowledge all day, ya ain't gonna score no cooze. The cheerleaders will think you're a nerd and won't spread their legs for you. 'Course, I ain't fucked a cheerleader yet 'cause I never impressed 'em enough. But I figger at least I got a chance if I don't turn into no nerd. Anyhow, Putnam High School been passing me in spite of my failing grades. The principal says I'm getting passed on probation 'cause the school don't wanna keep me around.

But I'm still gonna tell you this story about how I done *good* in school. That happened just last summer before I started my senior year. Ma said I won't get no diploma if I kept getting passed on probation, and if I don't get no diploma, I'll have to work at the Hillsdale Hog Farm. She says if I don't pay attention there, them hogs will gobble me up.

Well, Ma made me enroll in an American history course, which was being taught in summer school. She said American history oughta interest me 'cause it's fulla wars and stuff. Ma said she hoped I'd get a teacher like this fella called Mister Chips 'cause that dude knew how to inspire kids and bring out their full potential. See, Ma's she's always watching this DVD called *Goodbye Mister Chips*. It's about this teacher in England—a fella who couldn't get laid 'cause he was too fulla Latin verbs. It's kinda funny that teacher was played by an actor named Peter O'Toole.

*

Well, I started the course on the first day of summer in this classroom with no air conditioning. I was in there with three other farm boys who would rather be poundin' their pork. And the teacher we got—Mister Flanigan—weren't nothin' like Mister Chips. He was a nervous kinda fella and he had a sunken chest, and practically every time he spoke, he said the word *actually*. He said stuff like, "Actually, General McClennan wasn't that much of a general. He could have actually won the Civil War after the Battle of Antietam. But after winning the battle, he let the Confederate Army get away, so the war lasted three years longer than it actually should have lasted."

Every time that fella said *actually*, we all put marks into our notebooks. I wagered Bubba Little, this kid sittin' beside me, that Mister Flanigan would say it two hundred times before the first week of class was done. Bubba bet a copy of *Hustler* and I bet a Penn fishing rod, and before the fifth day of class was done, that copy of *Hustler* was mine. At first, Bubba said I got the count wrong, but I showed him all the marks I made, which I'd lumped into groups of five. There weren't no way Bubba could welch on the bet 'cause I took real careful notes.

Now Bubba he weren't too happy that I won his copy of *Hustler*, so he asked me to give him a chance to win his magazine back. He said if I would put up the *Hustler* and let him bet on Mister Flanigan, he would match the bet with a coupla condoms he been keepin' in his wallet. I asked him how old them condoms were and he said he'd had 'em four years, and I told him I didn't want no condoms that were probably too old to use. Bubba he said there ain't no such thing as a condom too old to use. He said

I could always fill 'em with water and pelt cars from Hostler's Bridge.

Well, Bubba he had a point, so I made him another bet, but that didn't matter nohow 'cause Mister Flanigan never came back to class. We was sittin' in the classroom the following Monday, after Bubba and me made our bet, and the principal came into the room and said we was changin' teachers. He said Mister Flanigan weren't coming back 'cause he had caught a case of the flu, and that we was gonna have a new teacher who knew history real good. He said his name was Doctor Nichols and he was educated at Oxford, and he told us to be on our best behavior and make him feel at home. Now I weren't too happy that I'd lost the chance to win some water balloons, but I sat up straight as a poplar and waited to meet our new teacher.

*

It weren't but a half-hour later when our new teacher walked into class. He was a short, skinny fella with bottle-thick glasses, and he had this little goatee. He was also wearin' a tweed jacket that looked too big for him, and he was walkin' kinda gimpy like maybe his shoes were too tight. I think I spotted him yesterday in downtown Putnamville. I was walking past the adult store after eating a Big Mac at McDonald's, and a fella who looked kinda like him came limping outta the store. But that dude had a hat pulled over his eyes, so I weren't completely sure it was him.

Anyhow, the dude limped to the blackboard and he picked up a piece of chalk, and he scrawled *Leonard Nichols, Ph.D*, in big ol' skinny letters. And then he spoke to the class in this real thin, reedy voice. It was a bit like the sound a balloon makes when ya let the air squeak out.

"Oh bum," he said as he looked us over. "Whatever have I gotten myself into?"

The dude had an English accent, but he didn't look like Mister Chips. He looked like he'd rather be back in that porn shop picking out dirty books.

Well, I raised my hand before speakin' to him 'cause I wanted to show respect. And I said, "How come they sent a doctor to teach us history?"

The dude grabbed the lapels of his jacket then rocked back and forth on his heels. It looked like he'd been thrown into an ocean and was clutchin' a life preserver. He then spoke as though he was apologizing for cutting a real smelly fart. "I'm a doctor of philosophy," he said. "I'm a doctor of world history too. When you're as frightfully educated as I am, lads, all you can do is teach."

I said, "How come ya gotta teach in a place like Putnam County?"

"Oh, me," he said. "Well, I travel a bit and sometimes I run out of money. Since teaching is all I am good for, you boys are stuck with me for the summer." He clutched his lapels even harder and the color went out of his face. "My goodness," he said, lookin' over the class. "This is really a sticky wicket."

"I guess what yer saying," I said, "is you don't wanna be stuck with *us*. I ain't gonna fault you for feeling that way 'cause we don't make too good an impression."

"I agree," he said in his squeaky voice, and he picked up one of our history books. "If you don't mind a bit of a warning, lads, things may not go very well."

I kinda liked the fella even though he was probably a pervert. And since Mister Chips weren't available, I guess he would have to do.

*

The fella he opened a history book and glanced at a couple of pages, then he shrugged and snapped the book shut as though he

130

was trappin' a fly. "Let's have a discussion, lads," he said, and his voice got even more squeaky. "Would one of you care to tell me what the American Civil War was about?"

We sat there like crows on a fence because we couldn't think of nothin' to say. There weren't none of us accustomed to having a teacher ask questions of us.

"Come, come," said the fella. "Would one of you tell me what the Civil War was about?"

Well, the silence was thicker 'an hogs at a trough, so Bubba he spoke up. "Them soldiers was fighting 'bout slavery," he said. "Ain't choo supposed to be teachin' us that?"

The fella he wrung his hands together as though they was covered with ants. He said, "Gracious, why would ordinary boys fight about something like that?"

Well, I think that fella had a point, but I don't think I was supposed to learn that. Shucks, if them soldiers were dumb as me, they wouldn't care about nothin' but cooze.

"My word," said the fella. "It's quite the riddle why those boys chose to fight. Especially when they wore uniforms that were itchy and beastly hot. You know, even the women who followed the camps gave them a pretty rum go."

"Who was them women?" asked Bubba.

"Prostitutes mostly," the fella said. "Now *they* had a reason to be there. They charged the troops three dollars to screw, which was a lot of money in those days. They also charged a dollar for handjobs if you can imagine that. A lot of soldiers *paid* for something they could have done for themselves."

Well, I don't guess there's nothin' stupider than paying for a handjob. But my hand shot up like a flushed-out quail because I wanted to know more about the subject. "They had handjobs in them days?" I said.

The fella he nodded and grinned like a possum; he seemed relieved to have found a new subject. "Of course," he said. "There were blowjobs too, but the whores charged two dollars for those. You know, some of them made so much money that they went home and opened up brothels."

He went on and told us a whole lot of stuff about what made the Civil War interesting. He said the term "hooker" originated in the Army of the Potomac—that's 'cause this general named Fighting Joe Hooker liked to bang him a whole lot of beaver. He said some of the whores sold the troops dirty photos and charged 'em as much as four dollars. And he said there was so much clap in them days that soldiers made their own condoms. But they made 'em out of sheep's gut, so they didn't work too well.

*

After class, I went home and told Ma that we had us a brand-new teacher. I said we was learning 'bout sticky wickets and it was real interesting stuff. Ma said it sounded like Doctor Nichols was an English gentleman, and she predicted my education was gonna expand a whole lot. Well, I was thinking about playing hooky and huntin' feral hogs, but I hurried on back to class the next day 'cause I wanted to learn more history.

Doctor Nichols spoke next 'bout westward expansion 'cause Mister Flanagan had skipped over that. He said a whole lotta screwin' went on in them wagon trains heading west. He said cholera, snakebites and Injuns killed so many of the pioneers that there was a gravestone for every mile along the Oregon Trail. He said the pioneers needed to sire new children to make up for those that died, so after they circled the wagons at night, most of 'em fucked like rabbits.

"It's a good thing those wagons were covered," he said, and he giggled like a drunk. "What went on behind the canvases would have made a degenerate blush."

132

"Was there golden showers?" I asked him 'cause I wanted to know more about those.

Doctor Nichols scratched his head then smiled. "There *are* no documented incidents," he said, "but I imagine they were quite common. Women who lost their husbands usually turned to prostitution, and there were so many of them turning tricks that competition was fierce. If a patron wanted a golden shower, I'm sure he had only to ask."

He went on to tell us about the mining towns out in California and Montana, about how them towns were built around brothels because the whores were smarter there. He said when payday came around, them miners all rushed to the brothels, and it weren't uncommon for a single whore to screw seventy men a night.

"I dare say it was rather ironic," he said, and he chuckled like a setting hen. "The men dug about in the dirt all day while the women were *sitting* on goldmines. The madams made so much money that they ended up running the towns."

"Did them prostitutes cum?" asked Bubba.

Doctor Nichols blushed then nodded. "The women had their pleasure," he said, "but it didn't come from their johns. You see, most of the whores had these steam-powered vibrators, which they used to keep themselves clean. A couple of minutes with one of those vibrators left them very satisfied."

"Them whores had it *good*," said Bubba.

"You would think so," Doctor Nichols replied. "But some of them tired of prostitution and married miners and ranchers."

"Bummer," said Bubba.

Doctor Nichols he shrugged. "Yes, it does seem a bit of a waste. But after those women retired, most became good wives."

Well, I was real happy to hear that 'cause I was still writing to Brandi. And Brandi she been writing me back and promising me real cheap rates. But, shucks, a woman as fine as her deserves much better than that. I decided that when I was finished with school, I would ask her to be my wife.

*

As the semester went on, Doctor Nichols told us a lot more interesting stuff. He said the dirty book industry got its start during the Roaring Twenties. He said *Lady Chatterley's Lover* was the novel that broke the ice, but the stuff that was published after that would have shocked even D.H. Lawrence. He said there was books about whips and midgets and books about lesbian orgies, and he said that a whole lot of taxable revenue was generated by them books. He also described the New York City blackout, when the city was plunged into darkness, and he said a whole generation of kids was sired in stalled elevators. And he told us all about Woodstock, which he called a cultural phenomenon. I'd never heard about Woodstock 'cause that's ancient history, but I wished I'd been born a hippie after Doctor Nichols told us about it. He said kids were sliding around in the mud and they didn't have to take showers, and girls were running around naked with their tits flapping in the breeze. He said you could have your choice of the girls 'cause the music made 'em horny, and ya didn't have to pay them—they gave it away for free. Well, I wrote a letter to Brandi and I told her all 'bout Woodstock, and Brandi she wrote me back and said that it sounded interestin'. She said she weren't sure it was ethical to give it away for free, but she was sure I had the potential to earn frequent-flier rates.

Well, I started taking my history book home, but it weren't too interesting. When I mentioned that to Doctor Nichols, he just patted me on the head. He said school books don't *have* real history in them and not to be wastin' my time.

*

Well, you probably know how this story ends up, so I won't take much more of your time. Especially since I don't think this story is making too good an impression. So I'll just give you a couple more details, and you won't have to read no more.

On the final day of the semester, we was waitin' for Doctor Nichols. We was hopin' he'd tell us a couple more stories before he gave us our final exam. And the principal he walked into the class like he was about to take a dip in a cesspool, and when we asked him where Doctor Nichols was, the principal said he was indisposed.

The principal handed out the exam papers, and after we answered the questions, he said Doctor Nichols was under arrest for contributin' to the delinquency of minors. Well, there *ain't* no mines in Putnam County as far as I'm aware, so I dunno where Doctor Nichols found any miners to corrupt.

Anyhow, I kept gettin' passed on probation all through my senior year, and I didn't get no diploma, so I'm working at the Hillsdale Hog Farm. And Brandi she said she won't marry me, and that's got me feelin' real down. But I got a C in American history, and I'm real proud of that.

How I Got Me
Some Standards

LIKE I TOLD YA, my name is Toby Dawes and I don't ask much of myself. I live on a small farm in Putnam County, which is in the middle of Indiana, and I been working at the Hillsdale Hog Farm since flunking out of high school last year. Now I'm real good at snagging buffalo catfish and shooting brown rats at the county dump, but Ma says them skills ain't enough to get me ahead in life. She said to me, "Toby, in a coupla months, you're going to be twenty years old. If you expect to make something of yourself, you're going to need higher standards."

Well, I thought my standards were pretty good when I asked Brandi to marry me last year. Brandi she's the prettiest whore in this cathouse in Michigan City—that's where Pa took me for my seventeenth birthday 'cause he was tired of me swiping his porn books. Pa was hopin' I'd leave them books alone if I got some mud for my turtle, so he drove me all the way to Michigan City so I could pop my cherry. I never shot no load in Brandi—I came while she was washing my johnson—but Brandi she covered for me 'cause she thought I was a real sweet boy. She told Pa I was a helluva cocksmith and that I made her cum three times, and Pa he patted me on the back and said, "That's my boy!"

Now Brandi and I been texting each other, but that stopped 'bout a month ago. That's 'cause I asked Brandi to marry me, and

Brandi she lost her temper. She said she would give me a bargain rate if Pa wanted to buy me another hour, but she weren't gonna marry no bumpkin who made a living slopping hogs.

Well, my life is kinda lonely now 'cause I don't have no pussy in it. All I do is work at the hog farm, slopping hogs and shoveling shit, and most nights I sit in our living room with Pa and watch *Wrestlemania*. I get paid pretty good at the hog farm—more 'an three hundred dollars a week—but most of the money I give to Ma to pay for my room and board. That don't leave me much money to have no social life, but I do go to Flakey Jake's now and then and have me a Michelob Draft. Flakey Jake's is this dive bar that's just half a mile from my home, and sometimes, when things are busy there, I help Flakey Jake serve drinks.

*

Now that you know a bit more about me, I'm gonna tell you this story. It's about how I got me some standards so I could do better in life. One Saturday night, I was sittin' in Flakey Jake's drinking a Michelob draft, and this woman I never seen before came walkin' into the bar. The woman she had on a tight, black dress that rode real high on her legs, and she was wearing a pair of stiletto pumps that looked sharper than paring knives. Her hair was brown with lotsa white threads and her tits were as small as apples, and her face had so many pockmarks that it looked like she'd lost a fight with a cat. She hadda be about fifty years old—which made her older 'an Ma—but I felt my willie expanding 'cause my standards ain't too high.

Well, the woman came right up to the table where I was drinking my beer and she said, "Hon, is this seat taken?" and my heart it started thumpin'. Before I could answer, she sat down beside me and patted me on the wrist. She said, "Hon, my name is Eve and I could use some company. My boyfriend is on the road tonight and won't be back until tomorrow morning."

I told her I weren't too good at making conversation, but that I was a hell of a cocksmith and a hooker could vouch for that. I told her that I'd made this whore in Michigan City cum three times.

The woman she just clucked her tongue. "Sure, you did," she said. All the time she was talkin' to me, she kept checking out the bar like maybe she was hoping Brad Pitt would come walking through the door. But there weren't nobody else in the bar 'cept Flakey Jake himself, and Flakey Jake he's a big greasy dude who don't look sexy at all.

The woman said, "Tell me more about yourself, hon," and her eyes kept searching the bar.

I told her my name was Toby Dawes and I worked at the Hillsdale Hog Farm, and that I was fond of shooting brown rats at the Putnam County Dump. I told her I was a real good shot and hardly ever missed.

The woman she pursed her lips like I'd put a bad taste in her mouth. "Do you mind if I call you Jackson," she said. "You look like a young Jackson Browne."

I told her it didn't make no sense for a dude to have two last names, but that I wouldn't have no objection if she wanted to call me Jackson.

The woman she squeezed my hand, and her nails bit my knuckles like red ants. "Maybe you *should* object, honey," she said, and her voice it got real testy.

I told her I don't object to much because I don't have very high standards, and the woman she got even testier and let go of my hand. She said, "In case you haven't noticed, hon, I'm a pretty attractive chick."

Well, the woman was starting to scare me some, and I felt myself starting to sweat. Whenever I get nervous, I sweat like a pig in a slaughterhouse. And it didn't help matters none when the woman took an iPhone out of her purse. "Let's pose for a selfie," she said, and that creeped me out even more.

But since I don't object to much, I said that would be okay, and she put her chin on my shoulder and snapped a photo of us. "Honey, don't look so shocked," she said as she put her iPhone back into her purse. "If you like, I'll make a copy for you. You can tuck it under your pillow. You look like the kind of boy who would like a racy photo under his pillow."

When I told her I already had lotsa racy pictures under my pillow, the woman she just yawned like a catfish gulping a minnow. I thought she was gonna get bored with me quick since I weren't makin' much conversation, but the woman she leaned back in her chair and started talking nonstop. She told me she worked part-time at this funeral home where she made cadavers look sexy, and that she'd recently served two years in state prison for possessing powdered meth. She told me she's now shacking up with a fella who cheats on her all the time—a dude who's an interstate trucker with a woman in every state. She asked me if I wanted to know how she met him 'cause that's a kinky story, and since I ain't got no standards, I didn't object to that neither. So she told me the dude contacted her on her website a coupla months ago 'cause he liked this selfie she'd posted where she was nude in a tub fulla Jell-O.

I said I was real fond of Jell-O when it's covered with Reddi-Wip, and the woman she just snorted and said, "Hon, you're missing the point."

I said Reddi-Wip oughta be the point 'cause it tastes better 'an vanilla ice cream, and the woman she asked me to pay attention because she had something important to say.

"He's the jealous type, hon," she whispered. "You don't want to mess with him. If I showed him that picture of us together, he'd punch you right in the nose. He'd hunt you down, wherever you are, and punch you right in the nose, then he'd beat me good and proper and take away my car."

"You don't gotta show him that photo," I said. "That way you can keep your car."

The woman she kinda blushed and said, "How about we bargain, hon? How about you come home with me and I won't show him that photo?"

Well, that sounded like a real good bargain, so I didn't express no objection. 'Cause gettin' some mud for my turtle was better than gettin' punched in the nose.

*

The woman she held my hand while she walked me out to her car, and her fingernails dug into my palm and they were sharper than catfish spines. Her car was a Ford Fiesta, and it had some dents in it, and it took her a coupla minutes to dig her keys out of her purse.

Once we was seated in the car, she put her hand on my knee. "Buckle up, Jackson," she told me. "We're in for a bumpy ride."

The woman she drove with only one hand—her other one was grippin' my knee—and the car it swayed like a drunk on skates as we rolled down Route 231. This Jackson Browne song called "The Great Pretender" was blarin' from her CD player, and the woman she kept singing along and she didn't miss a word.

Before the song was over, she pulled onto this narrow dirt road, and the road was fulla potholes and the woman musta hit every one. And every time I bounced in my seat, she gave my knee a squeeze, and her fingernails gripped me so hard that it felt like my leg was caught in a bear trap.

When we pulled up in front of this beat-up house, she let go of my knee. She said, "Keep the door shut once we're inside, Jackson. I don't want the cats to escape."

140

Well, I weren't in no particular hurry to follow her into the house, but my johnson it kept expanding like it had a plan of its own. So I unbuckled my seat belt, got out of the car and followed her into the house. The living room looked kinda cluttered 'cause there were cats all over the place, and the pissy smell of litter boxes hit me like a truck.

"Would you like something cold before we get started?" the woman said with a smile.

"Do you still got that Jell-O?" I asked her.

The woman she made a face and said, "Let's try to stay focused, Jackson. Take off your clothes and lie down on the couch. I'm going to fetch the worms."

The woman walked into this kitchenette and I heard her open a fridge, and since I don't object to much, I shucked off my shirt and pants. "Don't move a muscle," the woman called out as I lay down on the couch. "I'm going to be very cross with you, hon, if you don't stay as still as a statue."

She was holding a carton of fishing worms when she returned to the living room, and she dumped a handful of 'em into her palm and sprinkled them on my chest. Well, I weren't particularly partial to them wigglers on my chest, but since I don't object to much I lay as still as a stump.

"Don't move a muscle," the woman repeated. "I'm going to freshen up," and she sashayed outta the room while I lay real stiff on the couch. Well, I wanted to brush them worms to the floor but that wouldn't 'a' been polite—Ma she always told me that you gotta show women respect. But I weren't perturbed when some of them cats hopped up on the couch 'cause them cats they gobbled the worms offa me like I was a Bob Evans buffet.

When the woman returned to the living room, she looked like Frankenstein's bride. Her hair was piled up on top of her head, her eyes were smeared with mascara, and she was wearing this long white dress that puddled at her feet. She was making this creepy, moaning sound as she hobbled in my direction—her voice was so deep that it seemed to be coming from the bottom of a well.

Well, I didn't want to upset her 'cause she already looked wicked enough, so I lay as still as a road-killed buck as she ran her hands over my chest. After a while, she spoke to me and her voice sounded fulla gravel. "Act as though you're asleep," she said. "I don't want you looking at me."

Now I kinda wanted to leave the house and go back to Flakey Jake's, but I didn't have no permission to get off of the couch. But I opened my eyes when she told me that she had a job for me. She said she needed some punishing before we got down to sex.

Well, next thing I knew she was standing above me with a cat-of-nine-tails in her hand. "Flog me, Jackson, flog me," she said, and her voice was still gravelly and low. "Flog me like a carpet then I'll cover you with dirt."

"I ain't used to that kind of floggin," I said and I sat up on the couch, and I kinda hoped I could get out the door without letting no cats escape. I had pretty much decided that things couldn't get no worse, but that weren't a consolation for long 'cause things got a whole lot worse quick. I heard the sound of a truck pulling up outside front door then I heard this booming voice shout, "Baby, it's Jell-O time!"

"It's my boyfriend!" the woman cried, and she sounded more excited than scared. "He's come home early, Jackson. He's gonna kill us both!"

*

Since I still didn't have no permission to get up from the couch, I just sat in my tighty-whities while the woman opened the door. I could hear her talking with someone, and they was talking loud, then the biggest fella I ever seen came lumbering through the door. He looked kinda like Hulk Hogan but his face was sorta blank, and the dude he folded his beefcake arms and said, "How's it hangin', son?"

Well, my pecker was as slack as a bag of oats 'cause I weren't feeling horny no more, but I didn't think it would be good manners to mention something like that. So I told him my name was Toby Dawes and I worked at the Hillsdale Hog Farm, and that I'd be real partial to havin' some Jell-O with him.

The fella he said, "Excuse me, sonny. I would like to talk with Eve."

He took the woman by the arm and led her into what musta been the bedroom. She was panting as she followed behind him, but she didn't look scared at all.

After a coupla minutes, the woman came outta the bedroom. She had taken off her long white dress and was wearin' just her panties and bra, and she sat on the couch beside me and whispered in my ear.

"He wants to watch us, Jackson," she said, and her voice was as husky as corn. "He said he won't punch you in the nose if we'll let him sit there and watch."

"Does this mean we ain't getting no Jell-O?" I said.

The woman squeezed my pecker so hard that one of her nails broke its skin. She said, "Jackson, please pay attention. I'm *not* going to let him join in. That louse has women all over the country, so he's got this coming to him."

Maybe the dude had it coming to him, but I weren't in no shape to perform. My chub felt as poor as a drowned worm that was stuck on a fishing hook. And since there weren't no sense in hanging around to collect me a punch in the nose, I snatched up my clothes and jumped off the couch then jerked the front door open.

"Now you've done it!" the woman cried as I stumbled out onto the porch, and she started to howl like a thievin' dog that caught its paw in a trap. Well, I bolted as fast as a gut-shot stag, so I ain't sure what got her upset, but I had real strong suspicion that some of them cats got out.

*

I ran down Route 231 for a spell then I stopped and put on my clothes. There weren't nobody chasin' me, and I suspected that no one was gonna, so after I zipped my fly up and tucked my shirt back in, I strolled on over to Flakey Jake's and ordered a draft beer at the bar.

Flakey Jake he gave me a big thumbs-up 'cause he thought I had scored me some cooze, and I told him that woman was hurting so bad that I made her cum three times. Flakey Jake drew us both a beer and said mine was on the house, then he raised his mug above his head and offered me a toast. I guess I shoulda paid for that beer steada standin' there proud as a lord, but at least I had me some standards now and I felt real good about that.

Fact Check

HEY THERE, it's Toby Dawes again, and I hope ya ain't tired of me yet. I still live on a farm with my folks in the middle of Putnam County, and, like I said, the local folk kinda look down their noses at me. That's 'cause folks don't place no worth on all the stuff I'm good at. I'm good at shooting brown rats at the Putnam County Dump—I'll bet I've shot 'bout two hundred rats with this .22 Magnum I got. I'm also good at hogging buffalo catfish, which is kinda tricky to do. 'Less you grab them suckers by the gills, their spines will go right through your hand. And I'm really good at fuckin' though I ain't had much opportunity. But Pa took me to a cathouse 'bout three years ago when I turned seventeen. He thought if I had a taste of real pussy, I'd stop swiping his paperback porn books. So he took me to a brothel in Michigan City and bought me this young whore named Brandi. Brandi she's skinnier than an eel and she's got a nose like a beak—but she's got a nice disposition and she was real supportive of me. See, I never shot no load in her 'cause I jizzed while she was washing my willie, but Brandi she told Pa that I made her cum like a rabbit. Brandi wanted Pa to think I done good 'cause she could tell I felt real ashamed, and Pa he shouted, "Praise the Lord," and grinned like a henhouse fox. The madam of the whorehouse she smiled and pinched my cheek, and she said I had the potential to qualify for a discount rate.

Maybe I'm gettin' ahead of myself by saying I'm good at fucking, but I'll bet I *coulda* made Brandi cum if Pa had bought me another hour. You know, I've been texting Brandi on this iPhone Ma gave me for Christmas, and Brandi's been texting me back 'cause I guess she's kinda lonely. I told her I'm gonna drive up to see her, 'cause I just got my driver's license, and that I wanna take her to a tractor pull and maybe a McDonald's. I'm hoping she'll give up whoring and make an honest man out of me.

I guess all this stuff I'm telling you ain't making too good an impression. So I wanna tell you more good stuff I done before I get too far into this story. I've been workin' at the Hillsdale Hog Farm since flunking outta Putnamville High School, and the manager of the hog farm—his name is Cecil Baumgardner—he said I'm a real hard worker and I'm good at handling hogs. He said he ain't seen no one who can handle hogs better 'an me, and he said that someday soon he'll make me assistant manager. I told Cecil the secret to handling hogs is to let 'em know you care for them. 'Cept when they're eating each other, hogs are real sensitive critters, so if you scratch 'em behind their heads a bit, they'll become your friends for life.

I'm also real good at swipin' Pa's porn books—I still ain't quit that habit. See, Pa he's got them books alphabetized so he can keep track of 'em, so I take the covers off the books I wanna read, wrap them around paperback Westerns, and slip them Westerns into his collection so Pa won't know his porn books are gone. And once I'm done readin' the cock books I swipe, I just paste their covers back on 'em, and when I stick 'em back into Pa's collection, they look as good as new. I told Brandi all about that the last time I texted her. When Brandi texted me back, she seemed to be blown away. She wrote that I had the potential to become a famous spy.

Well, that purty much describes my life, and I guess it could stand some improvement. But I wanna finish this story 'cause it's

146

kinda interestin'. So I'm hoping you cut me some slack and let me get on with it.

*

My story it starts a coupla weeks before President Trump first got impeached, so I weren't surprised to see people demonstrating when I was walking to work. They was standing beside Route 231, holdin' up signs to the traffic, and one of them signs had a drawing of Trump that made his head look like a peach. Well, that got my mouth watering 'cause I'm real fond of yella peaches, and I kinda wish Ma had placed a coupla of 'em inside my lunch box. But when I got closer to the Hillsdale Hog Farm, I kinda lost my appetite. You can smell the farm before you even see it 'cause it's riper than shit in a diaper, but I'm inclined to take offense when folks complain about how bad it smells. The farm has a dozen long, silvery barns that are really beautiful, and it has this open-air lagoon that looks like a fishing pond.

But I don't wanna talk about the hog farm 'cause my story ain't about that. I don't wanna talk about Donald Trump neither—he said he'd done nothing wrong. I wanna talk about what happened after I got to work. See, this real uncommon bird was sittin' on one of the wheelbarrows. The bird was the size of a pheasant and its feathers were shimmery black, and it had this real long tail that looked like the train of a bridal gown. It hadda be the most beautiful bird that I have ever seen, and I kinda got the feeling that it was sittin' there waiting for me.

The bird didn't pay me no mind as I walked into one of the hog barns, so I put it out of my head while I was inseminating the sows. Heck, that bird was too dern beautiful to be hanging around a hog farm, and I figgered the smell of hog shit would send it on its way. But the bird was still perched on that wheelbarrow after

I quit for the day, so I suspected there hadda be something real special about that bird.

Well, the bird it musta been hungry, so I opened up my lunch box, and I offered it part of a bologna sandwich that I hadn't felt like eating. The bird it cocked its head like I had insulted it, but then it flapped its wings a tad and hopped up on my shoulder. I decided right then and there that I would take it home with me. It made me feel cooler than Long John Silver who owns hundreds of seafood shops. Long John Silver he's always got a bird perched on his shoulder.

*

When I walked into our farmhouse, with that bird squatin' on my shoulder, Pa was sittin' at the kitchen table, and he didn't look particularly happy. Pa was drunk on whiskey, but that ain't nothing unusual. What's unusual was that he was out of sorts 'cause he's usually a real happy drunk.

"Ya been stealing my cock books," Pa said to me the second I walked into the house.

Ma she blushed and said to me, "Toby, I hope that's not true. As long as Pa's pleasuring himself with those books, he won't be bothering me."

I said to Pa, "I ain't stole your cock books. I swear on a stack of Bibles."

Pa said, "How come them books are out of order if you ain't been plundering them? With that bird ya got on yer shoulder, son, you even *look* like a pirate."

I said, "Pa, I swear to God I ain't been stealing your cock books."

"Toby," Pa said. "I get real upset when you don't honor yer father. I was hopin' you'd do what the Good Book says after I bought you that whore."

148

Well, I weren't gonna make no confession 'cause Pa didn't have any proof, so I stood there lookin' purer than snow until that bird spoke up. "*Rrawwk*," said the bird. "*Fac chek*." and my ears they started buzzing. For all his beautiful feathers, that bird had a real annoying voice.

"What's he saying," Pa said.

"It sounded like fact check," said Ma. "And since you're acting suspicious, Toby, that's just what we're going to do."

So my folks went into my bedroom and Ma flipped my mattress onto the floor, and lying on the box springs were half a dozen of Pa's books. The books didn't have no covers on 'em, so I hoped that would give Pa pause, but Pa picked a couple of 'em up and read the title pages out loud.

"*Girls on the Prowl, Lesbian Lunch*. Yep, those are sure my books."

Ma said, "I think both of you ought to be real ashamed."

Well, Pa he weren't ashamed at all—he looked like a hanging judge. He told me I'd broken a whole bunch of Commandments, including taking the Lord's name in vain. He told me them books were sacred and I might just as well have stole from a church. He told me he expected better behavior from a boy who could make a whore cum, and he said that from here on out I was gonna have to live in the barn.

Well, I hadda respect the Fourth Commandment, so me and the bird went out to live in the barn, but I felt as poorly as Cain must have felt when he hadda live east of Eden. I texted Brandi and told her what happened, and Brandi texted me back. She said she was sorry I hadda live in the barn, and I shoulda hid those books better. She also said, if I wanted to come see her, she would give me a bargain rate. I texted her back and told her that, if she agreed to marry me, we could pool our money and rent a trailer in the Putnamville Mobile Home Park. Brandi said she wouldn't consider that until I improved my station in life, so I told her I would soon be promoted to assistant manager.

When I finished texting with Brandi, the bird hopped back on my shoulder. The bird spoke in my ear, and its voice made a sound like chalk draggin' over a blackboard. *"Fac chek, fac chek,"* squawked the bird and that got me to thinkin'. I decided it was time to have me a talk with Cecil Baumgardner.

*

Cecil Baumgardner he's got him an office shack that sits upwind of the hog barns, and when me and the bird got to work the next day, I knocked on the door of the shack. Cecil he let me into his office and said, "Son, what's on yer mind?" I felt real comfortable talking to him 'cause Cecil's a church-going man, so I told him how I hadda live in our barn 'cause Pa caught me stealing his cock books, and I told him I weren't cut out to be living in no barn. I also told him I wanted to marry this whore, so I won't have to live in no barn, but the whore weren't gonna marry me until I improved my station in life.

Cecil Baumgardner said, "I see, I see," and he leaned back in his office chair, and that chair squeaked like rats in a hopper because Cecil's a real heavy man. Cecil told me that Jesus our Savior got his start in a barn, and that living in a barn sounded a whole lot better than marrying some whore.

I asked Cecil when he was gonna promote me to assistant manager, and Cecil said I needed a livestock degree if I was gonna help manage a hog farm. "But that ain't the point," said Cecil as he rocked back and forth in his chair. "I ain't inclined to promote *no one* who's planning to marry a whore."

When I said I'd be saving the whore from sin, Cecil said, "Don't give me that. With that bird you got on yer shoulder, you look like a lecherous pirate."

Cecil told me how the Prodigal Son found the Lord while slopping hogs 'cause slopping them hogs helped him realize the error of his ways. He said if I was marrying just to fornicate, I was far from repentin' my ways, and I oughta keep slopping them oinker 'til I see the light of the Lord.

*

Well, I needed a way to show Cecil Baumgardner that I was already filled with the Lord. So I went online on my iPhone, and I found this real neat site. It was run by this fella called Luther Sunday who had saved a whole lot of souls, and it told me how I could become an ordained minister in just a few easy steps. Well, I filled out this form on the site and I got ordained right away, and the site promised to send me my certificate once I made a contribution. So I stuffed my last fifty dollars into an envelope and mailed it to the address on the site, and it weren't but a few days later that my certificate came in the mail. I was now a minister of the Lord and my name was now Reverend Dawes, and I was allowed to perform weddings and save unfortunate souls. Well, I texted Brandi and told her how I'd become a man of God, and Brandi texted me back and said she was real excited for me. She said when I came to see her to bring my certificate because that certificate entitled me to get fifty dollars off.

Well, I showed my certificate to Cecil Baumgardner and he weren't particularly impressed. He said he would never make no reverend an assistant manager. He said most preachers were nothing but thievin', conniving crooks, and it would be a cold day in hell before he trusted any of them with his hogs.

Well, since Cecil weren't gonna promote me, I did some real deep thinking 'cause it looked like I'd need another plan to get Brandi to marry me. So I decided to borrow Pa's truck and drive to that cathouse in Michigan City and save Brandi's soul from eternal damnation by bringing her into God's fold. After that, Brandi and I could get married and I could make her cum.

Well, I told Pa I needed to borrow his truck so I could save Brandi's soul, and Pa he's got too much religion to stand in the way of the Lord. So Pa he gave me the keys to his truck then he handed me a Bible. He said anyone who could pleasure a whore oughta have no trouble saving her soul.

*

With that bird perched on my shoulder, I drove to Michigan City, and it took me a while to find that whorehouse 'cause I had forgotten the way. So I drove through a buncha neighborhoods that were full of weedy sidewalks, and I hadda ask a cop for directions before I found the place. The whorehouse looked a whole lot worse than I remembered it to be. It had broken shutters, a collapsing roof and paint peeling off its walls. Some scary-looking kids were watching me while I was parking the truck, and I hoped that I would be able to save Brandi's soul before they snatched my tires.

I was holding the Bible Pa gave me when I knocked on the door to the cathouse, and this madam who looked like a schoolteacher opened up the door. She stared at me real suspicious like she didn't recognize me, so I told her that Reverend Dawes was here to pay a call on Brandi. The madam said she had never seen a reverend with a bird sittin' on his shoulder, and she asked me if I had an appointment because Brandi was her most popular whore.

Well, I told the madam I couldn't go nowhere 'til I saved Brandi from hell and damnation, and that's when that bird started squawking so loud that my eardrums started to pound. The madam she shook her head and said that preachers are lousy tippers, but that I was welcome to come inside if I kept that bird from squawking. So I scratched the bird behind its head and the bird it stopped making a racket then I followed the madam into this parlor that smelled of mildew and cats. The parlor was fulla whores and all of 'em looked older than Ma. They was lounging about on sofas and watchin' Donald Trump talkin' on television.

When Brandi came into the parlor, she looked like she'd just woken up from a nap. Her hair was kinda messy, she was rubbing at her eyes, and the lingerie she was wearin' looked like it needed ironing. When she noticed the Bible in my hand, she chuckled like a brook. "Toby," she said. "I hope you haven't come here to save my soul."

Well, I told her I hadda save her soul in order to marry her, and Brandi said she weren't gonna be saved by no one with a bird on his shoulder. She also said she wished I had texted her that I was coming to see her because she had plans to paint her toenails and maybe wash her hair. When Brandi said that, the bird looked at her and sorta cocked its head.

Brandi said it was really touching that I still wanted to marry her, and she said she just might change her mind once I'd paid her for an hour. The moment she said that, I kinda suspected that the bird was gonna speak up, so I weren't surprised when it ruffled its feathers and started squawking again. *"Fac chek, fac chek,"* the bird kept saying and Brandi she got real annoyed. She said if that bird didn't shut its beak, I could take my Bible and go.

I rubbed that bird behind its head, but that bird it wouldn't shut up, and Brandi she lost all her patience and told me I hadda go. She said, "I'm not going to marry a pig slopper who can't even control his bird."

Well, the bird it kept on squawkin', and Brandi she kept getting madder, so I concluded she weren't gonna marry me and that was the end of that.

*

Well, I was feeling kinda poorly after Brandi broke up with me, and I decided I needed to find me a place where folks respected religion. So a few days later, I hopped into Pa's truck and drove to this Donald Trump rally. Folks at them rallies are real religious and know how to treat a reverend, so I was pretty sure I could find me a church-going girl to marry.

The rally was being held at the Kellogg Arena in Battle Creek, Michigan. I'm real fond of Kellogg cereal, especially Rice Krispies with peaches, and I figured that was a real good place for Donald Trump to hold a rally. But when I tried to get into the arena, this guard turned me away. He said he weren't gonna let no one inside who had a bird sittin' on his shoulder. So I sat outside the arena with the folks who were tailgating, and I watched Donald Trump making his speech on a giant television screen.

After a while, a coupla women approached me and said they liked my bird. They patted the bird and made cooing sounds and remarked on how tame it was, and they said that it was the most beautiful bird that they had ever seen. They asked me if they could borrow the bird to show their families, and I told them that wouldn't bother me none 'cause my shoulder was feeling sore.

Well, the women carried the bird away, and that was the last I seen of it. 'Cause Donald Trump he kept ramblin' on, and them tailgaters was getting hungry, so a lot of them started milling around and lighting up outdoor grills. A few hours later, this janitor told me what happened to the bird. He said some of them tailgaters ate it with chitlins and barbecue sauce.

Pickup

I AM NOT IN THE HABIT of picking up women in bars, but habits are expendable when your life is topsy-turvy. So when I spotted her sitting alone in a corner of the Castleberg Lounge, I knew I was going to dispense with the tyranny of habit.

She was blonde, slim and finely-boned—much like a young Helen Mirren—yet she did not seem out of place in the seedy, local bar. The band was playing "Broken Lady," a Gatlin Brothers favorite, and this mournful ballad made her look accessible to me. As I walked towards her to ask her to dance, I hoped she was truly broken. If I could provide her with the illusion of support, we might share a few moments of touch.

"Madam," I said theatrically. "Would you spare this poor traveler a dance?"

She put down her drink and studied me in a manner that made me blush, and I prayed that her dating standards were as charitable as her looks. My recent divorce had all but convinced me that women expect too much.

"I don't like this song, but yes," she murmured. "I wish you had picked another."

When she rose from her chair, I felt as though I had passed a critical test, but she wanted to know more about me after I followed her onto the dance floor. "Please state your name and business," she said in a teasing voice.

She was obviously a regular, accustomed to getting hit on, and I knew it might be a challenge for me to outshine her pack of suitors.

"Tom Hemmings, soldier of fortune," I said as I carelessly stepped on her toes.

She winced and patted my shoulder. "Sally Potter," she said. "You know, I have an uncle named Tom. He got picked up for kiddie porn last year. He's locked up in that penal farm out on Highway 40."

"I start work there tomorrow," I said. "They hired me as a guard."

She arched her eyebrows. "How exciting," she said. "So what do you want with me, Tom Hemmings? I'm just a small-town girl."

"I'm new in town," I replied. "I could use a bit of company."

"A *bit* of company," she laughed. "Is that all you think I'm good for?"

Was she good for a one-night stand? I wondered as we stumbled around the dance floor. Ever since breaking the lockstep of a short, confining marriage, I had been feeling the need for an adventure to take me out of my funk. But the fruits of divorce implied more than the thrill of starting a job at a prison. I saw no harm if my bounty included a tryst with a barfly as well.

Reading my mind, she squeezed my fingers. "Don't get ideas, you fancy talker. I don't sleep with idle strangers."

"I'm not that idle," I told her, hoping to disarm her with my wit.

"Why? Did your wife just dump you?" she asked.

"How did you know that?" I said.

She smiled. "I'm familiar with self-absorbed men. I was married to a cop."

Some empathy seemed called for, so I pretended to be concerned. "I'm sorry he didn't make time for you."

"You're not sorry at all, Tom Hemmings," she said as the song droned to an end. "Besides, if I'd spent more time with him, it would only have made things worse. Cops are good for heroics, but they're pretty hopeless as husbands."

We left the dance floor. She again squeezed my hand. "Thank you for the dance," she said.

"Sorry I picked the wrong song," I replied as she sat back down in her chair.

She fished a tissue from her purse and dabbed at her mascara. "I enjoyed our chat, Tom Hemmings," she said. "Please ask me to dance again."

*

I sat at the bar for an hour, pretending to nurse a beer, and I watched as half a dozen men invited her to dance. She politely turned each of them down, and my hopes began to rise. I decided my chances of bedding her were considerable, after all. I did not attribute this to my appearance—I'm a plain-looking man who at thirty was probably five years younger than she was—but I had convinced myself that the bar's dim lighting made me look like a tall, mature stranger.

The band was playing "Not Fade Away," a classic hit from the fifties, and I abandoned my stool at the bar and approached her once again. The jaunty lyrics spurred my courage as I strolled across the dance floor. *"I'm a gonna tell you how it's gonna beee."* *Bumpa bumpa bum bum.* *"Yer gonna give yer love to meee."* Infused with the magic of Buddy Holly, I once again asked her to dance.

"What took you so long?" she said.

"I wanted to give you some space."

She frowned. "I have plenty of space, Tom Hemmings. I don't need any more."

"Would you like to dance?" I repeated.

She shrugged. "I don't think dancing's your thing. Please sit down, let's finish our chat. I'm not going to force you to dance."

We talked for almost an hour, and she told me about herself. Her story seemed rather provincial and maybe a little trite. She worked as a records clerk at the Castleberg Hospital, she had been married and divorced three times, her hobbies were going to the movies and reading romance books. She mentioned only briefly that she had left her home at the age of sixteen and had afterwards had an abortion. Since I suspected a family member had abused her, I did not pursue this subject. Instead, I kept our conversation light and was encouraged by her easy laughter.

When she asked me why I was taking a job at the Indiana Penal Farm, I said, "For the hell of it." This response more than adequately describes the milestones of my life. It applies to why I had dropped out of college and backpacked all over Australia. It applies to my short-lived marriage to a woman who had wisely discarded me. It explains why I had worked a bunch of odd jobs while trying to make it as a writer. If my life needed more introspection than that, I did not want to make the effort. "For the hell of it" was even the reason I was trying to pick her up.

"Tom Hemmings," she said, "you impress me as a rather shallow man."

"Would you prefer somebody profound?" I asked.

She smiled and sipped her drink. "I don't know about that," she joked. "You're too good at playing the clown."

"I'm not trying to sleep with you," I lied. "One-nighters aren't my thing."

She smiled. "Oh, how disappointing. I adore a one-night stand."

She crossed her legs and eased back in her chair. She seemed to be getting bored. "So where are you staying, Tom Hemmings, if you're so new in town?"

"The Holiday Inn near Highway 40."

"The Holiday Inn," she parroted. "I find that a little depressing. But if you've managed to keep your room tidy, you're welcome to take me there."

*

She held my hand as we walked to my room. There was no one around and the hallway was quiet, but she flinched when she heard the clanking of a noisy ice machine.

I escorted her into my hotel room, and she sat down on the queen-sized bed. Noticing a pile of books on the nightstand, she picked up one of them.

"*The Canterbury Tales*, my goodness," she said. "So that's why you talk like an actor. I had to read this in high school, and I haven't touched it since."

"It's a masterpiece."

"That's the reason," she said. She placed the book back on the nightstand. "I wouldn't survive in this boring town if I broadened my horizons too much."

She placed a pillow under her elbows then leisurely kicked off her pumps. Her shoes made a hollow clatter as they landed on the floor. "A prison guard that *reads*," she laughed. "You are full of surprises, Tom Hemmings."

"Does that impress you?"

"A little," she said. "but I'm not very hard to impress."

I sat down on the bed beside her. She rubbed the back of my neck. "I fall in love very quickly, Tom Hemmings. I hope you can keep up with me."

"Tell me about your uncle," I said. "The one who's serving time."

She interlaced my fingers with hers then rested her head on my shoulder. "He's where he deserves to be," she said. "But I could say that about us all."

"Was he the one?" I asked her.

She nodded. "His bedroom was right next to mine."

She told me about the incident as though she were describing a movie. Her voice was monotonic and without a trace of self-pity. It had happened only once, she said, after which she had left home for good and resided with an aunt. She had never reported the matter because she didn't trust cops or lawyers. "The system would have raped me again," she said. "One rape was all I could handle."

"I'm sorry."

She sighed. "Stop saying that word. It's *terribly* depressing. How can we enjoy what we came here to do if you're going to feel sorry for me?"

I touched her breast as though fondling a kitten. She pushed my hand away. "Let's be tidy about it," she said.

She rose from the bed, slipped off her dress and suspended it on the coat rack. Returning to the bed, she opened her purse and handed me a condom.

After we finished coupling, she shucked the condom off me then she retrieved a towel from the bathroom and meticulously dried me off. She seemed more intent on cleaning me than she had been on making love.

"Thank you for making me laugh," she said before falling asleep at my side.

*

I awoke to the clatter of the ice machine that was still laboring in the hallway. It was morning—she was already dressed and was perched on a chair sipping coffee. She looked like a commuter impatient to board a train.

"Will I see you again?" she asked.

"That might prove untidy," I said.

She handed me a hotel postcard on which she had scrawled her address. "I'm inviting you to move in with me, stud. I don't like living alone."

"Are you sure?" I asked her.

She blew on her coffee. "No, but that makes it exciting."

There was no time for discussion, so I simply gave her a nod. I was scheduled to report to the prison farm to begin my orientation.

"Some coffee before you go?" she said.

I nodded a second time.

"Cream and sugar?"

"Black."

She laughed. "You're such a basic man."

She manipulated the hotel coffee machine then brought me a cup of black coffee. "Don't look so shocked, Tom Hemmings," she said. "Haven't you shacked up before?"

"I've known you for just a few hours," I said.

"Maybe that's for the best."

"So why invite me to live with you?"

She placed her cup on a nightstand then sat back watching me dress. "Must everything have a reason?" she said. "All right, I'll give you a reason. The first thing I noticed about you is that you have nice fingernails. I've never been able to resist a man who takes care of his fingernails."

"That isn't much of a reason," I said.

"Well, I don't live in much of a place. It's a bungalow near the movie theater. The walls need a coat of paint. Maybe if you move in with me, you could give them a fresh coat of paint."

"Maybe you should shack up with a handyman."

She threw back her head and laughed. "You're handy enough for me, Tom Hemmings. Just keep taking care of your nails."

*

161

After I walked her to her car, I drove to the Indiana Penal Farm: an expansive penitentiary alongside Highway 40. I was in an especially buoyant mood after spending the night with her, and as I parked beside the arch gate, my cheerfulness endured. The barracks beyond the wire mesh fence reminded me of red-bricked fraternity houses, and the watchtowers hovering above them made me think of giant mushrooms. I was even seduced by the lettering painted on the arch. The message read, "Let he who passes through these gates renew his hope."

My orientation was held in a cramped conference room in the administration building, and I sat with a dozen strangers who had also been hired as guards. A short, excitable, training captain introduced himself to us then he paced back and forth like a wolf in a cage while he gave us a scripted talk. He told us his name was Harold Hawkins and he didn't tolerate fuckups, and if we expected to keep our jobs, we would have to learn how to say no to inmates.

"Ya can't be friends with these low-lifes," he barked. "They'll just take advantage of you. If I catch any of you cozying up to them, I'll fire you on the spot."

He went on to say we were all on probation, so we had better toe the line. "If I catch any of ya sleepin' on duty, I'll fire you on the spot. If I ever smell alcohol on you, I'll fire you on the spot. And if any of you sneak in contraband, you know what I'm gonna do?"

"You'll fire us on the spot," I said.

He gave me a withering stare then he hooked his thumbs behind his belt. "I saw ya last night in the Castleberg Lounge. You was bird-dogging Sally Potter."

"She know you?" I asked.

"I know *her*," he snapped. "The whole *town* knows Sally Potter. Son, didja come to your senses, or did you cross the line with her too?"

"I'll be living with her," I said. "Is that any business of yours?"

"It ain't," he replied. "I'm just doing you a favor. You need to know there ain't no percentage in messin' with Sally Potter."

During our lunch break, a shift sergeant approached me in the officers' dining hall. He said he'd heard about my altercation with Captain Hawkins, and that the captain was full of shit. "He ain't no judge of women," the shift sergeant assured me. "His wife ran off with one of the inmates a coupla months ago."

*

We spent the rest of the day watching some video training tapes. When the matinee was over, Captain Hawkins gave us some final advice. He suggested we go to Walmart and buy portable TVs. He said we were all going to spend two weeks at a correctional academy up north. "There ain't no entertainment there—just classrooms and a shotgun range. If ya don't wanna sit in yer room jacking off, ya better have a TV."

He said the next training cycle would start up in a couple of weeks, so we'd better start working the flab off and learn how to stay awake. In the meantime, we would get some on-the-job training at the Indiana Penal Farm. Tomorrow, each of us would be paired up with a seasoned officer, and if anyone showed up with booze on his breath he would be fired on the spot.

After returning to the Holiday Inn, I took a jog along Highway 40. Afterwards, I showered, checked out of the hotel and drove towards Castleberg. That I was about to act out of character did not seem important to me. There were probably a dozen good reasons not to shack up with Sally Potter, but the censure of a cuckold was certainly not one of them.

Castleberg, a gutted college town, was as barren as a moonscape. As I drove past the abandoned IBM warehouse and a dozen empty storefronts, it struck me that practically all of the streets had been named after famous poets. Names like Keats Lane and Tennison Way did nothing to salvage the town, which seemed too stark and ravaged to merit the nuance of verse.

She lived in a small house on Longfellow Street, a cottage with gray-panel siding, and I felt as though I were trespassing as I pulled into the driveway. She answered the door on my very first knock then invited me into the house. Although barefoot and wearing cutoff shorts, she seemed to be ill at ease. She bit her lip as I entered the house, and her smile did not reach her eyes.

"You're sweating," she said. Her voice was cool.

"I'm a jogger," I replied.

"Well, you might have jogged to a flower shop and picked up some roses for me. What kind of man sleeps with a woman then doesn't bring her roses?"

"A self-centered one," I joked.

She frowned. "You're *such* a primitive man. I guess I'm a sucker for primitive men, but some roses would also be nice."

"How about I go fetch some?"

She stiffened and shrugged. "How about I just fetch you a beer?"

Stung by her passive-aggression, I sat down on a cream-colored couch. *How could I have failed to bring her flowers?* I thought as I surveyed the room. The room lacked plants or artifacts, the carpet was threadbare and torn, and except for a metal crucifix, there was nothing on the walls. The barrenness of the room compounded my sin of omission.

She padded into a kitchenette then returned with two cans of Coors. Setting the cans on a coffee table, she curled up on the couch beside me. When she interlaced her fingers with mine, it seemed like an act of concession; the tension in her body suggested she had not gotten over her sulk.

"How was work?" she asked politely.

"I fought for your honor," I said.

"Oh really?" she laughed. "How medieval of you. Did you think I was worth defending?"

"Well the training officer trash-talked you, and I told him to mind his own business."

"That must have been Harold Hawkins. He's the laughingstock of the county."

"Is he?" I said. I shook my head, but the news did not displease me.

She released my hand. "You call standing up to that miserable gnome fighting for my *honor*? How can *anyone* take a man seriously whose wife eloped with an inmate?"

"Has he hit on you in the Castleberg Lounge?"

"What do you think, Tom Hemmings? He's a desperate little man. Cops and guards." She sighed like a kettle. "They just can't hang onto their women."

Using a remote on the coffee table, she turned on a television set. She flipped to a rerun of *The Mary Tyler Moore Show* then put the remote back on the table.

"Will you watch it with me, Tom Hemmings?" she said. "I never miss this show."

"I never miss it either," I fibbed.

"Stop teasing me," she muttered. "I don't find it funny at all."

We watched as Mary Tyler Moore's character broke up with her latest suitor. As the episode ended, Sally stretched like a feline and finished drinking her beer. "I'm *glad* she kicked him out," she said. "He was nothing but a *beast*."

"Mary lets all her men go," I said. "She's never satisfied."

"Maybe not," she replied, "but at least she has standards. I wish I could say the same."

"Is that why you let me pick you up?"

"*Must* you put it that way?"

"Well, why did you tell me you like one-night stands?"

"Why did you *believe* me, Tom Hemmings?"

"I found you pretty convincing," I said.

She folded her arms across her chest as though she were guarding her breasts. "How *easy* it was to convince you of that. I think you had better leave."

*

Bruised by her sudden mood change, I drove back to the hotel but not before parking at a KFC and picking up a box of fried chicken. In spite of my lack of etiquette, I was starting to ache for her—after all, she had given me sex and affection and had not expected too much. *How could I have forgotten roses?* I thought as I drove past the empty storefronts. *How could I have slighted a woman who had been more than generous to me?*

I was hoping a change of solitude would get her off my mind, so I asked the desk clerk for a different room, and he handed me a new key. But the total sameness of the room gave me little comfort. I could even hear the familiar clunking of the ice machine in the hallway.

Not feeling particularly hungry, I set the chicken aside. I wanted a stronger distraction than takeout, so I turned on the six o'clock news. Jimmy Carter, running for president, was addressing the American public, and I felt that he was scolding me when he promised he would never lie. I dozed for several minutes then awoke to the sound of thunder. To my annoyance, a *Brady Bunch* rerun had replaced the six o'clock news. The canned, robotic laughter made me feel like a washed-out clown, so I grabbed the remote from the nightstand and turned the TV off. Only then did I realize that someone was hammering on the door to my room.

I answered the door. She was standing there. Her hair was matted and wet. "It's pouring, Tom Hemmings," she gasped. "I need to dry my hair."

"Why are you out in the rain?" I blurted.

She sighed as though chastised then shook her head. "I *missed* you," she said icily. "Is that some kind of *crime*?"

She was still dressed in cut-off shorts, her blouse was untucked and disheveled, and swollen blots of mascara made her look like a panda bear. "Will you *please* let me use your bathroom? I *know* I look a mess."

"You look sexy to me," I murmured, and I regretted the remark right away. Her rumpled appearance had too quickly awakened the insensitive beast in me.

"Tom Hemmings," she snapped. "I will leave this *minute* if you don't let me tidy up."

Not wishing to vex her a second time, I invited her into the room. Seconds later, the bathroom door closed behind her and the hairdryer started to hum. My heart was racing like a sprinter's and I wanted to feign composure, so I picked up my copy of *The Last of the Mohicans* and pretended to be reading.

When she shuffled out of the bathroom, she was running a brush through her hair, and she looked at me as though I were keeping her from an appointment. "What a bookworm you are," she muttered. This time she did not seem impressed.

"Books keep me from getting lonely," I said.

"How *convenient* not to be lonely," she snapped. "Perhaps I should have read *Little Women* instead of coming here."

Hoping to change the subject, I offered her some Kentucky Fried Chicken.

"Is that what we're having for dinner?" she said. "Can't we go to a restaurant, at least?"

"Of course," I replied.

She laughed mirthlessly. "No, let's just have the chicken, I don't want to be an expense. Oh, how I wish I had standards—I'm *such* a bargain date."

As we sat on the bed, eating chicken and coleslaw, she started to relax. "I'm sorry I was such a bitch," she said. "It had nothing to do with you."

"I'm glad I wasn't the reason," I said.

She bit into a drumstick and looked at me pensively. "Don't get cocky, Tom Hemmings," she said. "You'll soon give me *plenty* of reason."

"How can you be so sure about that?"

"You're living life out of a suitcase, and you seem way too content with that. I know promising men when I see them. You aren't once of them, Tom."

The accuracy of her perception demanded an honest reply. "So why did you invite me to move in with you? Why not a more promising man?"

She finished eating the drumstick then picked up a paper napkin. After carefully wiping her fingers, she said, "Why do you think, Tom Hemmings? Feral men excite me. I know that's not much of a reason, but I don't have a better one."

Later, I lay under the bed covers, watching her undress. I was impatient to feel her body, but she moved as though in a trance. She slowly snaked off her shorts and blouse and smoothed them out on the bed, then she hung them from the coatrack as though they were works of art.

As she peeled off her bra and panties, she looked at me and smiled. "How come I want you so much?" she asked. "You're just using me, Tom Hemmings. I wish I wasn't enough of a tramp as to know that about you for sure."

"You've read me like a novel," I joked.

Laughing, she slipped under the sheets and fitted me with a condom. She then snuggled up beside me and threw her leg over my thigh. "You're more like a comic book, Tom Hemmings," she said. "Just be glad I'm a very light reader."

*

The following morning, I drove back to the prison to start my on-the-job training. Making love to Sally had exhausted me, and I did not feel up to being schooled. Why had she clung to me throughout the night like a cave dweller spooked by a storm? "Hold me, Tom Hemmings," she kept repeating. "I want you to hold me tight."

After donning the light-blue uniform of a correctional officer, I reported to the morning roll call to receive my first assignment. At roll call, Captain Hawkins assigned me to the dorm for laundry workers, and he introduced me to a short, wiry woman in her thirties who was going to be my mentor. Her name was Officer Dobbins, her hair was clipped into a buzz cut, and her alert brown eyes appraised me as though she were pricing a used car. "Keep an eye on him, Lou Ellen," Captain Hawkins remarked. "He's livin' with Sally Potter, so his judgment ain't too good."

"That true?" Officer Dobbins asked me.

I looked at Captain Hawkins. "Why do you keep bringing that up?"

The captain laughed and slapped my back. "Ya can't do yer job if you're pussy-whipped, son. That means ya dunno how to take charge."

"That true?" Officer Dobbins repeated. She seemed to be highly amused.

"Just show me my job," I replied.

Officer Dobbins told me to pay attention as we entered the laundry dorm, a cavernous barracks where a hundred inmates were on their bunks awaiting count. As she guided me through the count procedure, she kept trying not to laugh, and her chuckles caused me to miscount twice before our numbers matched.

Later, she demonstrated how to shakedown the bunks and inspect the footlockers, and she showed me how to test the window bars by striking them with a baton. "Do that every shift, hon," she said. "Make sure you hit them hard. That will discourage the inmates from trying to work them loose." She also told me to keep my cool if inmates started to fight. She said to call for backup and not get involved in the brawl. "Don't let the inmates distract you," she said. "Those fights are usually staged. That means they're planning to knife someone on the other side of the dorm."

When the shift was over, Officer Dobbins asked me to cut Captain Hawkins some slack. She said if she could take him more seriously, she'd report him for groping her. "But I just can't do it, hon," she said. "I feel sorta sorry for him. His wife ran off with an inmate, and he'll never live it down."

*

I spent a full week assigned to the laundry dorm under the tutelage of Officer Dobbins. She advised me to forget the captain's advice and to build some rapport with the inmates. "Don't get *too* friendly with them, hon," she said. "That will make them look like snitches, but it's okay to ignore minor infractions and to joke around with them some."

She demonstrated her humor one day when we were taking the mid-shift count—when an inmate tried to disrupt the process by meowing like a cat. "Will someone *please* feed that pussy," she said as she finished circling the dorm. The entire dorm rippled with laughter while we tabulated the count, and a couple of inmates told the joker not to mess with Officer Dobbins.

That evening, while sitting on Sally's couch, I described the incident to her. We were eating takeout pizza while watching *The Mary Tyler Moore Show*. I had waited for a commercial break before telling her the story.

She stared at me and nibbled her lip. "Is *she* your new girlfriend?" she snapped. "Are you tired of me already?"

"I think she's a dyke," I protested.

"Stop *lying* to me," she cried. "I've known Lou Ellen since we were in high school. She wants to get into your pants."

Her eyes teared up and she dropped her gaze and went back to watching the program, and I wondered if it was time for me to pack my bag and go back to the hotel. *This woman is crazy*, I reasoned. *This woman is out of her head. Why does she have to be beautiful? Why does that still turn me on?*

When the program ended, she rose from the couch then switched the television off. "Are you going to lecture me, Tom Hemmings?" she said. "The way you're looking at me, I feel a lecture coming on."

I chose my words as though they were pearls. "You're wrong about me and Officer Dobbins. I mean that in a nice way."

She carried our plates to the kitchenette and dumped them into the sink. Turning around to face me, she drew a ragged breath. "All right, I'm wrong, you're right," she said. "You've set the record straight. Do you really think that matters when you're just another man?"

"I don't want you thinking badly about me."

Shaking her head, she rinsed off the plates then shuffled back to the couch. She sat down beside me, picked up my hand and cupped it in both of hers. "You're living out of a suitcase," she said. "You're employed as a prison guard. If you want me to stop thinking badly about you, you're not making much of an effort."

"You told me I was exciting."

"Well, I'm telling you something else now."

"Do you want me to leave?"

She shook her head. "*No*, I don't want you to leave. Whenever things get difficult, men like you want to leave."

She kissed me as though she were sampling a dish at a buffet. "You taste like anchovies," she complained and turned her head away.

Despite her bewildering mood, I felt myself getting aroused. "Tell me what you want me to do," I urged.

"You should *know* what to do," she muttered. "Why is it my job to tell you?"

"I'm just a simple man," I said. "Consider it charity."

She dropped my hand and rubbed her eyes. "Will you *please* stop talking above my head? It's like you're laughing at me."

"Did I say something funny?"

"No, you just talk like you're read too many books."

"I thought that impressed you."

"It does," she said, "but not in the way you think. Talking with you is like meeting Mark Twain, and his writing is so blasé."

She rose from the couch and stared at me with wet, accusing eyes. "Why do you need to impress me at all? I'm just the local tramp. Ask anyone in town, they'll tell you the same. I'm only the local tramp."

"I'm sorry they think that."

She rolled her eyes. "That's *not* why you need to be sorry. How little I care what they think about me. I'd just like to meet a *man*."

*

"Count time," Officer Dobbins called the following afternoon.

The inmates retreated to their bunks, and we began the mid-shift count. Moving in opposite directions, we took individual tallies, counting each inmate quickly as we orbited the dorm. Our numbers matched on the very first go-around, and Officer Dobbins phoned the count in.

When the count for the entire prison cleared, the inmates filed out for lunch, and Officer Dobbins suggested I stroll around the dorm to keep from nodding off. We were seated at the officers' station, a horseshoe-shaped counter in the center of the dorm, and I could not ignore the severity with which she studied me.

"Does it show?" I asked.

"It shows," she replied. "Sally Potter is tough on her men."

"She told me she has no standards," I said.

Officer Dobbins shook her head. "She's a funny kind of woman if you want to know the truth. She'll live with a man for a month or two and then find fault with him."

"She's found fault with me already," I said. "It only took her a week."

"So why are you still shacking up with her, hon. You trying to prove her wrong?"

Before I could answer, a tall, tattooed inmate bellied up to the officers' station. He had blue, piercing eyes, a Roman nose and a smile that seemed carved on his face. Apparently, he had skipped lunch so he could chat with Officer Dobbins.

Leaning on the counter, he said, "Miss Dobbins, you look real nice today."

"Eddie Leach," she replied. "You're going to lose weight if you keep on skipping lunch. Didn't your mama teach you not to be missing meals?"

The inmate laughed, showing straight white teeth. "My mama taught me to watch over the ladies—make sure they get treated right. If any of these bozos start bothering you, I wantcha to let me know."

Officer Dobbins laughed and said, "Eddie, *you're* the only one bothering me."

"Aww, Officer Dobbins," the inmate drawled. "Why are you giving me a hard time today?"

She waved him away as though shooing a fly. "Get out of here, hon," she said. "Don't tell me about your hard time. You'll just have to find a Kleenex and take care of it yourself."

After the inmate ambled away from us, she glanced at me, shaking her head. "He's trying to soften me up, hoping I'll bring in drugs, but that's not going to happen."

"Why do you let him keep bothering you?" I asked.

She looked at me with serious eyes and replied in a patient voice. "Hon," she said, "if you're going to work here, there's something you need to know. It's the inmates that run the place—not the guards. The inmates just let us work here. Now they'll let you take count and do your inspections, they'll let you enforce the rules, they'll even allow you to write them up if you don't get carried away. But they can take your life any time they want, so you don't need to be a hard-ass. In case you haven't noticed, we're outnumbered fifty to one."

What have I gotten myself into? I wondered. *Do I really need this much adventure? Maybe it wouldn't be such a bad thing if Hawkins fired me.*

Aware of my thoughts, Officer Dobbins smiled and wagged a finger at me. "Just do your job," she said, "and don't be a prick about it. Hon, your chances are much better here than they are with Sally Potter."

*

I spent my next few workdays assigned to the visiting room, a sterile lounge with low tables, couches and several vending machines. I was working alongside a fleshless officer whose name was Henry Yoakum, a short, fawning man in his fifties with a poached, misshapen face. We were sitting at an officers' perch overlooking the room. The room was filled with inmates talking with wives and girlfriends.

The first thing Yoakum said to me was, "I take my hat off to you, guv'nor."

I told him, "I'm only a guard in training."

"No matter," Yoakum said grinning. "Hawkins told me yer living with Sally Potter, and that's a wunnerful thing. You gotta be a hell of a cocksmith to be pleasin' a woman like that."

"Why does that matter to *you*?" I said.

"'Cause you're way ahead of me, sir. I've tried to pick her up six or eight times, and she always sends me packing. She tells me she don't fuck fossils, and I need to stay outta her hair."

"So why do you keep trying?"

He cackled like a hen. "Guv'nor, she's balled half the men in town, including some married fellas. So I figger it's just a matter of time 'til she spreads her legs for ol' Henry."

"Can we end this conversation?" I asked him. "You're supposed to discuss this job."

"This job don't *need* discussin'," said Yoakum. "You can learn it in fifteen minutes. But holdin' onto a beauty like Sally is somethin' worth jawing about."

I insisted he show me the job, and he told me how to regulate visits. I was to check the inmate's visiting card when a caller came to the counter, and I was to deny visitation to anyone whose name was not on the card. Once an inmate entered the room, I was to log his time of arrival, and I was to terminate the visit once an hour was up.

"That's 'bout all there is to it?" Yoakum said. "But time is *flexible*, guv'nor. If the visitor is a babe with a nice set of tits, I might give her an extra half-hour."

"That sounds voyeuristic," I said.

Yoakum smirked. "This is a damn good *job* for a voyeur, sir, 'cause you're supposed to watch the babes close. Some of them bitches stick crack in their pussies and sneak that shit to their boyfriends. Usually, they go to the lady's room, so they can hide the balloons in their mouths, then they pass 'em off to their boyfriends by giving 'em a smooch."

"And that's when you write them up?"

Yoakum shrugged. "If I don't have a hard-on, I do. Ya gotta fill out a real detailed report steada admirin' tits and ass, and if the inmate don't shit a balloon, the brass will put *you* on report."

As I glanced around the visiting room, I saw several striking women. One of them was filing her fingernails while chatting with Eddie Leach.

"Why are so many women here?"

Yoakum winked like a firefly. "'Babes like bad boys—that's why," he said. "Don'tcha know nothin' 'bout women? Show a bitch a bad boy, and she'll stick to him like a leech."

Yoakum chuckled, pleased with his pun. "Now that fella you're watchin' got *three or four* broads, and he ain't even much of a crook. Far as I know, all he done was steal some iron from a construction site. But women are so hard up for bad boys, they'll settle for Eddie Leach."

*

The following afternoon, I received my orders to attend the training academy. I was to report to Westfield Correctional Facility, a combined prison and training institute a few miles south of Lake Michigan. I was instructed to pack loose clothing, sneakers and what medications I might need. The orders did not mention a portable television, but I picked one up at Walmart. Thanks to Sally, I had become addicted to *The Mary Tyler Moore Show*.

When I told Sally I was leaving for two weeks of boot camp, she looked at me stonily. "Boot camp?" she said. "How macho that sounds. And what am I supposed to do with myself while you're learning to be a screw?"

"It's only for a couple of weeks," I said. "I'll call you every night."

"Make sure you do, Tom Hemmings," she said. "I'll suffer while you're gone."

"You suffer when I'm *here*," I protested. "The break might do you good."

"So now you're deciding what's *good* for me. You're such a pig, Tom Hemmings."

Maybe it's time this ended, I thought as I started to pack my bag. *Or maybe it's ended already and only my willfulness is alive.*

A few minutes later, she came into the bedroom and gathered my hands in hers. "I'm such a bitch," she murmured. "I'm such a demanding bitch."

"Would it help if I were a bad boy?" I joked.

She let go of my hands and laughed. "A bad boy?" she said. "Just what are you saying? You're bad for me *already*, Tom Hemmings. You're *such* a narrow man."

*

The Westfield Correctional Facility, a sprawling, grassy acreage surrounded by watchtowers and fences with razor wire, did not stir my narrow soul. The prison contained dozens of Spartan-type buildings—barracks, garages, vocational shops—but there was no sign of habitation anywhere on the grounds. I was later to learn that the buildings were connected by a maze of underground tunnels, and that all inmate movements were conducted within these passageways.

I was assigned a tiny room inside the training building—a room that contained only a bed and a dresser, upon which I placed the TV. Training would not start until the next morning, so I had time to give her a phone call. Since I had some loose change, I made the call from a payphone in the hallway.

"I miss you," I said when I heard her voice.

"I miss you too," she said thinly.

When I told her I'd be back in just two weeks, I heard a sharp intake of breath. "How *nice*," she said. "Should that make me feel better? I miss you no less when you're *here*, Tom Hemmings, so please don't try to console me."

"I'll try to do better."

"Please *don't*," she snapped. "I don't want to be a bother."

"Would you rather I left you?"

"Of course not," she snapped. "I'm in love with you, you big dummy. But don't pester me with phone calls. You sound so cold over the phone."

I wondered again why I longed for her touch, being such a callow man, and why I was desperate for our conversation to end on a positive note.

"I miss you," I repeated.

"Oh, I miss you too," she replied.

The operator said, "Please deposit another fifty cents."

*

I phoned her two weeks later to let her know I was coming back. Along with forty other recruits, I had received my training diploma, and I had found the regimen undemanding and rather superficial. The class time consisted of glib observations about how to handle inmates—comments that in no way measured up to Officer Dobbins' sound advice. The self-defense coaching only filled a couple of afternoons, and I cringed to think how such training might fare against muggers and murderers. And peppering cardboard silhouettes with shotguns lacked the element of fear, an emotion sure to grip anyone forced to fire on rioting inmates. But if my liaison with Sally defined me, I had poor cause to complain. I should have grown used to embracing adventures I was unequipped to handle.

When she answered the phone, her voice was so tight that I wasn't sure I had the right number. "Is there something you want to tell me?" I said.

"Yes," she said flatly, "there is."

"What is it?"

She paused then spoke as though she had caught me reading her mail. "I happen to be in *love*, Tom Hemmings."

"I think I could love you too," I lied.

"You're not *listening* to me," she replied. "Everything is not about *you*. I have fallen in love with somebody else, and he's grown very dear to me. I believe I am truly in love for the first time in my life."

I felt no sense of betrayal as I processed this information. For a moment, I felt that my bogus diploma had made me unworthy of her. But her story seemed inauthentic—I had heard it many times. When women want to disown you, whatever the reason might be, they often say it's because someone dear has come into their lives.

Lacking a talent for outrage, I said, "I'm sorry I wasn't enough."

"Tom Hemmings," she said, "you were really *too much*."

Convinced that she was just cross with me—after all, she had dumped me before—I said, "Shall I drop by and pick up my things? There are only a couple of shirts."

"Don't be so condescending," she said. "Do you actually think I planned this?"

"What I think is that you're toying with me."

"*Must* you be cruel?" she murmured. "It really doesn't suit you. I want to remember you fondly, Tom Hemmings, so *please* don't pretend to be cruel."

"All right," I said. "You have my blessing."

"Your *blessing*?" she laughed. "My, that sounds so passé, but thank you anyway. Considering my luck with marriage, I could *use* a blessing or two."

"You're marrying him?"

"Yes, I'm marrying him. Does that surprise you, Tom Hemmings?"

"It would if I believed you," I said.

"Whether you believe me or not," she snapped, "please drop by and pick up your things. Let me know when you're coming, and I'll leave them on the front porch."

*

Driving south on Route 421, I decided not to pick up my things. This wasn't because I wanted to pout, but because her story was too unlikely. What prospects could she possibly have in such a diminished town? And, given her reputation, who would choose to marry her? I drove past the Castleberg turnoff and went back to the Holiday Inn. I wanted her to know where to find me once she was over her funk.

On Monday, I returned to the prison and met with Captain Hawkins. He had phoned the training academy to get my evaluation, and he seemed particularly eager to go over it with me. "You graduated at the top of yer class," he said, "but the report they wrote on you is bullshit. The instructors say you're capable of thinkin' outta the box."

"Why is that bullshit?" I asked him.

"Do I gotta spell it out, Hemmings? As long as yer ballin' Sally Potter, you ain't thinkin' outta the box."

When I asked him to stop projecting, he said he would give me a break. He said he had slotted me to work the laundry dorm on my own. He told me I would work the busiest shift, which was 4:00 pm to midnight, and that would give me a chance to prove that I wasn't pussy-whipped.

On my first afternoon in the laundry dorm, I remembered Officer Dobbins' advice. Treat them fairly and with respect, joke around with them a little and don't feel compelled to write them up for every infraction you see. My post orders stated I had to conduct three shakedowns every shift, so I selected the bed areas of inmates whom I believed would cause me no trouble.

The first inmate I chose was Eddie Leach who had always been friendly to me. "Go ahead, Mister Hemmings," he said, opening his footlocker. "You got a job to do." His manner was so obliging, his face so kind and composed, that I felt like I'd been punched when I found a balloon of white powder. It was tucked inside the cavity of a hollowed-out King James Bible.

"Eddie, what have we here?" I said, hoping to keep the matter light.

Eddie grinned. "Ya caught me, Mister Hemmings, so I guess I'll be losin' some good time. But don't feel bad about it, man. Yer only doin' yer job."

"I'm glad you feel that way," I said.

"We're cool, Mister Hemmings, don't worry. Man, I hope you'll still do me a favor."

"What is it?" I asked suspiciously.

He laughed. "It ain't nothin' illegal, man. Didja know I'm gettin' married?"

"After you get out of prison?" I asked.

"Naw, I'm gettin' hitched here," he replied. "The chaplain he's tying the knot tomorrow. Mister Hemmings, if you can manage it, I'd like you to be my best man."

*

It was not until after my shift had ended, and I was driving back to the Holiday Inn, that the most sobering thought I had ever had popped into my head. *Could it be?* I wondered. I shook my head. *No, how could it possibly be?* I watched the late news on television then fell into an exhausted sleep. The next morning I took an extra-long jog alongside Highway 40.

That afternoon, I arrived at the prison several hours before my shift. Eddie had actually given me an invitation, which he had printed on a scrap of paper. It said the nuptials would be held at 1:00 pm in the prison chaplain's office. The invitation did not mention the name of the bride, so I wondered again, *Could it be?*

This thought pounded my brain like a mallet as I entered the administration building. Walking towards the chaplain's office, I grew acutely aware of my footsteps. My soles thudded so loud on the uncarpeted floor that it felt as though I was being followed. So sharp was the hammering in my brain, so explosive the sound of my footsteps, that I was already stunned when I entered the chaplain's office and saw her standing there.

She was wearing a formal, white dress. Her hair was freshly-permed. Her face was so glacially composed that she looked like a mannequin. Eddie Leach was standing beside her, clad in starched prison blues, and the chaplain, a scrawny little man, was chatting with them both.

When Eddie introduced me to his bride, she smiled and squeezed my fingers. "Thank you for dropping by," she said then she looked away from me. Thankfully, her face did not betray a hint of recognition.

The group was still waiting for Officer Dobbins who was apparently the bridesmaid. She showed up a minute later, carrying a bouquet of white roses. Noticing me, she blanched and clutched the flowers to her chest. Speaking to Eddie Leach, she said, "Congratulations, hon."

*

I stood as though bound while the prison chaplain conducted the ceremony. That he seemed to be in a hurry was no consolation to me—after the vows were recited, after the rings were exchanged, he asked me to escort the newlyweds to the visiting room. The reception, if you wanted to call it that, would consist of a two-hour visit.

I delivered the pair to the visiting room then hurried away like a thief. Having grasped the true worth of my passion for her—a mawkish thing at best—I felt like a tawdry specter at the shoddiest of feasts. I was therefore surprised when Captain Hawkins stopped me in the hallway. As a phantom, I did not feel I deserved the concern with which he looked at me.

"I heard what happened, son," he said in a voice that could be poured over pancakes. "I wantcha to take a coupla days off. I'll arrange to cover your shift."

I did not want to suffer his sympathy. "She's just the town whore," I snapped.

"Never mind, son, it happens," he said, and he patted me on the shoulder.

I did not need a sermon—I needed a friend—so I broke off our conversation. Too feckless for flight, I retreated no further than the officers' dining room, and I felt that all eyes were upon me when I sat down at an empty table. I sat until Henry Yoakum, having finished his shift in the visiting room, came in, drew a cup of coffee and sat down on the chair beside me.

"Guv'nor," he said, "yer slippin'—there ain't no two ways about it. There can't be much lead in yer pencil if she swapped you for Eddie Leach."

"I'm one up on *you*," I joked cheerlessly.

Yoakum cackled and blew on his coffee. "I wouldn't be too sure of that, guv'nor," he said. "Eddie Leach has a year left to serve—he told me that anyhow. A woman like Sally won't keep her legs crossed while she's waitin' for *him* to get out."

"And that's where you come in, I suppose?"

"Well, she ain't no vestal bride—you know that as well as me. If I play my cards right, guv'nor, I'll be wettin' my turtle yet."

Since the room seemed oppressively warm, I told Yoakum I had to leave. The thought of sitting still any longer was more than I could handle, so I decided to take a cleansing jog alongside

Highway 40. I planned to exhaust myself running and then watch Mary Tyler Moore.

The shift change was beginning as I left the dining hall, and I had to push past a wave of officers showing up for the 4:00 p.m. roll call. Although I felt like a leper, none of them glanced in my direction—it was not until I escaped the building that I saw someone looking at me. Officer Dobbins was waiting at the edge of the parking lot.

*

"Hon," Officer Dobbins said, "you look like you need a drink. There's a bar a few miles from the prison—just follow behind my Jeep."

The charity in her eyes made me feel even worse. "It's early," I replied.

"Well, *I* want one," she said. "Will you keep me company?"

I got into my car and followed her Jeep to a bar on Route 231. The bar was a dive named Flakey Jake's, and its lot was filled with cars.

I accompanied her into the bar. We sat down at a small greasy table. The place was packed with guards from the prison who had just gotten off their shift.

Some kid with a bird on his shoulder, who seemed to know Officer Dobbins, automatically brought us a pitcher of beer and a couple of slippery glasses. "I come here a lot," Officer Dobbins explained. She filled both glasses with beer.

"How do you suppose they met?" I asked her.

"Probably through a church group," she said. "That's usually how it happens. Women come to the prison to bring the inmates to Jesus and then fall in love with them."

We talked no more about the wedding. We talked about jogging and softball— she belonged to a coed league. We talked about playing tennis, and she challenged me to a match. We even talked about fishing—she said the penal farm had several stocked ponds. "Just watch out for escaping inmates," she warned, and I laughed along with her.

By the time I had drunk several beers, I was a little in love with her. When I invited her to my hotel room, she said, "Not in your wildest dreams, hon. In case you aren't aware of it, that isn't the way I swing."

I apologized for my fantasy. I said I'd presumed too much.

Officer Dobbins smiled and said, "Dreams are dreams, aren't they, hon?"

*

A week later, while browsing in Walmart, I ran into Sally Potter. She was pushing a shopping cart that was full of men's clothing, and she blushed when she noticed me. Her face still wore the glow of a newlywed—she looked stunningly beautiful.

"Tom Hemmings," she said to me sternly, "you never did pick up your things."

"Will they fit Eddie Leach?" I asked her.

She laughed. "No, he isn't your size."

I wished her luck with her marriage. She smiled and folded her arms. "At least I know where to find him," she said. "Are you buying new jogging shoes?"

I confessed that I was. She shook her head. "You're such a runner," she said.

"So when is he getting out?" I asked.

"Not for eighteen months," she replied. "He lost six months of good time yesterday—that was because of *you*. Did you bust him just to spite me, Tom Hemmings?"

"I was only doing my job."

She told me my scheme was not going to work—she would wait for him anyway. She informed me he was the sweetest man that she had ever met, and that when he got out of prison she would make sure he was well-dressed. She said that wretched visiting room was no place for a honeymoon. They would honeymoon in Vegas, she said, and stay at a Holiday Inn.

A Diamond as Big as
a Black-Eyed Pea

WHENEVER I NEED ME some advice, I go see Flakey Jake. Flakey Jake he's a big, greasy dude who runs this bar near my folks' farm in Putnam County, Indiana. He's all the time giving advice to folks who get drunk in his bar, and whenever I go to his bar, which is 'bout every Saturday night, he looks at me with a possum grin and says, "How's it hanging, Toby?" That's his way of asking if I need me some advice.

A week ago, I asked Flakey Jake how come he's always trying to straighten folks out? I asked him how he would feel if he gave a fella advice, and that fella got into trouble 'cause it didn't work out too good. Flakey Jake chuckled like a setting hen, and said he don't got to worry about that. He said none of the drunks who come into his bar are inclined to take his suggestions, so he can hand out all the advice he wants 'cause there won't be no consequences. I said to him, "Jake, if yer advice is that worthless, I ain't gonna ask for no more." Well, Jake he flashed me his possum grin and said, "Toby, ya got nothin' going for you. You work at Cecil Baumgardner's hog farm, you live at home with yer folks, and you're all the time pining for some whore ya met in Michigan City. Son, the way I see it is you need all the advice you can get."

Flakey Jake was referring to Brandi who ain't really a full-time whore. I met Brandi 'bout five years ago in this cathouse

187

in Michigan City—that's where Pa took me on my seventeenth birthday so I could become a man. I never did shoot no load in her 'cause I came while she was washin' my johnson, so we played checkers instead of fucking and she told me all about herself. She told me she was taking classes so she could become a paralegal, and that she only worked part-time in the cathouse even though she was the most popular whore there. She also said she was lonely 'cause whorin' had put her off men, so she hoped I'd keep in touch with her 'cause she needed a friend. Brandi she's as thin as an otter and her nose is too big for her face, but I fell in love with her anyhow 'cause she's got a heart of gold.

Ya see, after my hour with her was up, she told Pa I'd pleasured her good, and Pa he said, "Praise the Lord," and he slapped me on the back. He said, "Now that you've had the real thing, Toby, I expect you to stop stealing my porn."

I still ain't had sex with Brandi, but we're all the time texting each other. Brandi keeps saying I'm a real sweet boy and she really likes texting with me, and if I wanna try to pop my cherry again, she'll give me a bargain rate. I've asked her to marry me a few times, but I don't do that no more. Most times, when I asked her to marry me, Brandi she lost her temper. She said she ain't gonna marry no bumpkin who makes his living slopping hogs, and that if I keep on raising that question, she won't text with me no more.

Now that I've toldja 'bout Brandi and me, I'm gonna tell you this story. Wouldja believe that a month ago, she *almost* married me? A few weeks before that happened, I was more inclined to take Flakey Jake's advice, and I'd told him I needed some know-how about how to win Brandi's heart. Flakey Jake told me the heart of a whore is a heart that ain't worth winning, and that Brandi had done me a real nice favor by refusing to marry me. When I told Flakey Jake that weren't no kind of favor, he kinda humored me. He said the key to winning a woman's heart is to give her an unexpected gift at an unexpected time.

Well, I remembered Sean Connery saying that in a movie called *Finding Forrester*, and I told Flakey Jake that he oughta be ashamed to be plagiarizing his advice. Flakey Jake said I don't deserve better if I'm hopin' to marry a whore. He said I oughta go find me a church-goin' sort of girl, and if I decided to marry a church-goin' girl, he'd give me better advice.

*

A day after Flakey Jake gave me the advice he stole from *Finding Forrester*, I got to thinkin' about it. And I decided that just 'cause he swiped the advice didn't mean it wasn't worth takin'. So I asked Pa and Ma about what they thought about me taking Flakey Jake's suggestion. I asked them if they thought I would win Brandi's heart if I surprised her with a gift. Pa said whores don't deserve no gifts though it's okay to give 'em tips, and that, since I'd made Brandi cum, she ought to be tipping me. Ma she said it was time I stopped obsessing about that girl. When I told her how Brandi's been nice to me 'cause she has a heart of gold, Ma said that, if whores had hearts of gold, they'd have pawned 'em long ago. Ma she told me what I oughta do is open my heart to the Lord, and that if I put my trust in the Lord, He would provide me with all I needed.

Well, I went to church the following Sunday, and I opened my heart to the Lord 'cause I was hopin' the Lord would provide me with a gift I could give to Brandi. See, Brandi she's a real young whore—she ain't much older 'an me—so I figgered she hadn't had enough time to pawn her heart of gold. And the Lord He musta known that 'cause he provided for me quick. Just the next day, when I was at work shoveling hog shit, my shovel scooped up what looked like an expensive diamond ring. It had a gold band that was just the right size to fit over Brandi's ring finger, and the band was attached to a clear, sparkling stone as big as a black-eyed pea.

The stone sparkled even brighter after I hosed it off, so once I left work, I went to this jeweler in Putnamville to get the ring appraised. When the jeweler said the stone was 'bout half a carrot, I felt real disappointed, and I told him I didn't want no ring that weren't worth more 'an a carrot. Well, the jeweler said he was only referring to what the gemstone weighed. He said that I had me a diamond ring that was worth maybe two thousand dollars. He asked me where I got the ring, and I told him the Lord had provided, and he said I didn't look like no Prodigal Son even though I smelled like hogs.

Well, after I'd been to the jeweler's, I went to Flakey Jake's bar, and I showed Flakey Jake the ring that the Lord had seen fit to give me. Flakey Jake he suggested that someone might have lost the ring, but I told him that didn't make no sense 'cause I found it while I was scooping up hog shit. I said that no one who could afford a ring that expensive would be hanging around a hog pen, so the ring hadda be a gift from the Lord 'cause I'd opened my heart up to Him. I said I was gonna give Brandi the ring so she'd think about marrying me, and Flakey Jake said, "Toby, folks reap what they sow" 'cause he likes to quote the Bible.

Well, since the Lord had listened to me, it was time to get on with His plan, so right after supper, I went to my room and called Brandi on my iPhone. I told her I'd like to come see her and that I had a surprise for her, and Brandi said she loved surprises but I still hadda pay for an hour. Brandi said she would charge me just three hundred dollars 'cause that was her bargain rate, and since I had that much in my bank account, I told her I'd pay for an hour. I asked her if I could come see her next Sunday 'cause I wanted to honor the Lord, and Brandi she said that would be just fine and she was lookin' forward to my visit.

When Sunday rolled around, I asked Pa if I could borrow his truck. I told him I was gonna go see Brandi 'cause I had some sowin' to do, and Pa he said it don't hurt a young buck to be plantin' his wild oats. Pa he grinned like a rattler, and he gave me the keys to his truck then he patted me on the shoulder and said, "Give her a poke for yer pa." So with that diamond ring in my pocket, along with three hundred dollars, I hopped into Pa's truck and drove to Michigan City.

*

When I spotted the cathouse in Michigan City, I started to have second thoughts. The place looked kinda scary even though I'd been there twice before. I was there on my seventeenth birthday, when I tried to pop my cherry, and I was there a coupla years ago when I showed up toting a Bible. I'd been hopin' I could bring Brandi to Jesus by quotin' some scripture to her, but Brandi she got real mad at me 'cause she didn't want to be saved. She told me I had no business showing up without an appointment 'cause time is money for hookers and I was just wasting her time.

As I pulled Pa's truck into the parking lot, I started to feel even more nervous, but at least I had an appointment this time, so my visit wouldn't be no surprise. Flakey Jake he may be right about giving a woman an unexpected gift, but if the woman's the most popular whore in a cathouse, you don't wanna show up unexpected. Course Brandi couldn't have been that busy 'cause the parking lot was empty. I guess that's 'cause none of her other customers were inclined to honor the Lord.

Well, I sat in the truck for a while 'cause I was half an hour early, and it wouldn't a been too classy of me to show up ahead of time. I also wondered if I oughta take her to a restaurant instead of fucking her. Flakey Jake says women will love you if you take 'em out to dine. Now I only had three hundred dollars, which was the money I already owed her, but if she agreed to give me another discount, I could take her to a Cracker Barrel.

I was thinkin' about grits and collard greens when I knocked on the door to the cathouse, but the madam who answered the door weren't inclined to negotiate. "That'll be three hundred dollars upfront, young man," she said in a schoolteacher's voice, so I gave her all the money I had and she led me into the parlor. The parlor was still fulla aging whores who didn't have no customers. They was lounging around watching *Jeopardy* on television like they had nothing else to do.

"Brandi will need a few minutes," said the madam. "She's a bit out of sorts today." Well, the parlor it stank of cat litter and the whores looked sadder than scarecrows, so I hoped it wouldn't be too long until Brandi sorted herself out.

After a coupla minutes, Brandi came into the parlor, and she looked like a mare that been put away wet after being ridden all day. Her hair was as wild as a bird's nest, her mascara was streaked down her cheeks, and her nightgown was so rumpled that it looked like she'd wrestled in it. "How nice to see you, Toby," she mumbled, and her voice sounded kinda raw. She didn't look like she'd taken no time to get herself sorted out.

"I gotcha a surprise," I said.

"Did you?" she muttered. She looked at me strange like she'd forgotten I was gonna surprise her. "Let's get this over with, Jasper," she said. "After that, I'll let you surprise me."

Brandi she took me by the hand and she led me down this hall, and we entered a room that had nothing in it but a bed and a chest of drawers. And, instead of inspecting my johnson, Brandi sat down on the bed, and she covered her face with both of her hands and started to bawl like a cat.

"Toby, this is my life now," she said after she had cried for a spell. "Those women you saw in the parlor—all of them have given up. Well, today, for the first time ever, I knew I was gonna be one of those women."

Brandi she went on to explain that she'd just earned her paralegal certificate, but she had been to all the law firms in Michigan City and none of 'em wanted to hire her. Most of the lawyers recognized her, and a couple of 'em told her point-blank that it ain't good public relations to be giving jobs to whores. Brandi said she tried to explain that she was only a part-time whore, and they told her that didn't mean squat as far as public relations went. Them lawyers also said law firms do background checks on folks they're fixin' to hire, and if she'd ever been busted for turning tricks, the feds had a record of that. "I've been busted for turning tricks, Toby," she said, "so all I can be is a whore. And, to make matters worse, I'm too damn depressed to even be *much* of a whore."

I told her I'd take her to a Cracker Barrel if she weren't up to being a whore, and Brandi took my hands in hers, and her fingers were wet from her tears. "Do you mind if we just play checkers?" she said. "I don't feel like dressing up."

Well, Brandi she went to this closet and came back with a checker set, and we set the board up on the bed and I let her have the first move. After we'd played a coupla games, which I think she let me win, she said, "Toby, no wonder I love you. You're just a sweet, sweet boy."

After we'd played checkers a while, Brandi looked up from the board. She said, "Toby, I almost forgot. What's this surprise you have for me?"

Well, I reached into my pocket and I handed her the ring, and her eyes got as big as doorknobs and she gasped like a broken pump. "Toby, what did this cost you?" she said.

I told her the ring was worth two thousand dollars, but I hadn't paid for it. I told her the Lord had provided the ring so she'd think about marrying me. Well, Brandi flared her nostrils 'cause she ain't too fond that subject, and I thought she was 'bout to lose her temper and call me Jasper again. But instead, she threw her arms 'round my neck like maybe she was drowning, and her breath was softer 'an moonlight when she whispered in my ear.

"Oh, Toby, Toby, Toby," she sobbed. "Of course I'll marry you."

*

Well, Brandi she wanted to get married quick, so she told me to come back in a week. She said we was gonna get hitched in the whorehouse, 'cause she had clients to see that day, and that she was gonna give up whorein' for good once we tied the knot. The ceremony wouldn't cost nothing, she said, 'cause she was friends with the minister, but I hadda pay her another three hundred dollars 'cause it would take up an hour of her time. I didn't have no three hundred dollars so I asked Pa for a loan, and Pa he said he would give me the money if I promised to stop swipin' his porn.

The night before our wedding, I went to Flakey Jake's bar, and I invited him to come with me to the cathouse 'cause I needed a best man. Flakey Jake said he wanted nothing to do with that kind of foolishness, and he told me to take some advice from him and not trust in the oath of a whore. Well, I asked him where he swiped that advice, and he said it came from King Lear, and I told him it weren't smart of him to be plagiarizing a king.

Flakey Jake frowned and said, "Toby, I don't think you've thought this thing through."

I told Flakey Jake that, when the Lord provides, you don't gotta think things through. After I drank me a coupla beers, I went home to get me some sleep, and when I woke up on my wedding day, I weren't thinkin' bout nothing but cooze.

Well, I wanted to give Brandi a phone call in case she had changed her mind, but I remembered her saying it'd be bad luck to phone her before the ceremony. But Brandi she called my phone instead 'cause the bad luck had already happened. She told me she had just been arrested and was in the LaPorte County Jail.

Brandi she told me she got arrested 'cause she tried to sell the ring. She said she needed some extra cash to pay for a wedding dress, so she tried to sell the ring to this jeweler in Michigan City. But the jeweler he examined the ring and said it had been reported as missing. It turned out there was this laser inscription on the girdle of the ring, and the ring belonged to a woman who lived in Putnamville. The jeweler he called the city police and the police had put Brandi in jail, and she was scheduled for a hearing that afternoon in the Michigan City Courthouse. Brandi said she needed me to be there as a witness because, since I had given her the ring as a gift, she couldn't have known it was missing. All the time Brandi was talkin' to me she kept on calling me Jasper. I said maybe the judge could marry us as long as we was in court, and Brandi said she weren't in a marrying mood and to meet her in Superior Court Four.

Well, I drove Pa's truck to the Michigan City Courthouse, and I went to Superior Court Four, and I sat down in the gallery and waited for Brandi's case to be called. And Brandi she was wearing an orange jumpsuit and was sittin' with her public defender, and that woman was chatting away on a cell phone and paying no attention to her. Brandi she turned around and looked at me and her eyes were as cool as a cod, and after a while, this judge entered the room and this bailiff shouted, "All rise!" Well, the judge, this big fella with a lazy eye, sat himself down at the bench. "The clerk will call the case," he said once everyone else sat down. The clerk, a woman 'bout ninety years old, shouted, "The People versus Wanda Fry." At first, that kinda puzzled me 'cause there weren't no one on trial but Brandi.

I remembered Flakey Jake telling me that there shouldn't be no surprises. He said folks only got surprised when they was slow to see things like they were. Well, while I sat in the courtroom, I started to see things how they were. How they were was that Cecil Baumgardner's wife had probably dropped that ring in the hog pen. How they were was that Brandi weren't likely to stay in a marrying mood for long. How they were was that Brandi weren't even Brandi—she's a woman named Wanda Fry.

Well, Brandi—I'm still gonna call her Brandi 'cause I'm in the habit of that—Brandi she sat like a dog on a chain while her public defender spoke to the judge. And this nervous-looking district attorney fella, he joined the conversation, and after a while, the judge looked at Brandi and said, "Will the defendant please stand?"

Well, maybe there oughtn't to be no surprises, but I was surprised by what happened next. What happened next was Brandi told the judge she weren't gonna take no plea deal. What happened next was Brandi fired her public defender and argued her case herself, and she told the judge she weren't guilty of nothin' 'cause she'd been given the ring as a gift. And then Brandi put me on the stand so I could testify, and when I told the judge how I'd found the ring, the judge he chewed me out. He said any reasonable person woulda known the ring belonged to someone, and I shoulda turned the ring over to the police steada using it to bribe a whore. Well, Brandi she told the judge that I was just a dumbshit boy, and that I was gonna pay her three hundred bucks so that she would marry me. She said anyone who would do a fool thing like that weren't no kind of reasonable person, and the judge he shook his head and told Brandi she had a point. Well, the district attorney fella said I still oughta be charged with theft, but Brandi said, "Hey, don't I know you from somewhere?" and he didn't say nothing more. The judge said he was washing his hands of us and to get ourselves outta his courtroom, and he said we both oughta go to church to repent our despicable ways.

Well, after Brandi was let out of jail, I drove her back to the cathouse, and Brandi she didn't say nothin' until I walked her to the door. And, while we was standin' at the door, she punched me hard in the face, and lights started hoppin' in front of my eyes like flashbulbs going off. "Toby," she said, "Don't *ever* ask me to marry you again."

While I was driving back to Putnamville, I got to thinkin' 'bout things. And I wondered if Brandi woulda married me if she had been able to keep the ring. But there weren't no point in thinkin' too much 'cause I hadda look after Pa's truck. My eye was swollen up so bad I could hardly see the road.

*

Well, that's the story about how Brandi almost married me. But I gotta tell you one more thing 'cause it's interesting to know. Yesterday, I got this text from Brandi, and she told me not to come lookin' for her at the cathouse anymore. She said she was giving all her customers notice that she weren't gonna be there much longer 'cause she had rented herself an office near the Michigan City Courthouse. She said that, by handling her court case herself, she had built up her confidence, so she was gonna do paralegal work for whoever wanted to hire her. She also said lawyers were nothing but prostitutes themselves, so it weren't too big a transition for her to be practicing law as well. Brandi she thanked me for helping her build her confidence, but she said she still weren't gonna marry me 'cause I'd helped her by accident.

Well, I went to Flakey Jake's bar and I showed him Brandi's text, and Flakey Jake poured me a beer on the house and said I done a good thing. When I told him Brandi shoulda paid me back by helping me pop my cherry, Flakey Jake said not to worry 'bout that 'cause she already paid me back twice. She had saved me from going to jail for not turning in that ring, and she had also saved me three hundred dollars by refusing to be my bride. Flakey Jake said I oughta thank her for taking such good care of me.

Well, I'd have rather gotten my cherry popped, but Flakey Jake had a point. And I guess I done Brandi some good even though it was accidental. Brandi she got herself outta that cathouse and into a better class of whoring, and that wouldn't have happened if I hadn't given a diamond as big as a black-eyed pea.

Krispy Kremes

SIX MONTHS AFTER Joe Biden replaced Donald Trump in the White House, Joshua McIntyre, founder of the Brawny Lads, addressed a crowd of his fellow citizens in Putnamville, Indiana. Speaking from the courthouse steps, Joshua, also known as the General, spoke in a loud, measured tone. He was a veteran of both the Iraq War and the January 6 siege of the United States Capitol Building, and his voice rang with the authority of one who is battle-tested. After reminding the crowd that American jobs were still being shuttled to China, he said that his spies had informed him of the deep state's latest plot. According to his spooks, the U.S. government, having deemed the American worker expendable, was planning to eliminate the middle class entirely through a sterilization campaign. "Neighbors," he boomed from the courthouse steps, "that China virus is no more dangerous than the flu, but those vaccines are laced with antineoplastic agents that will keep you from havin' children."

"Do they poke you in the butt?'" shouted Toby Dawes, a simple-minded farm boy who made his living inseminating hogs. "If they poke you in your butt, Donald Trump oughta be told."

The General shook his head stoically—he was not a gullible man. "Toby," he said, "there's no point in confiding in Donald Trump. Didn't that coward turn tail and run after ordering us to attack the Capitol Building?"

"Maybe he had an appointment to go to," Toby cried hopefully.

The General sighed like a punctured tire. "More likely, he set us up," he muttered. "The government is busting us in droves since they have us all on film—and now Donald Trump is claiming that we acted on our own. You know, it wouldn't surprise me if he was part of the deep state himself."

Were the General a less-respected man, this comment would have drawn hoots of derision. Instead, the townsfolk stood as though hog-tied and muttered among themselves. It was a dawning of sobriety, an awakening of pawns. If the General was right, their Mussolini was just a hot-air balloon.

A few plaintive shouts of "USA" erupted from the crowd, but these scattered voices faded when the General bowed his head. He made no further mention of Trump, his expression said it all. Putnamville had married the wind, and now the wind had stalled.

*

The General went on to inform the crowd that the deep state's campaign was accelerating—that government agents, armed with the vaccines, would soon be going from door-to-door.

"Them shots gotta hurt!" shouted Toby who had turned as gray as a corpse.

"Ah, they're only a scratch," said the General, "but they're enough to do the job."

Billy Babbitt, a reporter for *The Putnamville Gazette*, suspected the General had paraphrased Shakespeare to get his point across. Although the General's claim seemed shopworn, he was an educated man. Before founding the Brawny Lads Militia, he had been a high school English teacher. It disturbed Billy Babbitt to know that the Capitol raiders were not just knuckleheads—that doctors, lawyers and teachers were included in the mix.

Hoping to harness the General's better instincts, Billy Babbitt spoke up. "Joshua," he said, "the county hospital is filled to capacity. Dozens of people on ventilators are gasping their lives away."

The General drew a labored breath. "Billy," he said, "we're a people at war. It's not a war that we asked for, but it's one that we may as well fight. Since the government plans to make us extinct, the virus can't hurt us that much."

No further comments were necessary. How could one not be aware that the time had come for true citizens to make a final stand? But since it was clear that the Donald was not going to fight the arrests, it was implicit that passive resistance would now be the order of the day.

When Toby Dawes piped up again, he was speaking for them all. "I ain't gonna take no injection," he cried, "if they stick you in the butt."

*

After the rally, the General and Billy had a beer in Flakey Jake's Bar, a dive on the outskirts of Putnamville where locals drank away their government checks. Both were town-trapped men in their forties whose lives had not come to fruition. The General had once tried to publish a tell-all book he had written about the Iraq War, but the corporate-run publishing houses had shown no interest in printing hard truths. Billy Babbitt had once tried to write literature, but he had no true genius for that, so now he was covering trivia for *The Putnamville Gazette*. The men had been friends since college where they had performed for the drama club, and it was an intimacy fostered by Ibsen and Chekov that enabled Billy to speak candidly.

"Joshua," Billy said, "why did you lie to them? You know they'll believe anything."

"A lie may set them free," said the General.

Billy salted his beer. "If you're going to start an insurrection, I think you should stick to facts."

"Facts!" said the General. He spat out the word as though it had blistered his tongue. "The fact is the country's been stolen and a lie might help folks get it back. I don't mind blowing smoke in their eyes if it gives them a rallying point."

"Well, this is the only revolution I know of where the rebels are killing themselves."

"Naw, I saw plenty of that in Iraq. Suicide bombers blowing up servicemen who were conned into being there."

"You take that war too personally, Joshua. You left Iraq ten years ago."

"It's not personal," shrugged the General. "Hell, my feelings are broader than that. You know, the only occupation that makes sense to me was when we took over the Capitol Building."

"It's not like you stormed the Bastille," Billy said. "Your brawny boys were in there for less than an hour, and then they got bored and left."

"Insurrections fall apart," said the General. "Governments fall apart too. Hell, what's happening in America happens to all countries sooner or later."

"Maybe you're too keen to pick a fight, and any lame cause will do."

"All insurrections are lame," said The General. "All of 'em follow the same stupid script, and they're all betrayed sooner or later. Hell, I'm just a clown in a comedy that was written long ago."

*

If the General's script had been written a long time ago, it soon suffered in translation—perhaps because he was diabetic and feared being put in jail. And since firing up crowds was conspicuous work that might expedite his arrest, he decided to make no more speeches to citizens of Putnamville. Convinced that a printed slogan would better serve his campaign, he confined his clarion call to placards the Brawny Lads passed around. *Go away, government goons*, read the signs. *We don't want Doctor Fauci's ouchy*. Before too long, these placards appeared on all of Putnamville's lawns.

After a Brawny Lad handed him one of the placards, Billy Babbitt dropped by his friend's house. "Joshua," he sighed, "has it come to this? My god, you taught high school English."

The General blushed and shook his head. "I don't wanna preach over their heads," he muttered.

"No danger of that," said Billy. "Your message demeans even the stupid ones, including Toby Dawes."

"Don't overestimate 'em," the General said, and his cynicism proved correct. None of Putnamville's citizens removed the signs from their lawns, which deterred the government from sending its goons out to knock on people's doors. A month later, when a fleet of refrigerated vans pulled into the hospital parking lot, it was clear that the General's slogan was working very well.

But the government was not to be stopped by a bunch of dumbed-down signs. The following month, the mayor of Putnamville, who was obviously in league with the deep state, issued a mask proclamation. The order read that public buildings and restaurants would be barred to anyone not wearing a mask. To facilitate the order, the mayor arranged for a special delivery. Trucks from the National Guard Armory roamed the streets of Putnamville, and drivers tossed boxes of masks onto the lawns of unsuspecting citizens.

Incensed by this tactic, the General ordered that all the masks be destroyed, so the Brawny Lads strolled from house to house, retrieving boxes of masks. Within a matter of hours, the Lads rendezvoused at the town dump where they soaked the boxes with gasoline and set them aflame. Weeks later, when more refrigerated vans squeezed into the hospital lot, it was clear that incinerating the masks had been a huge success.

While sitting in Flakey Jake's with the General, sharing a pitcher of beer, Billy Babbitt asked him why he had ordered the burning of the masks. "What's the point?" Billy snapped. "Those masks can't do any harm."

"Don't you see?" said the General. "It's a matter of folks keepin' their faith. They need to believe that God will protect them—not those fucking masks."

"But those vans are packed with cadavers, Joshua, and God is just letting it happen."

"All that matters," the General said, "is for folks to think that God's on their side. If they put too much trust in the government, they won't take their country back."

"How many will live to *take* it back?" Billy muttered. "You must have thought of that. And why are you trying to liberate people you hold in such contempt?"

The General belched like a cannon then topped off his glass of beer. "Billy, you're too damn logical. Let's talk about something else."

*

Putnamville's death toll continued to climb and townsfolk grew irritable, and the deep state tried to exploit their displeasure with yet another ploy. In a sneering attempt to blunt the resolve of those who had lost family members, it set up vaccine information clinics in the high school and the fire station. Adding insult to injury, the deep state also mailed out fliers, informing the townsfolk that a trip to these clinics would lay their fears to rest.

Not to be outdone, the General drew up a message of his own. *Beware the Zombie Apocalypse*, his fliers boldly announced.

Those vaccines are laced with pesticides that are going to destroy your brains. With the speed of Minute Men, the Brawny Lads dashed through the town, stuffing the notices into mailboxes and shouting the alarm.

Toby Dawes, a fan of *The Walking Dead,* a popular Netflix series, was quick to add his voice to the chorus. "I don't wanna be no zombie!" he hollered to anyone who would listen. "If the government turns you into a zombie, they'll get to shoot out your brains!"

Sensing their friendship ebbing, Billy Babbitt again challenged the General. They were sitting in Flakey Jake's again, drinking whiskey sours, and Billy made no effort to hide his irritation. "When fighting the FDA," he sniped, "be sure not to become a pill."

"Leave the puns to Shakespeare, Billy. I don't think that's very funny."

"But a zombie apocalypse? My god! And the sad thing is they'll buy it. What's the point in them owning the country if they're dumb enough to believe that?"

"I think they know it's a lie," said the General. "It's just one they want to believe."

"What about the Dawes boy? You scared him shitless, Joshua. He really thinks that the deep state is planning to turn him into a ghoul."

The General shrugged. "All rebellions have collateral damage, Billy. If all that gets damaged is Toby Dawes, we're getting off pretty cheap."

"The poor, stupid kid," said Billy.

"Let it go," the General replied. "If the rumor doesn't work, I'll take Toby aside and tell him it was a lie."

But the fliers proved effective in keeping suspicions high, so it made no difference whether or not the town truly bought the lie. Nobody went to a government clinic where he might have been propagandized. Even the thought of becoming a zombie was more than the townsfolk could bear.

*

The next tactic the deep state used was comical to a fault—a ploy so desperate that the General could only laugh. One day, a fleet of Krispy Kreme trucks invaded Putnamville, and loudspeakers, perched on top of the trucks, offered the townsfolk a Faustian deal. Simply put, those Putnamville citizens, willing to compromise, would be given a donut in exchange for rolling up their sleeves. *"They're fresh and creamy and sticky,"* the loudspeakers declared, an artless attempt to entrap the good people into devaluing their souls. Sadly, this tactic had some success. Although the General spread the word that the donuts contained tracking devices, a handful of Putnamville's citizens, who had reached their tipping point, chose to receive a vaccination in exchange for a sugary snack. Among them was Toby Dawes who seemed indifferent to being collateral damage. The General spotted the boy near one of the trucks, munching a Krispy Kreme. He had apparently forgotten the deep state's plan to turn him into a ghoul.

"You too, Toby?" The General exclaimed.

Toby smacked his lips. "Them donuts are mighty tasty," he said.

The General rolled his eyes. "Toby, you disappoint me. I thought you had principles."

"Principles don't got cream filling," Toby replied, and he went on stuffing his mouth.

Sensing capitulation, the deep state pressed the donut campaign. *"Bliss in every bite,"* the loudspeakers now proclaimed. Several days later, the deep state doubled the price it would pay for a soul. The loudspeakers announced that residents, willing to take both shots, would, upon receiving either vaccine, get two of the tasty treats. This piping-fresh deal was enough to unravel Putnamville's waning resolve. Overwhelmed by the tangy smell of fresh donuts, more townsfolk crowded the trucks where they stood like storks while paramedics jabbed them in the arm.

When he met with Billy Babbitt again in Flakey Jake's honky-tonk, the General sadly conceded that he had given up on the town. "My neighbors have let me down, Billy," he said. "I don't think I asked them for much."

"You're not to blame," said Billy. "You gave them your best shot."

"That I did," The General sighed. "I gave 'em my best shot. But principles don't have cream fillings, and I should have realized that."

Contempt

WHEN BILLY BABBITT received a subpoena from the House Select Committee, his first thought was that the committee had made a terrible blunder. The committee was investigating the January 6 riot in the U.S. Capitol, and Billy had no interest in coups and had never even been out of Indiana. Yes, he was friends with Joshua McIntyre, the self-appointed general of a local militia group called the Brawny Lads, but he felt that Joshua and his boys had only been playing soldier when they "stormed" the Capitol. Didn't video clips, posted on Fox News, show them milling around in the Rotunda like sheep? Hadn't Joshua told him that he and his "soldiers" got bored after an hour and left? And hadn't the entire incident happened over ten months ago? Yes, the FBI had busted Joshua last month for obstruction and indecent exposure, but he had been released on his own recognizance, and his trial was yet to be scheduled. Joshua was confident he could plead to a charge of trespass and get off with misdemeanor probation.

Billy and Joshua, both in their forties, were leading constricted lives. They were lifelong residents of Putnamville, a small Indiana farm town, and they met most evenings in Flakey Jake's Bar and shared their discontent. Billy, once an aspiring novelist, had not found a publisher, so he had settled for being a reporter for *The Putnamville Gazette*. Joshua had taught high school English after serving a stint in the Army, but he had been fired after a CNN video showed him vandalizing the Capitol. Although his arrest had shaken him up, Joshua reveled in being a "general." "Why teach about Jay Gatsby and Ahab," he joked, "when I can be an antihero myself?" Both men had honed their love for the arts at Butler University, a nearby college from which they had graduated twenty years ago. During their college days, they had performed in the drama club—Joshua because of his abiding love of Beckett's and Ibsen's plays, Billy because his serve was too weak for him to make the tennis team. Billy had starred and performed passably in a couple of Shakespearean dramas, and it was with the Bard's flair for the underdog that he showed his subpoena to Joshua. The two men were again sitting in Flakey Jake's, lamenting the state of the country, and both were feeling the flush of too many Heineken drafts.

"They can't be serious," said Billy, thrusting the summons under Joshua's nose. "They say I've been seen keeping company with a notorious saboteur."

"Really?" muttered Joshua as he pushed Billy's hand aside. "In case you don't remember, I'm a peace-loving kinda guy."

"So why did you drive to Washington and piss on the Capitol floor?"

"I must have got bored," shrugged Joshua, and he took a long sip of beer. "Or maybe I saw too many buddies die when I served my tour in Iraq."

Billy shook his head. "That was over ten years ago."

"Is that supposed to make me feel better?" said Joshua, staring into his beer.

"Well, since you're the one with the goddamn grudge, what do they want from me?"

Joshua looked at Billy as though he were indulging a child. "What do ya think? They'll want you to say that I confided in you. They'll want you to say I told you I was obeying an order from Trump."

Billy groaned then folded the subpoena and stuffed it into his pocket. "I don't want to embarrass you, Joshua, by bringing up something like that. Not when Trump ran off and hid after ordering the mob into battle."

"Yeah," said Joshua, lowering his voice as though he were confessing a sin. "After telling us to take back the country, he tucked his tail and ran."

Joshua's voice bore the timbre of a man whose dog had been run over. He had lost all belief in Trump after Trump let his followers down, and he sincerely hoped the Left would rise up and put the coward in jail. But the Left had done nothing but bury itself in the House Select Committee, an assemblage that seemed less like a posse than a high-school debating team. It was clear that justice, however deserved, was not going to catch up with Trump.

"Those jokers should throw him in jail," Billy groused, "steada bugging me with this subpoena."

"Billy," said Joshua, "you expect too much from dog-and-pony shows."

"He incited sedition on *television*. How much more evidence do they need?"

"This is not about evidence," said Joshua, pausing to top off his beer. "It's more like a half-assed production of *Waiting for Godot*."

"Trust Congress to do things halfway," Billy muttered.

"They usually do nothing at all—that's why their building got trashed. Hell, doing things half-assed is kind of a step-up for them."

Billy shrugged. "I've got half a mind to tell them where to shove their subpoena."

"They'll call that contempt and put you in jail."

"Sometimes, contempt is deserved."

Joshua sighed like a broken pump then took a measured breath. Despite his pique, he had no wish to put his friend at risk. "Billy, you've been summoned to testify. Now I've had your back all my life, so I'm suggesting you go to Washington and get it over with."

*

After rethinking the subpoena, Billy took his friend's advice. He bought a Greyhound bus ticket to Washington, D.C. then he purchased a blue blazer and a red tie to wear when he testified. As he stepped aboard the Greyhound bus, his pulse began to flutter, and he suspected that facing the Select Committee would be the most exciting moment of his life. Of course, this was only a measure of the mundanity of his life, his inherent inability to rise to an occasion. While in college, he had not made the tennis team because he could not beef up his serve. "Take a deep breath," his fool coach kept insisting, "then pretend that your arm is a whip." But Billy could not relax his arm and his serves barely cleared the net, and when he failed to make the cut, he smashed his rackets upon the court. "You're way too inhibited, Billy," said Joshua who was rooming with him at the time. "If you want to be a varsity athlete, you gotta let it all hang out." Since Billy had lost his tennis career because of a volatile temperament, Joshua suggested that the drama club might prove to be his element.

It took several pep talks from Joshua to pull Billy out of his funk, but eventually, Billy relented and joined the drama club. A diva by nature, Billy was given a shot at playing Hamlet and Henry the Fifth, and his performances, on occasion, drew polite applause. Still, a critique in the college newspaper accused him of overdramatizing these roles, and Billy lacked all capacity to take criticism in stride. After he read the review, Billy snarled like a cornered dog. "Dammit," he wailed to Joshua. "*No one* deserves reviews like that."

Billy vowed that he never again would strut upon a stage. This was not because being a thespian was more than he could handle, but because he did not want his talent dependent upon somebody else's script. After graduating from Butler with a Bachelor of Arts in world literature, Billy wrote a three-hundred-page novel while supporting himself with odd jobs. His novel was deeply influenced by James Joyce's *Finnegans Wake*, which had captured Billy's imagination despite its garbled prose. He entitled his novel, *The Sweat of the Sun*, and he sent it to dozens of agents, but the agents returned the manuscript with form rejection slips. One of them scrawled at the bottom, *Dear Mr. Babbitt, Why are you emulating a writer in his period of decline? Only academics read* Finnegans Wake, *and even they cannot agree on what the book is supposed to mean. You show ability in your ambition, but your book has no storyline. I strongly suggest you find your muse in less esoteric work.*

Tiring of being a penniless author, Billy put his book aside and took a job as a reporter for *The Putnamville Gazette*. His job was to cover high school sporting events and other local news, tasks that he hoped would prove banal enough to tame his stormy soul. But a life of quiet desperation did not suit his temperament either, and he looked forward to damning his critics whenever he got drunk in Flakey Jake's. In his conversations with Joshua, he described his detractors as common sinks. Coaches, directors and literary agents had all become sinks to him. "These are prosperity's seawalls," he cried. "Lackies and charlatans—all. They are no more able to fathom my depths than a sink might contain an ocean."

Having found his identity in martyrdom, Billy could now pretend that never again would he suffer the barbs of insubstantial men. And so, his subpoena amounted to an ill-timed irony—a charade he could only endure if he put his inquisitors in their place. Would he rise to the occasion? Would he set aside his doubts? Would he finally manage to take a deep breath then it all hang out?

*

We know you're a snitch.
We're coming to get you.
We're going to feed you to dogs.

Billy re-read the texted threats on his iPhone as the bus rolled towards Washington. Since these threats had been signed with pseudonyms, they had obviously been written by cowards. Still, Billy was annoyed that the Select Committee had not kept his name from the press—that its notion of justice did not extend to protecting witnesses from kooks.

Snitches get stitches.
There's no place you can hide.

These threats went on and on. Was there any chance that one of them might prove to be sincere? And, if so, should he spend the rest of his life looking over his shoulder?

Billy recalled an incident that had happened a week ago in Flakey Jake's—an event that suggested that he was at least a match for those who might feed him to dogs. The incident took place because Billy could not shake his love for the Bard, and was in the habit of boozily quoting Shakespeare to patrons in the bar. On this particular occasion, he was delivering his favorite speech: the Saint Crispin's Day soliloquy from *Henry the Fifth*. No sooner had he reached "band of brothers" when a lazy drawl interrupted him. "Who's brother mightcha be, dingle dork?" the slurry voice called out. The outburst had come from a fleshy fellow wearing a MAGA hat, a beer-bellied meathead who appeared to be eager for a fight. "Why don't you ask your mother?" Billy snapped. "We might be related, you know." Had Billy's insult been less transparent, the brawl might not have happened. The clod might not have leaped from his chair and slammed Billy against the wall, and Billy might not have broken his beer mug over the Neanderthal's head. Nor might Billy have plunged his fist into the fellow's crotch, nor driven his heel into the man's belly after he dropped to the floor. It was not until Joshua wrapped Billy in a bear hug and pulled him away from the man, that Billy realized that he had come out on top for the first time in his life.

When the police arrived and placed Billy in handcuffs, the brute chose not to press charges. Clearly, the man did not wish to admit that he'd been thrashed by a skinny dork with a bad haircut. So after the cops uncuffed him and said he was free to go, Billy was able to relish the joy of having finally vanquished a boor. The fury with which he had captured the moment seemed to harbor a life of its own—the strength of a guardian angel that had commandeered his soul. It was a stranger he wished to know better, a presence he wanted to court—a lionhearted paladin that would save him from assassins and louts. Perhaps, if he gave the hero a name, they might form a more intimate union. Had Charlemagne not bonded with his sword by giving it a valiant name, and was Billy's new counterpart any less worthy of being christened as well? Borrowing from Shakespeare once again, Billy named his avenger Macduff.

*

The following morning Billy, wearing his brand-new blazer and tie, strolled into the Capitol Rotunda to keep his appointment with fate. Having spent a sleepless night in a Holiday Inn near the National Mall, he was feeling especially picked upon and was in no mood to testify. The majesty of the Rotunda did nothing to improve his mood: the towering paintings lacked nuance, the statues seemed blandly heroic, and the Romanesque painting on the ceiling produced only a pain in his neck. He remembered

Joshua's favorite quote from *Waiting for Godot.* "'There is no lack of void,'" Joshua was fond of repeating during their discussions in Jake's. As he studied the paintings and sculptures that so effectively distanced the past, Billy better understood what Samuel Beckett meant.

Fifteen minutes later, Billy entered a House hearing room, a surprisingly small chamber with mustard-colored walls. Pushing his way past the clerks and reporters, Billy sat at the witness table. He was relieved to discover that he would not face the Select Committee alone—that half a dozen other witnesses were sitting at the table. They were a passive-looking bunch with dazed, incurious eyes, but he could easily imagine them wearing MAGA hats and cheering on Donald Trump.

When the members of Congress filed into the room and seated themselves on the dais, Billy was surprised to see that their number had increased. He then remembered an article he had read in *The Washington Post* that morning. For some obscure reason, the Republicans had ended their boycott of the committee, so the committee now included an even mix of both parties. In all, there were fourteen House members perched upon the dais, and Billy could not dismiss the thought that they were ganging up on him.

The chairman of the committee, a spinsterish woman from one of the blue states, opened the hearing with a twenty-minute monologue. Her speech, which included the usual forebodings, struck Billy as insincere. If the pillars of the republic were crumbling, if the coup had almost succeeded, if democracy was still under siege, why wasn't Donald Trump in jail? As the chairwoman finished her sermon, Billy felt a profound sense of loss, and his last conversation with Joshua took on additional weight. Yes, he had been expecting too much from a dog-and-pony show.

As the vice-chairman, one of the Republicans, made his opening statement, Billy fidgeted impatiently. The man's rich, booming voice filled the entire room, yet his speech was so robotic that he seemed to be reciting a script. In an effort to reassign blame, the man degraded the Capitol Police, insisting the committee needed to know just why these cops were so ill-prepared. The man's prepackaged outrage bordered on comedy, and if Billy had a sense of humor, he might have laughed out loud.

After the vice-chairman finished his speech, the chairwoman introduced the witnesses, inviting each to make a statement before the questioning began. All, except for Billy, declined the invitation, and Billy would have also stayed silent had he been able to control Macduff. But Billy felt so beaten-down that Macduff again hijacked his soul and then spoke with all the abandon one might expect from a Highland chief. The fearless Scot was too battle-hardened, too principled and bold, to cede the moral high ground to undeserving souls.

And so began a back-and-forth between the committee and Macduff. Macduff labeled the Republicans purveyors of lies and eaters of broken meats. He called the Democrats geldings, and cried out, "You're all jack and no jizz!" The term traitor he applied equally to the brokers of either party, unconcerned that a term so overused could have no lasting sting. But at least Macduff could not be singularly accused of overdramatizing his role: every glare he received from the dais, every inauthentic shout, every wallop from the chairwoman's gavel was theater at its worst.

"The witness will answer the questions!" the chairwoman repeatedly shouted.

"This committee will answer to history!" Macduff bellowed again and again. The Scot's eyes did not waver or soften as they traveled from member to member. Whether one was a traitor to truth or courage made too little difference to him.

But after Macduff finished his tirade, Billy felt utterly alone—a reminder that swashbuckling fantasies could only go so far. As he returned the stares of the other bad actors with whom he had shared the stage, an impenetrable silence descended upon the room. It was a silence so overpowering that it mocked them one and all. It was a silence that said that so fruitless a play did not merit a curtain call.

*

Hoping to find some peace of mind after getting thrown out of the hearing, Billy returned to Jake's and sat with his lifelong friend. He had ridden the bus back to Putnamville in a deep, abiding trance, and it was only by force of habit that he had found his way to the bar. Joshua, who had watched the hearing on television, poured them each a Budweiser draft.

"Chum, don't look so glum," he joked. "You brought that committee together."

"What do you mean by that?"

Joshua chuckled. "Every one of its members voted to hold you in contempt."

"Why do you find that amusing? Aren't you facing prison as well?"

"Naw, my lawyer finalized my plea bargain while you were making a fool of yourself. I'll cop to a charge of vandalism, and I'm gonna get three years probation."

"Probation," sighed Billy. "I could settle for that."

Joshua topped off Billy's beer. "Don't get your hopes too high," he said. "All I did was piss in their building. You had to go tell 'em the truth."

A month later, a team of FBI agents took Billy into custody. He was brought to the D.C. District Court where he opted for a bench trial, and the judge found him guilty of contempt and gave him a year in prison. Billy was placed in the Federal Correctional Institution near Otisville, New York, a pastoral facility with several tennis courts. He was assigned to shelving books in the library, which was only a part-time job. This allowed him several hours a day to work on improving his serve.

The Keeper of the Abyss

CHILD MOLESTERS WERE rarely harassed at the Indiana Penal Farm, a medium-security prison where I once worked as a guard and a counselor. This revelation surprised me at first, but it now seems rather redundant. Molesters are masters of disguise, so their dark deeds are not on display, and many have the sort of job skills a prison is likely to value. Most of the inmate plumbers and carpenters were convicted child molesters as were a lot of the clerks in the prison law library. Passive and well-behaved, they blended seamlessly into the inmate population, respected for their abilities rather than damned for their crimes.

But abusing a child does not lend itself to internal solitude. For this reason, some of them spoke candidly to me after I was promoted to job of counselor. They would often admit their modus for courting and seducing minors, and they sometimes volunteered the fact that they were child-abuse victims themselves. I would listen to them politely in the privacy of my office. I felt as though I had fallen into the role of a confessional priest.

Accustomed to discretion on the part of molesters, I was not prepared for Dan Geegax—a serial pedophile from Muncie who ended up on my caseload. Shortly after he arrived at the penal farm, he sent me a request slip. His request was written in a childish script, so I was surprised by his artful language.

To: Thomas Hemmings, Dorm 12 Counselor
Date: July 21, 1979
From: Daniel Geegax, DOC-982251
Location: Law Library
RE: Request to be transferred.

I look forward to meeting you, Mister Hemmings. Sadly, I need a friend. Excuse my penchant for puns, but I'm hoping you'll do me a solid. As an intellectual, I must admit that I am out of my element here. I'm not saying an honor camp would be much improvement, but in my current position, I am willing to settle for scraps. Please toss me a bone, Mister Hemmings, and I will forever be your amigo.

I could have ignored his presumptuous request, but I decided to call him into my office instead. Since he had just been placed on my caseload, I needed to prepare his visiting list. Besides, as an aspiring wordsmith myself, I looked forward to having a chat with someone so able to turn a phrase. The penal farm was as bare as a moonscape where culture was concerned.

I sent a pass to the law library where he had been assigned to work as a clerk. Minutes later, he entered my office and sat down on the chair by my desk. He was a tall, boney man in his sixties with large uneven teeth, and his clear-blue eyes were enlarged several times by a pair of bottle-thick glasses.

He squinted as though he were looking at me from the bottom of a well, then he smiled solicitously and handed me a pamphlet from the American Man-Boy Society. "Son, don't look so shocked," he said in a cheerful, reedy voice. "When karma catches up with a fella, a mission will set him free."

I tossed the pamphlet into my wastebasket. "I wouldn't be circulating these," I warned. "Some of our inmates are touchy when it comes to sex with children. One of them might get pissed off and beat the shit out of you."

"Wouldn't be the first time," he laughed.

"Maybe not. But prison is not a good place to make enemies."

"Point taken," he said with a wink. "You seem a bit self-righteous, buddy, but I won't hold that against ya. I'm always happy to listen to what a young fella has to say."

"Then hear me out," I said. "I can't recommend you for honor camp."

"How come?"

"You don't qualify. They don't take pedophiles there."

He slapped his chest as though wounded. "Can'tcha pull some strings, Mister Hemmings?"

"No, I can't bend the rules quite that far."

He snorted. "You don't seem like the sort who gets off on enforcing rules."

As a child of the turbulent sixties, I had no fetish for rules. I had smoked my share of pot, I had protested the Vietnam War, I had even been arrested during the '68 Siege of Chicago. But rules were not unappealing to me when it came to Daniel Geegax.

"In your case, the rules have their place," I admitted.

He sat back in the chair and chuckled. "If you're supposed to be my guru, buddy, what *can* you do for me?"

I shrugged. "I can make out your visiting list."

"That ain't gonna cut it," he said. "Why would I want *anyone* to come see me in a place like this?"

"That's up to you."

He studied me as though he were taking notes. "Save yer paper, son," he laughed. "Go scribble a story on it."

"I've written a few short stories," I confessed since he seemed to know this already. I was not surprised by his astuteness—child molesters are excellent profilers. Still, it made me uncomfortable to make this admission to him.

"Short stories," he scoffed. "No money in them—they're like contemplating your navel. What are you, some kind of idealist?"

"I just like to write," I muttered.

"Well, write for money—that's what I do. Don't end up like Herman Melville. He hadda work in a custom house because no one bought his book about whales."

"So what do *you* write?"

"I write porn," he said proudly. "My pen name is Hardy Peters. You've probably read some of my books if you're into that sort of stuff."

"I hope you're not talking about kiddie porn."

He narrowed his eyes like a gunfighter and stared at me woodenly. Whatever his depth of depravity, he was not without limitations. "I would *never* write porn about children," he snapped. "Kids are sacred to me."

"What then?" I asked him, shaking my head.

"Just run-of-the-mill, standard-issue porn. I used to be a journalist, but smut pays a whole lot better. I make two thousand dollars a book, and I can write one in three or four weeks. Jesus, I've written dozens of 'em and my publisher keeps asking for more."

"You've written dozens of books?" I said. I could not help but be impressed.

"Naw," he said. "When it comes to porn, there's no room for variety. Basically, I wrote the *same* fucking book a coupla dozen times. Sometimes, I just changed the title and the book sold anyhow."

"Impressive," I said sarcastically.

He rolled his eyes and shrugged. "Those books are nothing to brag about. I've done better work writing screenplays. Didja ever see *Lesbian Lunch*? That won a Flint award."

That the movie was actually familiar to me made me blush to the roots of my hair. Sensing my embarrassment, he patted me on the wrist.

"It ain't as good as *Deep Throat*," he said, "but I'm proud of it anyhow. It was my first stab at a screenplay and it won a Flint award."

"I haven't seen *Lesbian Lunch*," I lied.

"No, I'm sure you haven't," he laughed. "But I got hope for you, buddy. If you ever need an editor, I'll be happy to look at your stuff."

*

After Dan Geegax left my office, I felt a deep despair. Had I given up too much when I became a civil servant? A decade ago, I had dropped out of college and spent seven years roaming Australia. I had herded cattle in the Northern Outback, I had traveled with a carnival, I had even worked on lobster boats off the rugged coast of Tasmania. Had these adventures so exhausted me that I now craved moderation? Was I content to sit in an office all day and make out visiting lists? It was clear that Daniel Geegax pitied me and that his pity had some foundation. My menial scribblings could hardly compete with his many publications, and my waning sense of adventure was dwarfed by his cavalier recklessness.

I was also perturbed that my warning had had no effect upon him. When I walked through the prison yard later that day, I spotted him handing out his pamphlets to inmates. *It won't be long*, I thought, *until someone beats the shit out of him*, and the anticipation of this gave me a hollow satisfaction.

But months went by and nobody held Daniel Geegax to account. This was probably due to the skill he displayed as a hearing advocate. I chaired a conduct adjustment board when I wasn't making out visiting lists, and most of the inmates facing disciplinary hearings asked that the law library assign them Dan Geegax to help them present their cases. He was remarkable at reviewing writeups and spotting the seams in them, and he was frequently successful in getting charges reduced or thrown out. "Yeah," he might argue, "Ol' Bubba here was caught jacking off in his bunk, but the officers who work the midnight shift let him get away with it all the time. If you're gonna run a prison, ya gotta have consistency."

Daniel also turned out to be a very reliable snitch—a role for which the prison recruited him after he had been there only a week. To avoid suspicion, he reported to me instead of the office of the investigation sergeant. After providing information about drug trafficking, which I relayed to the investigator, he would give me his car salesman grin and tell me about his day. Once, he said, "Ya know, Mister Hemmings, I think I've made a few converts."

"We have enough pedophiles here," I said, "without you recruiting more."

"I'm a man on a mission, son," he boasted. "Are you going to fault me for that?"

"Why do you need to have converts?" I said. "Can't you whitewash your crimes on your own?"

"Do you really think I believe that line about teaching boys how to make love?"

"Don't you?" I asked.

"Naw," he replied. "I'm just a fucking pervert, and I'm willing to live with that."

"So why do you pass out those pamphlets?"

"Ya ever read *The Scarlet Letter*, son—that eighteenth-century chestnut about an adulteress named Hester Prynne. You seem like a literary fella, so I shouldn't have to spell it out for you."

"What's Hester Prynne got to do with it?"

"Be true to yerself—that's the sage advice with which Hawthorne ends the book. If you wear your sins upon your chest, they're easier to bear."

"It seems you've thought this through," I said.

"Exactly," he replied. "Hester Prynne was a sinner—not that adultery is much of a sin—but she was also the type of person who helped out other people. Now the whole damn town poo-pooed on the bitch for stepping out on her husband, but even those Puritans loved the slut for all the good deeds she did. 'Be true, be true'— Hawthorne had it right. But be true to your total self. If you keep your sins secret, yer conscience will punish you a lot more than other people will."

"Incredible," I said. I was almost impressed. "You're a modern-day Hester Prynne."

"I wouldn't go quite that far," he laughed, "but I wanna be true to myself. If it's good enough for ol' Hester, it's good enough for me."

*

As a prison informant, Daniel spent a great deal of time in my office. He was a constant source of knowledge regarding inmates smuggling in drugs, and, of course, he bartered this information for personal favors. I allowed him to use my office phone to call his publisher and his attorney, and soon he started to treat me as though I were at his beck and call. So great was his sense of entitlement that one day he asked me if I wouldn't mind storing his pamphlets inside my desk.

"Do me a solid and hide 'em," he said. "If a dorm officer shakes down my footlocker, he might think they're contraband."

I handed the pamphlets back to him. "No big loss," I replied

"Like hell," he said with a chuckle. "I *need* my scarlet letter."

Having reread *The Scarlet Letter*, I decided to challenge him. "Your analogy is crap," I said.

"What are ya saying, buddy?"

"Hester Prynne was beautiful, but you're not much to look at. She also felt genuine guilt. I'm not so sure you do."

"That all you got?"

"There's more," I replied. "Hester Prynne wasn't a snitch. The Church wanted her to name her lover, but she protected him. She had too much integrity to throw anyone under the bus."

"Didja just read that book again, Hemmings? It sounds like she gave you a hard-on."

"They punished her way too much," I snapped. "That hardly applies to you."

Dan cracked his knuckles one by one. "*All* analogies are crap," he said. "How come you're picking on mine?"

"I'm your counselor," I said, "and it's obvious you don't know how to serve time."

He stuffed his pamphlets back into his shirt then looked at me curiously. "You're not much of a guru, Hemmings. Ya talk like you've lost your nerve."

"Maybe so, but don't look to Hawthorne to sanctify your hubris. After her bust, Hester lived out her life in a shack at the edge of town. She didn't run around preaching adultery and putting her life on the line."

"Are you suggesting I pick another book? Like maybe *Don Quixote*."

"I'm suggesting you check into our segregation dorm before somebody bumps you off."

"Now who's exaggerating?" he laughed. "You're starting to sound like Tom Sawyer."

"You're serving four years," I reminded him, "and you're drawing the wrong kind of attention. If you keep living in a novel, you'll be deader than Mark Twain."

He looked at me as though I were a stranger then drew a labored breath. "Ya mean well, Hemmings," he said. "I'm grateful to you for that. But I ain't gonna take no advice from a fella who hides in his office all day."

*

Almost a year went by, and Geegax kept serving his time recklessly. He cheerily dropped a dime on inmates possessing pot and cocaine—inmates he later defended in front of the conduct adjustment board. He argued that contraband found in footlockers was no evidence of possession—that the stuff could have easily been planted to set an inmate up. This argument was so persuasive that I threw out dozens of cases, which eventually earned me a letter of reprimand from the warden.

Geegax bragged to me that he charged his clients up to ten dollars a case. These fees were payable in cigarettes and homemade hooch, and he was not above accepting blowjobs from some of his younger clients. When I remarked that these sounded like petty returns for a man who made two grand a book, he laughed and said, "Hemmings, it's about the hustle. It ain't about the prize."

We were sitting in my office, having one of our chats, and our conversation once again drifted to the pitfalls of doing time. "If you want to serve easy time," I said, "why don't you just read Proust?"

He pinched his nose as though I had farted. "I'm sure you know all about easy time, Hemmings, but don't bother bending my ear. I don't believe in serving time. I think time oughta serve me."

"A great book will serve you as well as a hustle, and you won't have to watch your back."

"I've read all the great books, Hemmings," he said, "so don't bother suggesting one. Especially not Proust—that long-winded fag will put a fella to sleep."

"What about Hemingway?"

"Overrated. His writing's too damn thin."

"Steinbeck?"

"Too fucking preachy. He makes me feel like I'm in church."

"Have you read Nabokov?"

"I slogged through *Lolita*. I thought it had racy parts. But there wasn't a bit of sex in the book—it just dragged on and on about nothing."

I shrugged. I was out of suggestions.

He said, "Why don't we talk about you? Ya married, Hemmings?"

"No."

"Have ya ever been in a fight?"

"Not lately."

"Ya ever had a roll with a hooker or fucked yer neighbor's wife?"

When I told him I'd rather go fishing, he snorted then grinned like a ghoul. "So whaddya do when the fish ain't biting? Do ya sit in the boat reading Proust?"

He laughed when I didn't reply and said, "Ya don't gotta answer that question. Ya strike me as the sort of fella who's read a whole lot of Proust."

*

My next conversation with Geegax took place in the Special Housing Unit, a starfish-shaped building at the core of the prison where unruly inmates were kept. His dorm officers had shaken his bed area down and had found a shank under his mattress—a footlong piece of metal that had been ground to razor sharpness. I suspected one of the guards had been ordered to plant the shank, but there was nothing I could do about it. Geegax had appeared in front of the conduct adjustment board while I was attending a training session, and the board had found him guilty of possessing a deadly weapon. The board had recommended that he be confined to a cell pending a transfer to the Indiana State Prison. The hearing report described him as a dangerous predator.

After his hearing, Geegax had sent me a request slip asking me to pay him a visit. Although deemed a dangerous predator, his message was typically light.

To: Thomas Hemmings, Counselor Dorm 12
Date: June 23, 1980
From: Daniel Geegax, DOC 982251
Location: SHU
RE: I told you so.
Hemmings, I hope you're not the sort to say, "I told you so." Not when my saboteurs showed no originality at all. Why couldn't they have planted a penis stretcher instead of a fucking knife? I'm not well-hung for a predator and could use a couple more inches.
Anyhow, I hope you drop by and see me. I'm in A Range, Cell 17. I'd like to summarize Proust with you before I head for the big house.

As I waited for him in the conference room of the Special Housing Unit, I wished I had picked a better time to stop by for a visit. Some A-Range inmates had blocked up their toilets, which had flooded most of the range, so it was an hour before an officer fetched Geegax from his cell. His hands were linked to a waist chain, he was wearing ankle irons and he stumbled like a drunk as the officer herded him into the room.

He stood as still as a statue while the officer removed his restraints, then he sat on a chair by the conference table and sadly shook his head. "I guess my being a snitch ain't enough for this fucking place."

"Being a snitch may have bought you some time, but you were bound to get set up."

"Spare me the lecture, Hemmings," he said. "I knew it was gonna happen."

"If you saw it coming, why didn't you bail. Why did you keep winning cases?"

"Why did you let me keep winning them, Hemmings? If you had been a hardass conduct board chairman, I wouldn't have rocked the boat."

"I hope you appeal the decision."

He stretched like a feline and smiled. "Your guilt won't save ya, Hemmings, so let's just talk about books. I ain't gonna waste my time bucking a frame-up that the warden probably ordered."

"Shall I bring you something by Proust?" I joked.

"Naw, I'm rereading Ken Kesey's book. The chaplain slipped me a copy of *One Flew Over the Cuckoo's Nest*."

"I'm sure it will keep your attention. It's got plenty of taboo sex."

"You're missing the point," he laughed. "The point is the hero had enough balls to shake up a looney bin. Get yer mind out of the gutter, Hemmings, if ya wanna discuss a great book."

"Listen," I said, "when you get to the State Prison, don't act like the guy in that book. They kill known child molesters there, so keep out of the main population."

"Why are you telling me this?" he said.

"You need some sage advice."

"Ya ain't acting like a counselor, ya know. You're acting like a pal. Just 'cause I have a good side don't mean I wantcha to be my pal."

"I'm just doing my job," I insisted. "There's something you may not know. Every week, we transfer trouble makers to the Indiana State Prison. Most of them know you're a pedophile and they're bound to spread the word. A reception will be awaiting you the moment you step into the yard."

"Hemmings, ya got noble intentions," he said, "but you're giving me pussy advice. If you wanna turn me into a wimp, I won't letcha be my pal."

"I'm trying to save your life," I said.

"By making my life not worth saving? What kind of friend are you?"

"You won't last a day if you don't check into segregation. There's going to be a bounty on you."

He arched his eyebrows in mock alarm then laughed as though watching a skit. "A bounty, my, my. That sounds so cloak-and-dagger, but don't let it getcha down. At least my life will have value if I end it in the yard."

*

The following week, I stood by the watchtower inside the main sally port, and I watched Geegax trip toward a transport van bound for the Indiana State Prison. He was draped in so many chains that he looked like Marley's ghost, a compatible image since I had little doubt that he was a dead man walking.

He noticed me standing there and grinned. "Hemmings!" he called. "I'll write cha, and I'll come see ya after I get out!"

I nodded warily and watched him slip into the van. I wondered, *How will it happen if they don't get him in the yard? Will they corner him on a catwalk? Will they trap him in his cell? Will they gang-jump him in the showers after diverting the guards?* I only knew that the hit would be quick—he wouldn't see it coming—and the knife would be passed off several times before his heart stopped beating.

I relived our last conversation as I watched the van pull away. He had actually had the temerity to recite Nietzsche's most famous quote. "Hemmings," he'd said, wagging his head. "What am I gonna do with you? You know, if ya stare into the abyss, the abyss stares back at you."

How unsettling it felt to know that I had opened myself to the abyss and that, despite its villainy, the abyss was just toying with me. "So what did you see?" I muttered.

His face was full of pity, and he dropped his probing gaze. "Son," he said, "don't take this wrong, but you're a hopeless case."

*

Three weeks later, my prison mail included a letter from Geegax. That he had lived long enough to write it suggested he might have listened to me. I did not particularly want to credit myself for salvaging his life, and when I read the letter, I was relieved to discover that this had not been the case.

July 23, 1980

Hemmings,

I have to say this about karma: it doesn't sting with precision. From everything you told me, I should be a specter by now. I don't want to upset your apple cart because I'll bet you're disappointed, so let's just say that the Birdman of Alcatraz hasn't got much on me. He was a pedophile too, you know, and he thrived like a fucking weed.

They've assigned me to the prison library, so I won't be arguing any more cases. But that's just as well because it gives me time to court my randy muse. Watch out D.H. Lawrence— that's all I've got to say. I know I can write much classier smut than Lady Chatterley's Lover—*that book is so repetitious it almost put me to sleep.*

Do you remember our talk about The Brothers Karamazov? *I just read that monster again—the library here has a copy—and I've got to say that maybe you got it wrong again, bucko. You said those three brothers were existentially different, but my guess is they're all Dostoyevsky. Ivan he's Dostoyevsky's mind— his powerful, unflinching mind. Alyosha he's the D Man's heart because he keeps getting led astray. And Dimitri, that lecherous fucker, has got to be the loins. You're kind of like Alyosha, a well-meaning ideologue. Me, I'm more like Ivan, but I like Dimitri best.*

Hemmings, don't bother writing me back—I don't want the brass slapping your wrist. I'll drop you a line from time to time if my muse abandons me.

Daniel

It was almost two months before he wrote me again, so his muse must not have strayed far. But how he had managed to stay alive remained a mystery to me. His letter did not show a hint of concern that someone might cut his throat. Like the canny protagonist in *The Shawshank Redemption*, he was making his time serve him.

September 14, 1980

Hemmings,

Today I'm down to ten months. If you factor in the good time I'm earning, that's all I've got left to serve. That means I'll disenthrall myself a whole lot sooner than you will—I'll bet you've got twenty years to go before you can fish all day.

I'm the head librarian now, so the guards don't watch me much. I wish they would because I'm buying and smoking too much goddamn weed. Pot blunts my creativity, you know, and my muse is getting lonely.

Yesterday, I took a break and reread The Old Man and the Sea. *The book is way too sentimental, but I'll give ol' Papa a pass. With all the brain cells he zapped with his boozing, I'm surprised he could write it at all. The book's supposed to be a tragedy, but I say the old man was blessed. Hell, the marlin was way too big to be lashed to the side of a skiff, and that graybeard was too damned stubborn to cut that fucker loose. If the sharks hadn't been peckish that day, the skiff would have probably sank, and the dumb piscator would have ended up in Davey Jones' chest.*

I ain't quite sure what I'm saying, bucko, but I think there's a deep message here. And since you're so fond of fishing, I'm hoping you'll figure it out.

Daniel

Although it had deemed me a charity case, the abyss was baiting me still, but I saw no enduring reason to keep on playing the game. Having never fished for anything bigger than crappies and bass, who was I to speculate on the agenda of the abyss?

Five weeks passed before I received another letter from Geegax. *He keeps popping up like a jig bait*, I thought as I tore open the envelope.

October 20, 1980

Hemmings,

On a pedestrian note, I'm going to clue you as to what's been happening here. Some con shanked a guard and the prison is on lockdown, so I've been stuck all week in my cell. The guard was a newbie who was stupid enough to try to be friends with the inmates, and a gang leader must have ordered one of his soldiers to take the asshole out. Most inmates don't want a guard for a pal—it makes them look like snitches—so take heed, bucko. Don't make a habit of overstepping your bounds. Still, I wish the gang had just warned the guard instead of knocking him off. Having to sit in my cell all day long is giving me cabin fever.

I'm still the head librarian here, and I've managed to hang onto my good time. I've even adopted a cat—can you believe that, Hemmings? The cellblocks here are crawling with cats, so it's not too hard to adopt one. She's a marmalade-colored tabby and I call her Molly Bloom. I won her over by feeding her guppies from my aquarium. Most cells here have aquariums, but the brass is now hauling them off. It's too easy to hide a shank in one—you just stick it under the sand. We get to keep our televisions though, and the World Series starts today. I've bet an ounce of weed on the Phillies—they oughta win it in six games.

Hemmings, I wish you hadn't told me your favorite book is Paradise Lost. *I dug a copy out of the library just to see what the fuss was about, and I had to blow off three layers of dust before I could open it up. Be honest, is this really your favorite book, or are you just trying to show off? My god, the dead language and Hebraism could drive a reader nuts. I will say this about Milton, though: He knew the Church was corrupt, and that it's better to be a law unto yourself than to let some priest fuck you up. I just don't see how that pertains to you—it's not like you're bucking the system. If you want to have a favorite book, Hemmings, stick to* The Scarlet Letter. *Don't start quoting from* Paradise Lost *because I think you'll be out of your depth.*

I've got to go, for now, Hemmings. My fish-watching days are up. Some guards have stormed the catwalk, and they're taking the aquariums out. All the damn racket they're making has upset Molly Bloom, so I'm going to feed her the rest of the guppies and hope that improves her mood.

Daniel

Three months later, I received yet another letter from Daniel. He had sketched a harpooned marlin on the back of the envelope, and underneath the marlin, he had written, "The jig is up." The letter was short, the writing looked hurried and his nonchalance seemed forced.

January 20, 1981

Hemmings,

"Ask for me tomorrow, and you shall find me a grave man."
Mercutio couldn't have said it better after Tybalt ran him
through. But don't bother asking for me, Hemmings—I have
no more tomorrows. By the time this letter reaches you, I'll be
pushing up daisies too.

I'm not going to tell you the details—that's something you
don't need to know. Let's just say that the interest is due on all my
borrowed time. Now I ain't a fellow to dodge his debts, so I'm not
going to check into seg. Hell, what would old Milton think of me if
I took the coward's way out?

Once the piper is paid, and I've been planted in the ground,
I'm hoping a flock of fallen angels will give me a livelier home.
I'm not saying a lake of eternal flame is a perfect place to dwell,
but given how fucked-up heaven must be, I'll be happier in hell.

Daniel

*

Six months passed, and I did not receive another letter from
Daniel. Given his compulsion to taunt me, I could only conclude
he was dead. I did not have enough of Alyosha in me to regret his
leaving this world, but I did hope the hit had come quickly and he
had not lingered in death.

I found myself watching for Daniel's ghost when I fished the
pond at the prison's north quarter, a forested preserve where
prison staff was allowed to picnic and fish. I compulsively looked
for ghosts when I fished there, having recently seen a couple.
Staff suicides were not uncommon at the Indiana Penal Farm,
and over the years, two guards had drowned themselves in the
pond. Their ghosts had approached me a month ago while I was
casting from the shore and had gazed at me like gophers before

236

wandering away. Since these shades were without an agenda, I chose to contain my fear. Although chilled by this glimpse of the netherworld, I went on with my fishing.

On a hazy afternoon, six months after Geegax had written me last, I was casting a jig from a dinghy, which I had rowed to the middle of the pond. Since the fish were not biting that afternoon, my eyes drifted toward the shore, and that's when I spotted a misty figure standing on the dock. The form was as stiff as a sentry and was watching me like a voyeur, so I dipped the blades into the water and pulled toward the dock. It unnerved me to think that this presence had unfinished business with me, but the fog was so thick and cottony that I rowed as though I were drugged.

"Hemmings," a reedy voice shouted as the prow of the boat touched the dock, "if you're catching lotsa fish, I hope you're tossin' the little ones back."

"For a spook, you sound rather cheery," I quipped. I chastised myself as I spoke, hoping the Great Beyond would not fault me for feigning a lack of respect.

The dinghy swayed like a pendulum as Geegax eased himself into it. "Hemmings, don't be so smug," he said as he seated himself at the prow. "If I'd had the option to haunt you, I'd have done it before now."

His face lacked the insularity I associated with ghosts, and the potbelly he had developed suggested he still had a grip on this world. When I realized he was still alive, my pulse began to race. I would have been far less startled if he had come to me as a spook.

"You're real!" I exclaimed. I started to sweat.

He saluted me and laughed. "Didja have me dead and buried, Hemmings? Yeah, I'll bet ya did."

"You told me your time had run out. You *put* that in your last letter."

"A moment of weakness," he shrugged. "We all have 'em now and then. I finished serving my bit last month, and now I'm out on parole."

"When your letters stopped, I thought your time had run out long ago."

"Naw, I just got tired of writing you, bucko. You kind of bore me, ya know?"

"So what are you doing here? This is private property."

"I see ya still have a hard-on for boundaries," he laughed. "Well, I did drive up to the prison to see you, but the shift captain said you'd gone fishing. He said if I wanted to talk to you, I'd have to hunt you down here."

"How?" I said.

"How do you think? I turned off Highway 40. Some local kid in stinky bib overalls directed me to the pond."

"I mean how did you last a whole year in state prison? There had to be a bounty on you?"

He shook his head and snorted. "There *was* one for a while. When I wrote ya last, it was after some dickhead lunged at me with a shank. But a coupla shot callers grabbed the fucker and pulled him away from me. They said the gangs would protect me as long as I shared my lewd writing with them."

"Did you share it?" I said.

"Of course I did, and I wrote 'em a whole bunch more. Since ya can't buy cock books in prison, my work was in high demand."

"So you gave them smut and they gave you your life."

"Hemmings, they gave me more than that. Pot, blowjobs, commissary snacks—whatever I wanted was mine. Just as long as I used the library printer to launch a new book every month."

"It sounds as though you were inspired."

"How could I *not* be, Hemmings? I was writing for my life. Watch for new titles by Hardy Peters because I snuck those books out on disks."

"Amazing," I said.

He grinned like a jackal. "I guess you could call it that. Those books are the best damn writing that I have ever done. Fully-fleshed characters, powerful imagery, stunning metaphors. D.H. Lawrence and Nabokov are gonna be turning in their graves."

Given my weakness for boundaries, I struggled to catch my breath. It felt as though a steel cable had tightened around my chest. "It's amazing you're still alive," I muttered. "That's what I meant to say."

"Don't ever go into politics, son, if you think criminals can't be bought."

"But you bought them with books you call *literature*?"

"Well, the subtext went over their heads. But as long as I put lots of smut in those books, the dipshits ate 'em up."

"So why are you here?"

He looked at me sternly—as though I had stood him up. It was then I remembered his pledge to come see me after he got out.

We sat for a minute in silence then he climbed back onto the dock. Standing above me, he arched his eyebrows then chuckled like a clown. "Go back to yer fishing," he teased. "It seems I'm rocking yer boat. Anyhow, I won't get my books on the market if I stay here gabbing with you."

He pushed the boat away from the dock as though ridding himself of a load. I watched as the fog reclaimed him, and then I started to row.

About James Hanna

JAMES HANNA wandered Australia for seven years before settling on a career in criminal justice. He spent twenty years as a counselor in the Indiana Department of Corrections and recently retired from the San Francisco Probation Department where he was assigned to a domestic violence and stalking unit.

James' familiarity with the criminal element has provided fodder for much of his writing. His debut novel, *The Siege*, depicts a hostage standoff in a penal facility; his book, *Call Me Pomeroy*, chronicles the madcap adventures of a street musician on parole who seeks fame by joining the Occupy Oakland Movement of 2011; and his novella, *The Ping-Pong Champion of Chinatown*, follows the blunders of a Gertie McDowell, a naïf who is lured into sordid activities by unscrupulous hustlers. James is also the author of many short stories, some of which are consolidated in his anthologies: *A Second, Less Capable Head and Other Rogue Stories* and *Shackles and More Gripping Tales*. His stories vary from weirdly sci-fi to the equally bizarre world of the criminal mind.

Fact Check and More Probing Tales is James' sixth book.

www.ingramcontent.com/pod-product-compliance
Lightning Source LLC
Chambersburg PA
CBHW050411260626
47156CB00003B/970